'Our b̶̶̶̶̶̶ ̶o̶r̶r̶e̶s̶t̶ ̶l̶o̶v̶e̶s̶ ̶̶ ̶t̶h̶e̶s̶e̶ days'
– Hank slapped down a copy of the *Manhattanite*, the glossy
tabloid her cousin, Clara, had used to make Gloria an icon of
flapperdom – 'you're both. He'll be drawn to you like a fly to
honey. And you'll figure out what his secret is.'

Gloria glanced again at the photograph in her hands. This
boy certainly didn't look like a criminal. He actually reminded
her a little of her best friend, Marcus – she'd be willing to bet
that, like Marcus, Forrest would have dimples when he gave a
real smile.

But thinking of Marcus led her to thinking about a far handsomer, darker-skinned man: Jerome.

It had been an agonizing month and a half apart, but one
day soon she hoped to hold him, kiss him, and stare into those
deep-brown eyes of his that said he knew her better than anyone
she'd ever met. She still sang as much as she could – jail cells
actually had pretty swell acoustics – but she desperately missed
Jerome playing piano beside her. If sh̶ ̶̶̶̶̶̶̶̶̶̶̶̶̶̶̶̶̶̶̶̶ dirt on
one wealthy, handsome ̶̶̶̶̶̶̶̶̶̶̶̶̶̶̶̶̶̶̶̶̶̶̶̶̶̶̶̶̶̶̶̶̶̶̶̶ t back
into Jerome's arms, wel̶̶̶̶

'If I do this, and I ge̶̶̶̶̶̶̶̶̶̶̶̶̶̶̶̶̶̶̶̶̶̶̶̶̶ I go
free?'

Also available in The Flappers series

VIXEN

INGENUE

THE FLAPPERS

DIVA

JILLIAN LARKIN

CORGI BOOKS

THE FLAPPERS: DIVA
A CORGI BOOK 978 0 552 56506 6

First published in the United States by Delacorte Press, an imprint of
Random House Children's Books, a division of Random House, Inc., New York

First published in Great Britain by Corgi,
an imprint of Random House Children's Publishers UK
A Random House Group Company

Delacorte Press edition published 2012
This edition published 2013

1 3 5 7 9 10 8 6 4 2

Copyright © 2012 by The Inkhouse

Song lyrics: 'I Ain't Got Nobody', music by Charles Warfield and lyrics by David Young,
published in 1914. ''Tain't Nobody's Business If I Do', by Porter Grainger and Everett
Robbins, published in 1922.

All rights reserved. No part of this publication may be reproduced, stored in
a retrieval system, or transmitted in any form or by any means, electronic,
mechanical, photocopying, recording or otherwise, without the prior
permission of the publishers.

The Random House Group Limited supports the Forest Stewardship Council® (FSC®), the
leading international forest-certification organisation. Our books carrying the FSC label are
printed on FSC®-certified paper. FSC is the only forest-certification scheme supported by
the leading environmental organisations, including Greenpeace. Our paper procurement
policy can be found at www.randomhouse.co.uk/environment

MIX
Paper from
responsible sources
FSC
www.fsc.org   FSC® C016897

Set in Granjon Roman 11.5

Corgi Books are published by Random House Children's Publishers UK,
61–63 Uxbridge Road, London W5 5SA

www.randomhousechildrens.co.uk
www.totallyrandombooks.co.uk
www.randomhouse.co.uk

Addresses for companies within The Random House Group Limited can be found at:
www.randomhouse.co.uk/offices.htm

THE RANDOM HOUSE GROUP Limited Reg. No. 954009

A CIP catalogue record for this book is available from the British Library.
Printed and bound in Great Britain by CPI Group (UK) Ltd, Croydon, CR0 4YY

To Julie and Jenny –
for filling our house with music and laughter,
and for loving Carol Channing
every bit as much as I do.
(Raaaspberries!)

♦♦♦

The pleasure of your company is requested

at the marriage of

Anastasia Juliet Rijn

to

Mr. Marcus Edward Eastman

on Saturday the twenty-seventh of September

at four o'clock

at the Plaza Hotel

in the City of New York

♦♦♦

PART ONE

Ain't got Nothing

'Things are sweeter when they're lost.
I know — because once I wanted something and got it.
It was the only thing I ever wanted badly, Dot.
And when I got it it turned to dust in my hand.'

— Anthony Patch, in F. Scott Fitzgerald's
The Beautiful and Damned

Chapter 1

JEROME

All his life, Jerome had dreamed of crowds screaming his name. But this wasn't what he'd had in mind.

'Jerome!' they yelled from outside, the sounds barely audible where he was standing – onstage with the rest of the band in the newest and hottest club in Greenwich Village. A strong spotlight shone in his eyes and a microphone craned over the keys of the glorious baby grand in front of him. The Chaise Lounge was the swankiest joint he'd ever played – and with places like the Green Mill and the Opera House on his résumé, that was saying something.

'Come fight like a man!' called a fellow built like a freight truck.

'Yeah, you lousy piker!'

Some of the folks were visible through the brand-new glass windows, but most stood in clumps down at the corner of the street, blocked off by bodyguards and rope.

'Spade punk!'

Jerome winced. Even empty, the club gave off an air of smoky luxury. Black vines climbed up the flocked lavender wallpaper toward the high ceiling. A few autographed photos hung over the silky, wine-colored booths – candid shots of glamorous folks like film actress Barbara La Marr and boxing champ Jack Dempsey.

There was no bar – the booze came up from the basement through a carefully hidden dumbwaiter in the back. But Jerome knew from experience that the Scotch around here was older than half the club's patrons.

Apparently, scandal was good for business. After that heart-stopping night at the Opera House weeks earlier, when Carlito Macharelli had died, clubs had been scrambling over themselves to be the first to showcase 'notorious killer' Gloria Carmody's colored beau. Jerome had never dreamed the Chaise would want him. A clear line ran through Manhattan at 110th Street, a line that blacks were supposed to stay north of. You had to be a star like Duke Ellington or Bessie Smith to be allowed to perform all the way down in Greenwich Village.

And yet here Jerome was.

Little Joe, the surprisingly fat manager, had been nothing but welcoming. 'Take your time putting together something worthwhile,' he'd told Jerome. 'I know everyone wants you because of your girl, but I want you because you're also one of the best pianists in town.'

So Jerome spent three weeks practicing with the band and knew they had a stellar show. Part of him wished Evan could have been his trumpet player, just like old times, but his friend was too busy making Jerome's little sister, Vera, happy. And that was just fine – better than fine, really.

His horn player, Roger, certainly wasn't Evan, but he had a nice smoothness to his style. Jerome had thrown himself into arranging 'Rhapsody in Blue' for the band to play at their debut. He'd caught one of the Paul Whiteman Orchestra performances of the piece over the summer and been thunder-struck. It wasn't classical music but it wasn't quite jazz, either – it was something new, something American. It could have only happened here. Just like him and Gloria. Jerome had promised himself that if he ever had the opportunity, he'd lead his band in his own take on the piece.

The rest of his band was top-notch. But none of the pending success made up for how Jerome had gotten here in the first place: because his sweet, beautiful fiancée was in prison for shooting a man – a man who'd been about to shoot Jerome dead. He hadn't been allowed to see her once since she'd been pried away from him.

Now Gloria was stuck under glass, though hopefully not for much longer. Her cousin, Clara, had promised to use her column at the *Manhattanite* to rave at the injustice of it all until Gloria was released. In the meantime, Jerome planned to work as many gigs as he could. He wanted to save enough money so that somehow, somewhere, he and Gloria could get married.

The *Manhattanite* had been selling like hotcakes these past few weeks. So many New Yorkers were rooting for him and Gloria. Jerome knew that many people were eager to see him play, but ten times that number were keen to hear Gloria. And those were the people he hoped would help free her from the big house.

But this crowd was different.

Jerome glanced out the night-darkened windows of the

club again and saw that some of the people were holding up
signs:

RACE MIXING IS COMMUNISM!
GO BACK TO HARLEM WHERE YOU BELONG!
CHAISE IS FULL OF NEGRO LOVERS!

And those were the nice ones.

Jerome glanced at his band. 'Looks like a different sort of
audience tonight, fellas.'

The men's eyes flicked to the windows and back. No one
said a word. Arnie, the young bassist, crossed himself.

Little Joe waddled into the lounge from his office, looking
natty in a custom-made black suit and matching bowler.
He walked up to the windows and stood for a minute without
moving.

'Boss?' Jerome called. 'When you want to start letting the
birds in?'

Little Joe turned and pulled off his bowler. He combed
his fingers through the few gray hairs on his head. 'Jerome,
you're a gifted musician – we both know that. And I don't care
about the color of your skin. Talent is talent. But this . . .' He
looked back out at the protesters. 'It's not something my club
can handle right now.'

'What about the show?' Jerome asked.

'Ain't gonna be one. Not with that mob out there. We'd
have a riot.'

Jerome clenched his fists. Couldn't Little Joe see that

stopping the band's performance was exactly what those monsters wanted? But then he glanced at his band. They were all breathing deep sighs of relief, and Arnie wiped sweat off his brow. The boy was barely old enough to shave. 'I understand,' Jerome said with a curt nod.

'C'mon, I'll sneak you out the back. I'll take you one at a time – that crowd's bound to notice if you all leave at once.'

Little Joe led Jerome into the backstage area, which was strewn with wooden chairs, half-empty bottles of hooch, and overflowing ashtrays. 'I'll wait while you get out of that straitjacket.' In the band's dressing room, Jerome changed out of his smart white suit and back into his tattered trousers and short-sleeved button-down. His suit looked forlorn where it hung on the rack in the corner. He'd have to come back and get it later.

At the stage door the manager counted a few bills from a fat roll. 'Something for your trouble, kid.'

A year ago Jerome wouldn't have accepted it. He hadn't even played! But money had been scarce since Gloria got locked up six weeks before. Thanks to Puccini De Luca's arrest and Carlito Macharelli's death, Gloria and Jerome had never gotten their promised payment for performing at the Opera House.

And now this. Jerome didn't know how he was going to make the rent at his roach-infested boardinghouse.

So Jerome thanked Little Joe and crammed the bills into his pocket. Then he slipped out the back door and into the night.

The stage door led to a deserted side street. Jerome pulled

his hat down and turned left in the direction of the subway a few blocks away. He'd nearly reached the corner of the street when he noticed the man.

The man was leaning against a car far too expensive to be parked anywhere in this neighborhood. He was dressed immaculately in a tan suit and blue silk tie, his graying russet hair shining in the light from the streetlamp. Jerome had only met the man once, but he'd have recognized him anywhere.

Lowell Carmody. Gloria's father.

Jerome crossed the street and walked up to the fat black car. 'Mr. Carmody, what are you doing here?'

'Came to see your big show.'

Jerome gestured down the street. 'You're welcome to join my eager fans.'

'I'm a lot more welcome than you.' Gloria's father squinted. 'Looks like a few have figured out what happened to their favorite piano player.'

Startled, Jerome turned and looked. The street was dark, and he didn't see anyone. Then, before he realized what was happening, Lowell Carmody had opened the back door of the car and shoved Jerome inside.

Jerome brought his hands up too late to stop his shoulder from hitting the car's plush floor mat. Gloria's dad picked him up by the feet and heaved him the rest of the way, then got in behind him and slammed the door. 'Drive!' he barked out.

The chauffeur shifted the car smoothly into gear and took off with alarming speed.

Jerome climbed up from the floor and settled back on the leather upholstery. He found himself sitting across from a steely-eyed goon whose muscles strained beneath his black suit jacket. Lowell Carmody slid onto the seat beside Jerome. He fished a handkerchief from his jacket pocket, mopped at his face, folded the handkerchief, and put it away.

'I don't mean any disrespect, *sir*,' Jerome said, 'but what in the hell do you think you're doing?'

Mr. Carmody said nothing, just turned and stared out the tinted window.

With a resigned sigh, Jerome joined him in watching the world pass by. Minutes passed, then more minutes, and soon Jerome realized they were no longer in Manhattan. Instead of sleek skyscrapers, they were surrounded by sprawling, flat warehouses and rusty cranes and rigs. In the distance Jerome could see a skyline that was a sad imitation of what they'd left behind on the other side of the Hudson River. A clock hovered over one of the many factories, next to a billboard painted to look like an enormous tube of toothpaste, COLGATE emblazoned across it in big white letters.

For so many musicians, playing in Manhattan was a dream – the hopping clubs, the twinkling lights. It was easy to forget that a smog-belching nightmare like New Jersey was so close by.

Mr. Carmody finally turned to Jerome. 'I'm tempted to just push you out of the car and have Elroy here shoot you.'

Jerome swallowed hard.

'But I don't have to do that,' Mr. Carmody went on with a

self-satisfied smile. 'I've got the law on my side. I've had Gloria declared my ward, since she is clearly incapable of making her own decisions.'

'What's that supposed to mean?' They veered away from the main highway and their surroundings became increasingly rural, with rows of corn and dilapidated barns on either side of the road.

'It means I control her life and her world. And you are no longer a part of it.' Lowell Carmody's smile had turned sinister. 'If you come near Gloria and I hear of it, I will have you arrested. I'll have the cops throw you into a cell where no one will ever find you. Or I'll have you killed.'

Jerome looked desperately out the window, but the only signs of life he could see were a few matted, feral-looking barn cats slinking through the night.

Mr. Carmody exhaled and glanced at Jerome with a smug twinkle in his eye. 'That bigoted mob back there? That was *my* doing. I'm the one who leaked where you were playing to the Klan, and I'll do it again, and again. Pretty soon there won't be a club in Manhattan that will risk hiring you.'

The car turned onto a barren stretch of road with nothing but dirt and dying grass on either side. 'So from this day forward, you will have nothing to do with Gloria – or New York City – for the rest of your life. Or else I will make sure there's no life for you to have. Understand me?'

Jerome opened his mouth to respond – how could Gloria's father be so cruel? – but Mr. Carmody waved him into silence. 'I'm serious.' With a nod, he signaled the scowling thug sitting across from them. The goon seized Jerome's arm with a hand like a steel cuff.

'I can't say it was nice to see you, Jerome Johnson. Elroy?'

The thug threw the car door wide open, banging it against the chassis so that it swung violently to and fro on its hinges. Jerome could hear the gravel crunching under the car's tires and the wind roaring by. 'This is where you'll be leaving us,' Mr. Carmody said.

Jerome thrashed as hard as he could against Elroy's grip and managed to connect one of his feet with Mr. Carmody's face. But then both men grabbed him and heaved, and then Jerome was airborne.

He was aware of the door slamming behind him, aware of tires squealing and of the bright full moon above him, bathing the grubby marshland alongside the road like a spotlight . . . and then he hit the ground. Hard.

He didn't even have time to summon one last memory of Gloria before darkness engulfed him like a black velvet curtain rushing across a stage.

Chapter 2

GLORIA

Cushy leather chairs didn't belong in federal prison. But then, neither did Gloria.

Surprisingly, her cell was a lot better than where she'd been living in Harlem. Her new desk was made of varnished wood rather than steel, she actually had a mattress with springs, and the three meals they brought her each day weren't half bad. Before her mother went home to Chicago, Beatrice managed to use her connections to have Gloria moved from the county jail to a holding cell in the FBI headquarters. Thanks to her, being incarcerated was a lot less miserable than it might have been.

Now Gloria sat at a long cherrywood table in an empty bureau conference room. The smell of burnt coffee hung in the air. She wasn't sure why Hank had called this meeting.

Special Agent in Charge Hank Phillips walked through the door carrying his briefcase and a cardboard box. He wore his usual crisp black suit, white collared shirt, thin black tie, and smart pair of oxfords. His dark hair, light brown eyes, tanned skin, and muscled build made it easy to understand how her ex-best friend, Lorraine, had fallen for him.

Of course, Lorraine had thought Hank was a bartender – not an undercover FBI agent. That's how stupid Lorraine was. She'd probably thought Hank stayed in such fantastic shape by bench-pressing bottles of hooch instead of barbells.

14

Without even a hello, Hank set the box down and then laid its contents out on the table. There was a black garment bag and a velvet jewelry box. A pair of long white gloves and a pair of silver T-bar heels. When Hank pulled out a beaded lime-green clutch, Gloria finally spoke up. 'That would really bring out the green in your eyes, Hanky.'

'My eyes are brown!' Hank glared. 'If you call me that again, I may just have to bring one of the other jailbirds to this party.'

'There are parties in jail? I wish I'd known. I would've worn my best dress. You know – the one with only three holes in it.'

He snapped open the clutch to reveal something a much more interesting shade of green: a wad of cash, more twenty-dollar bills than Gloria could count. 'Now, is the comedy act over?'

Gloria gave a silent nod, her eyes wide. Hank opened the garment bag as well. Gloria could see a sparkling bodice that matched the clutch perfectly. After a month and a half of wearing gray prison rags, the bright dress almost hurt her eyes.

'You're going to the Hamptons to help us figure out the story on a business mogul called Forrest Hamilton,' Hank said.

He opened his briefcase and handed Gloria a photograph. It was a candid photo taken at a party. A man puffed on a cigar while watching an exquisitely beautiful blonde spread her hands, probably in the midst of telling some wild story. His suit was classy in the way only simple but extremely expensive material could be. The man was very handsome, with dark hair slicked away from his face and even darker glittering eyes. He had a sharp, straight nose and a square jaw and could easily have been in motion pictures if he wanted to.

'Business mogul?' Gloria said doubtfully. 'He looks awfully young.'

Hank nodded. 'He's a Broadway producer, and he can't be older than twenty-five. The guy just turned up one day, saying he's from the Midwest, and went from penniless nobody to moneybags somebody in three shakes of a lamb's tail. He's got a servant who looks like he hurts people for fun, and a big swanky house he's renting. We don't know his game – he's produced nothing but flops and yet he keeps raking in the dough. Until we find out where that cash is coming from, he's just a person of interest.'

'But what does any of that have to do with me?'

'Our boy Forrest loves singers and celebrities, and these days' – Hank slapped down a copy of the *Manhattanite,* the glossy tabloid her cousin, Clara, had used to make Gloria an icon of flapperdom – 'you're both. He'll be drawn to you like a fly to honey. And you'll figure out what his secret is.'

Gloria glanced again at the photograph in her hands. This boy certainly didn't *look* like a criminal. He actually reminded her a little of her best friend, Marcus – she'd be willing to bet that, like Marcus, Forrest would have dimples when he gave a real smile.

But thinking of Marcus led her to thinking about a far handsomer, darker-skinned man: Jerome.

It had been an agonizing month and a half apart, but one

day soon she hoped to hold him, kiss him, and stare into those deep-brown eyes of his that said he knew her better than anyone she'd ever met. She still sang as much as she could – jail cells actually had pretty swell acoustics – but she desperately missed Jerome playing piano beside her. If she had to dig up the dirt on one wealthy, handsome young fool to free herself and get back into Jerome's arms, well . . .

'If I do this, and I get you what you're looking for, can I go free?'

Hank nodded. 'We'll cut you a deal, I promise. But let me be clear: If you fail to turn up dirt on Forrest, you're going back into the big house. And not these cushy FBI digs. Nothing your parents do or say will help you then. You'll have to serve *real* time.'

Gloria glanced at the box and sighed. Really, she didn't have to think about her decision for too long. 'Have you got a garter in there somewhere? No self-respecting flapper would leave her prison cell without one.'

'Oh, congratulations, darling!' the pixielike woman in the silver Chanel dress gushed. 'You have *no* idea how utterly elated my girlfriends and I were when we saw the news in the *Times*.' The woman stood across from Gloria near one of the tiny tables covered in fine blue tablecloths that were arranged around the dance floor at the Conch Shell, a hopping beachfront restaurant. The life preservers, colorful shells, and anchors that hung on the wood-paneled walls were a playful nod to the ocean lying just beyond the restaurant's back patio.

17

'We toasted your release right then and there at the newsstand!' the dame went on, practically yelling over the roar of the band playing hot jazz on the stage beyond the dance floor. 'Champagne would've been best, but at nine in the morning, a flask of gin had to do.'

The woman speaking was a tiny wisp of a thing – shorter than the petite Gloria, even – and very, very beautiful. Her dark brown hair was pinned to the side to reveal spectacular diamond earrings and even more spectacular cheekbones. Her nearly black eyes glowed with an aloof sophistication.

A year before, a woman this glamorous wouldn't have been caught dead talking to a bluenose deb like Gloria. But now she was one in a long line of starlets, journalists, and artists all eager to congratulate Gloria on her sudden release from prison. Gloria felt an instant sense of *belonging* among these impossibly charismatic flappers and swells. A far cry from the first time she'd entered the Green Mill back in Chicago, when she hadn't even bobbed her hair.

Before Gloria reached the mahogany bar when she first arrived, a black man in a crisp white shirt, black vest, and blue bow tie had appeared beside her with a dirty martini. 'Giggle water's on the house for you tonight, darlin'.' He gave her a nod. 'It's a brave thing you done for Jerome Johnson,' he whispered. 'Something none of us'll ever forget.'

'Thank you,' Gloria had said. She had finished the drink quickly and set the glass down at the bar – just in time for a handsome man in a seersucker suit to sweep her to the dance floor, where she moved through the steps of the Baltimore

Buzz, amazed she could remember them. Gloria glanced at the sparkling dancers around her, smoke filling the air and spinning in endless curlicues as it flowed up to the ceiling fans above. There was glitter, glamour, and music – and Gloria was at the center of it in her brilliant Paquin dress and flawless makeup. What else could a girl ask for?

Well, besides her fiancé.

It had only been when she'd caught the eye of the only grim-faced fellow in the crowd that she had remembered she *didn't* belong here. She had come here with a bureau chaperone, and she had a mission: Find Forrest Hamilton and grill him for information.

The man, Terzy, had tapped his watch and continued scowling at Gloria. She'd excused herself from the dance floor and started to search for the handsome host of the party, but enthusiastic admirers like her pretty new friend here weren't making the task easy.

'You're such a darling, darling,' a young brunette not much older than Gloria said to her while sipping from a silver flask.

'As are you,' Gloria replied.

'Well, I know. But really, you're truly a dear.' The brunette had a heart-shaped face and almond-shaped eyes. She swayed back and forth, the fringe from her dress swishing ever so slightly.

'And your name is . . . ?' Gloria asked.

Just then, a curmudgeonly man stepped out of the crowd to stand next to her new acquaintance. His light brown hair was shot through with gray, and his wrinkles made him look ten years older than he probably was. He seemed old enough to be her father.

'Ruby, I told you not to go wandering off like that,' he said in a gravelly voice.

A bit of the light went out of Ruby's sparkling eyes. 'Oh, sorry, dear.'

The man sniffed and straightened his brown bow tie. 'Just remember that these are *your* friends.'

'You're in the theater business, too, Marty. It's not like producers and actors are different animals.'

'No, they're different *species.*'

Ruby suddenly seemed to remember Gloria. She gave a bell-like laugh and her cheeks got rosy. 'Oh, how rude of me! My darling, dear new friend, this is my husband, Marty Hayworth. Marty, this is Gloria Carmody. You know. *The singer.*'

Marty acknowledged Gloria with a gruff nod. 'From the tabloids.'

'You're a Broadway producer?' Gloria couldn't imagine Marty with such a glamorous job; he was about as flat and dull as his wife was incandescent. 'Have you produced anything I would've seen?'

Ruby smiled graciously. 'Well, he produced my first show. We finished our run a few weeks ago. Maybe you've heard of it – *The Girl from Yesterday.*'

Oh my! Gloria had read all about the show in the *Manhattanite*s Clara religiously sent her, one every week. Ruby had received nothing but love-letter reviews for her portrayal of the ingenue Violet, a fierce but vulnerable young ballerina-turned-cancan-dancer in Gilded Age Paris. Ruby was a bona fide star at the beginning of an exciting career.

This brunette who'd had too much to drink and thought Gloria was her newest and dearest friend was Ruby Hayworth?

As much as Gloria hated to admit it, she was insanely jealous.

Her chaperone, Terzy, stared at her from across the dance floor and twitched in an alarming way. Was he trying to wink? Finally Terzy beckoned with his pudgy arm.

'I've heard fantastic things about that show!' Gloria smiled at the Hayworths. 'You'll have to excuse me – but I promise to be in the front row when your next musical opens.'

'I'm not sure when or what that will be,' Ruby replied. 'But I'll make sure the box office boys set aside a ticket for you, darling.'

Terzy narrowed his eyes at Gloria when she reached him in the middle of the crowd. 'What are you cooling your heels with the starlet for?' The short, stout FBI agent hunched over his glass of seltzer and glared at the riotous guests. 'Just talk to this Forrest character so I can get home and go to bed.'

'Have you seen him?' Gloria had taken every possible chance to scan the room for the man from the picture since she'd arrived, but she hadn't caught sight of him yet.

Terzy hooked his thumb over his shoulder. 'Open your eyes.'

Through the open back doors, Gloria saw a few couples at patio tables, loudly toasting the sea. Beyond them, sitting alone at one of the smaller tables, was Forrest. He was bent over a little notebook, scribbling, his brow furrowed in concentration.

Gloria took a deep breath, more nervous than she'd ever been onstage. Her entire future with Jerome hinged on her ability to get Forrest to spill his secrets. She took her red lipstick out of her purse and smoothed it over her lips. Every battle required a little war paint.

With a nod to Terzy, Gloria walked out onto the candlelit patio. After the noise of the party, the clacking of her heels against the flagstones seemed too loud. Gloria could hear the waves crashing in the distance but couldn't see them; it was dark out here. A wind blew her dress taut against her legs.

Forrest smiled as she approached. He was even handsomer in person. Gloria had been right about the dimples.

He quickly stretched a black ribbon across the binding of his leather notebook and closed it. 'It's a bit embarrassing, I know, sneaking out to write at my own shindig. But I always get my best ideas when I'm at parties.' He cocked his head toward the dancers inside. 'How much closer can you get to a musical in the real world?'

It was the sort of thing Gloria would think but stop herself from saying, worried she'd sound pretentious. But with his earnest gaze, Forrest didn't seem like a phony.

'Aren't you a little young to be a Broadway producer?' Gloria asked. Up close, he looked barely older than she was.

'Nope. Being a producer only has one job requirement: money. And you can get your hands on that at any age. If you're

22

smart.' His brown eyes skimmed right over her sparkling green dress up to her face. With a black silk headband over her newly waved and bobbed hair and chandelier earrings, Gloria knew she looked good. 'Aren't you a little young to be an ex-con?' he asked.

'Trouble's a lot easier to find than money,' Gloria countered. 'And unlike money, sometimes trouble comes looking for you.'

'Ah, but yours is a special kind of trouble that only a special kind of dame could get into,' he said, laughing. He pulled a chair out for her. 'Have a seat, rest your gams. I guess we can skip over introductions and right into congratulations. To you on your release from the big house and to me on the new show I'm financing.'

'You're producing a new show?' she asked as she settled in beside him.

'That's why I threw the party.' He lit a cigar with a gold-plated lighter, and the spicy smell of it filled the air. Cigar smoking was a habit Gloria had always associated with older men, but it suited Forrest just fine. 'It'll be called *Moonshine Melody*. It's my third show, and *hopefully* my first success.' His gaze drifted away from her and back toward the crowd.

'What makes you think this one will be any different?' she asked, her tone playful.

Forrest pointed through the back door: Ruby was dancing with a young, good-looking fellow in a white suit. When she danced, Ruby had a charisma that made everyone else within ten feet disappear. '*That's* what,' Forrest said.

'Ruby Hayworth?'

'The one and only. Manhattan would pay good money to watch Ruby Hayworth read the paper.' There was more than artistic admiration in Forrest's face as he spoke.

'Stars like that don't come cheap, I bet,' Gloria said. 'You sure you can afford her?'

'Money's no object for me, I'm happy to say.'

'But how is that true, if your other shows weren't successful?' She'd hoped to be a little craftier about working this question into the conversation, but if she didn't get Forrest talking, Terzy was going to drive her straight from this party back to prison.

Forrest's dark eyes narrowed, but his face lost none of its good humor. 'Why so interested? Are you thinking of becoming a producer?'

'Sure,' Gloria said with a flirtatious smile and a silent apology to Jerome. 'Sounds like a pretty great gig, especially if I could be rich whether or not my shows did well.'

'It doesn't really work that way. I haven't been able to make much money at all off my shows.' He stretched his arms behind his head and gave a lazy smile. 'I've actually lost a lot. But I've got to keep trying, right?'

'Why, though, if you're losing money?'

'What else should I spend my wealth on? Why use money to buy useless baubles when I can use it to *make* something?'

'Most men your age think parties and baubles are more worthwhile than musicals.'

'Well, they're free to think that. But personally? I love musicals,' Forrest proclaimed.

'But if you're not making money off them, then where does all your wealth come from?' She scooted her chair closer to him. 'It's nothing illegal, is it?'

Forrest gave her a pitying look. 'Oh, Gloria, you're not very good at this at all, are you?' Gloria blinked, and he gave her another dimpled smile. 'Tell you what, after this a bunch of us are driving out to stay at my mansion in Great Neck. It's got so many rooms that I don't think I've seen them all yet. Why don't you join us?'

Gloria raised her eyebrows and looked at Terzy where he leaned against the doorjamb wearily. He glanced over at her and Forrest frequently and obviously.

Forrest laughed. 'I know why you're here, honey – the feds sent you and that stuffed shirt over there to spy on me.' Gloria swallowed hard. How did Forrest know? 'But I don't care about that; I've got nothing to hide. You're a singer, right? And you seem like a swell dame who's been cooped up for the past six weeks and could use a spot of fun. What do you say?'

Gloria glanced at Terzy, then back into Forrest's good-natured eyes. If she went back with Terzy now, she'd have a whole lot of nothing to tell Hank. Jerome wouldn't like her staying at another man's house, but what better opportunity would she get to learn more about Forrest and free herself and Jerome of Tony Giaconi's murder for good?

She stuck her hand out for Forrest to shake. 'Count me in.'

Chapter 3

CLARA

Something was seriously wrong when not even the Charleston could raise Clara's spirits.

She'd spent hours doing the trendy knee-banging dance with her friends under the crystal chandeliers, trying to let the jazz pulse through her blood as it always had. Her friends whirled around her in their best glad rags – Coco in a gold-and-white Madeleine Vionnet and Leelee in a pink velvet dress that barely reached her knees. Most of the boys were in tuxedos, while Arthur had donned a pale blue suit. Clara could feel every pair of eyes in the ballroom peering toward her group.

But all she felt was fatigue and irritation.

She left the dance floor and headed toward her table. The Terrace Ballroom of the newly opened Roosevelt Hotel was posilutely gorgeous, with its high ceilings, moldings, and large arched windows. A roaring band played on a makeshift stage beyond the gleaming dance floor. The crowd was adorned in their best sparkling flapper attire. The haze of cigarette smoke gave each flash of diamond earring or beaded purse a dreamy, fantastical quality. The party was good, it was perfectly fine: it was just like all the others.

And that was why Clara hated it.

She found her seat and returned to a love that never failed her: whiskey. Clara 'borrowed' her friend Arthur's flask and emptied it. She didn't realize he was standing right behind her until he cleared his throat.

'All that liquid courage might not feel so nice come morning, Clarabella.'

'Morning? What's this "morning" you speak of, good sir?' Clara replied. These days, Clara stayed up until the sun just began to peek over the Manhattan skyline . . . and didn't awaken until her hangover receded, which was usually not long before sunset.

She could admit it: She was trying to drink away her boredom. She'd grown so sick of it all – the women with their black spider-lashes and too much rouge, the way they manufactured every laugh, every smile, so that they forgot what the real things felt like. The men in their fedoras and debonair suits were exactly the same, but even less interesting. Maybe it was because they lacked the mascara and rouge.

But who was Clara to judge? She was no different in her sleeveless Paul Poiret, a pretty number that darkened in tiers from sunshine yellow to burnt orange; more silver necklaces than she could count wound elegantly around her long neck; her perfect golden bob without a single errant strand.

She was the Flapper Queen once again. But now that was just another gilded cage.

'Clara, darling?'

She squinted across the table at her friend Julia Spence, Arthur's older sister. One would never guess that the statuesque redhead was related to rakish, larger-than-life Arthur. Leelee, Coco, Arthur, and Clara's old friend Nellie had settled into the other gold-cushioned chairs around the table.

'What is it, loves?' Clara asked.

'Are you all right?' Nellie asked, her usually joking expression serious.

'Never been better,' Clara slurred.

'You're hitting the juice pretty hard tonight,' Coco observed. With her sleek, dark bob and flawless rings of black kohl around her exotically slanted eyes, Coco was utterly committed to being the most sophisticated modern woman in the room. Clara's ex-roommate leaned close. 'That new twit of Marcus's doesn't mean anything. She's nothing but a cheap replacement for a custom Chanel like you.'

Not Marcus again. It had been weeks since their breakup, but the thought of his golden hair falling into his eyes after hours of dancing, his electrifying blue eyes, his stupidly adorable dimples – it all still pierced Clara's heart as if no time had passed at all. She downed the rest of someone's glass of whiskey to dull the pain.

'They're *engaged*,' Clara replied in a low voice. 'After a *month*. If he's able to fall for someone new so quickly, what does that say about his feelings for me?'

'Nothing, sweetie,' her other old roommate, Leelee, replied. 'He fell for her because he's heartbroken.'

I'm heartbroken, too, Clara wanted to say. She hadn't spoken to Marcus since Gloria's debut at the Opera House weeks earlier. Marcus had already broken up with her by that point. Clara had thrown herself into writing her articles about Gloria and convincing herself that she wanted as little to do with Marcus as he did with her. That she was better off on her own. By the time

28

Clara realized she'd been wrong, Marcus was already engaged.

She imagined telling her friends that she missed Marcus terribly, that she'd made a mistake . . . but what was the point of making herself even more depressed? Were her friends right – was this new girl just a rebound? But then why had he asked her to *marry* him? A rebound was a weeklong fling; marriage was forever. And Marcus had decided that he wanted to spend his forever with somebody else.

So really, what good was it to talk about it now?

'What's done is done,' Clara announced. She gave them all a wicked smile, putting on her bravest front. 'What we *really* need to talk about are those stiffs next door.'

Vicious grins appeared on her friends' faces. 'What did you have in mind?' Arthur asked.

Clara and her friends had come to the Roosevelt that evening solely to attend the event next door in the hotel's finest ballroom: the Grand Ballroom. No one at *that* party would have to pretend to be clever. *Their* party was being thrown by the Algonquin Round Table – Franklin Pierce Adams, Dorothy Parker, Robert Benchley, and more of the most brilliant literary minds Manhattan had ever seen. There was even a rumor the Fitzgeralds were home from Paris and would make an appearance.

But instead of letting Clara's crowd in, the bouncer had scoffed. 'Only *real* press are allowed to attend this event, Miss Knowles. Not baloney spinners like you.'

Clara had flinched at that. So what if the *Manhattanite* was known more for its celebrity gossip than its hard-hitting journalism? She'd still done real, *important* work there.

Hadn't she?

So they'd stormed off in a huff and crashed this less-than-classy party next door instead.

'Did you figure out a way to sneak in?' Julia asked now, casting a glance at the wall as though she could see right through it and into the exclusive world beyond.

'Why bring ourselves to the party,' Clara asked, 'when we can bring the party to us?'

Moments later Clara, Coco, and Leelee were in the corridor, gathered around two servers who had been working the Round Table event. Clara had spied the men steering carts piled high with covered trays toward the hotel's front entrance.

'What have you got there?' Clara asked with a sideways glance.

Both men raised their eyebrows. They looked Clara and her girlfriends up and down. Oh, this was going to be eggs in the coffee. 'Just some food,' the blond one replied, bashful.

'We can see that, honey,' Coco purred. 'She was wondering what *kind* of food.'

'Um,' replied the other, a brunette with glasses, 'shrimp, cucumber sandwiches, assorted cheeses . . .'

'Oh, I *love* cheeses!' Leelee exclaimed with a giggle. 'Especially when they're assorted.'

'Sounds much tastier than what they've got in the Terrace Ballroom,' Clara said, working hard not to slur. 'The Round Table party – now, *that* seems like a classy bash.'

The blond chuckled. 'You don't know the half of it, doll face. Pretty soon all the guests are heading downtown to ride a *yacht* around the Hudson. We were just taking these hors d'oeuvres out to the car so we can meet the captain at the dock before the guests arrive. Some life, am I right?'

Coco gave him her most beautiful smile. 'That sounds completely jake! Our girl Leelee has never been on a *yacht* before. Have you, Lee?'

'What is that? Is that some kind of boat?' Leelee asked, her already large eyes even larger with feigned wonder.

'What would Leelee do,' Clara said, touching the blond lightly on his wrist, 'to go for a ride on an actual boat!'

'We'll never know,' Coco said sadly.

The two waiters looked at one another. 'Actually, the captain's an old buddy of mine,' the brunette said. 'So maybe there's a way to find out . . .'

While Leelee followed the waiters to a convoy of Packards parked at the curb, Clara and Coco dashed back into the ballroom to gather the gang. They could only locate Julia and an amused Nellie.

'It's even swankier than we thought!' Clara exclaimed. 'There's a yacht!'

'A yacht whose captain just happens to be a mutual friend of *our* new waiter friends!' Coco added.

Nellie grinned. 'Fantastic! Maxie and Arthur heard that they're planning to bring fireworks on the yacht, too. Because, really, what's a yacht without fireworks?'

31

'No . . . ,' Clara and Coco said with barely suppressed glee.

'Arthur and Maxie are out with some boys who know how to make 'em work right now,' Nellie confirmed. 'It should only take them another minute or two to convince those boys that we are *far* more deserving of fireworks than the stuffy old birds next door.'

Clara and Coco leaned toward one of the arched windows, through which they could see the paved courtyard with its marble fountains and decorative vases of roses. Maxie stood silently laughing while Arthur gesticulated madly in front of two young hired hands in coveralls. A stack of wooden crates sat on the ground between them.

Clara's smile grew. 'Let those dreary literary types enjoy their party. I can't wait to see their faces when they realize we stole the most exciting part of their evening right out from under them!'

Even as she spoke, she knew the prank wouldn't dim the sting of the earlier rejection. Deep down, Clara knew that bouncer had been right. She wasn't a *real* writer. She wrote biting but meaningless stories that only pleased people as boring and empty as Clara had become.

If you want to write, write about something that matters, Marcus's voice rang through her mind. *If you want to write trash, then find someone else to love, because I won't be waiting around.*

Ever since Clara had written about Gloria and had seen what an effect a real story could have, she had wanted to write about more than catty fights between teenage heiresses.

Clara had thought about asking her editor if she could

switch to writing something else, but she was sure he'd say no. Parker bragged to everyone who would listen about how Clara's column had helped to make the *Manhattanite* the most popular gossip rag in town.

Maybe her articles about her cousin had been a fluke. Maybe salacious drivel was all she was really capable of. And yet Clara was beginning to realize that she wanted to go to college, where she could hone her skills. She wanted exactly what Marcus had wanted for her. He'd been right about everything, and she couldn't run into his arms and tell him so because his arms were full – with another girl.

She felt a tap on her shoulder and turned. Standing next to her was easily the handsomest man in the room. He wore a tan pin-striped suit and a pale blue tie. Even with a healthy dose of Brilliantine, the soft waves in his dark brown hair were visible. His strong jaw was the sort a girl always wanted to run her hands over, and his bright green eyes oozed intelligence and charisma. Most girls would consider Parker Richards, the young and attractive editor of the *Manhattanite,* one of the biggest catches in town.

But those girls weren't fresh off losing the loves of their lives. And Parker Richards also wasn't *their* boss.

'Coco and Julia, you go find Leelee and the boys waiting outside. And Nellie, you go tell Arthur and Maxie the plan, and invite their new friends, too. We don't want to burn the yacht down trying to set those fireworks off on our own. I'll meet you out there in ten.' Clara turned to Parker. 'Now, what can I do for you?'

'What are you and that gang of hooligans up to now?' Parker asked, squinting through the arched windows.

'Well, we couldn't get into the Round Table party next door, so now we're stealing their food and their yacht. And hopefully some fireworks.' Just then, she heard a loud *boom*. She looked to see Arthur, Maxie, and Nellie running through the courtyard with crates in their arms, smoke wafting in their wake, and what looked to be hotel security guards running after them.

'Looks like the fireworks are a go,' Clara said.

Instead of congratulating her on what a fantastic *Manhattanite* column this would make, Parker shook his head. 'Clara, that's a terrible idea.'

Clara's anger was sharp and immediate. She jabbed a finger into Parker's chest. 'I'm doing exactly what you wanted! You said if I wanted to work for you, I needed to dance on tables and lead toasts with my flute of champagne! Or don't you remember?'

A few guests looked in their direction.

Parker straightened his tie and took a step back. 'Yes, but you're talking about theft, Clara. Theft from people who *matter*. Your articles helped keep that cousin of yours out of prison! Now's the time to be careful with your reputation – you should be trying to *impress* the folks at that other party, not rob them.'

Parker was right, Clara realized. What would this stunt do other than convince New York's literary giants that Clara didn't deserve to be taken seriously?

He put a hand on her arm. 'How about you ditch the yacht and come out with me? There's a new place called the Chaise

Lounge downtown that's supposed to be the cat's pajamas.'

'Ah, I see. Your sudden concern for my career is just a way to ask me on another date.' Aside from a near kiss and the pseudo-date that had ended in Gloria's getting arrested, nothing had happened between them. But that hadn't been for lack of trying on Parker's part. Barely a day had gone by since that night at the Opera House without Parker inviting her to some new club or play. Clara always said no.

But why shouldn't she go out with Parker? Marcus certainly wasn't waiting around for her, was he? 'Tell you what, boss. I'm in. Just give me a second to visit the ladies'.'

Parker gave her his usual self-assured smile. 'I'll be waiting for you in the lobby.'

Even the bathroom in this joint was swanky, with plush couches where girls could rest their sore gams, wide mirrors where they could line up to reapply their lipstick and gossip about hemlines, and sinks made of the finest marble.

Clara was really feeling her liquor tonight. It took an embarrassing amount of time to fish her lipstick out of her silver clutch – good thing no one was around to see. Once her lips were ruby red once again, she searched in her bag for something to blot with . . .

. . . and retrieved a card she'd been carrying around for the past two weeks.

The pleasure of your company
is requested at the marriage of
Anastasia Juliet Rijn . . .

35

There was a photograph in the invitation. That must have cost a pretty penny – but then, the Eastman family had many pretty pennies to spend on things like engagement photos.

Marcus's betrothed, Anastasia, was a remarkably pretty girl with delicate bone structure and large pale eyes. She looked about as interesting as an ankle-length skirt. Clara couldn't guess the girl's hair color from the black-and-white photo – only that it wasn't blond like her own. Standing next to his bride-to-be and looking happier than Clara had seen him since he'd moved to New York was Marcus. Had he ever looked so delighted with Clara, even in the beginning?

Clara folded the invitation in half and raised it to her mouth. Even though she hadn't had it for long, it was creased and worn. She looked up at herself in the mirror. Even hours into her evening, she still looked flawless and sexy. Maybe she wasn't the prissy debutante in the photograph, but who would want to be? She'd never been that girl, good as she'd been at pretending back in Chicago. Instead, she was a flapper, which was a hell of a lot more interesting.

So she didn't have Marcus anymore. So what?

She crumpled the invitation and threw it in the trash.

'Out with the old,' she slurred.

Chapter 4

LORRAINE

Bills, bills, bills, and a reminder of her next dentist appointment – how could a woman as deliciously intriguing as Lorraine accumulate such a dull pile of mail?

She really needed to send out a change of address notice. Lorraine was a Barnard girl now, and had moved from Greenwich Village to Morningside Heights; her friends and admirers needed to know where she was so that they could reach her at a moment's notice. What if she missed an invitation to a fabulous party or a moonlight stroll with some of the Columbia boys? For all Lorraine knew, she had already received dozens of these invites, only for them to be lost on the long, arduous journey uptown.

But the most exciting letters in this stack were the regular correspondence from Lorraine's parents. And those might as well have been addressed 'To Whom It May Concern.'

> *Your father and I went to Minnie Wilmington's engagement party this weekend. She's had the hardwood floors varnished. They look lovely.*

Lorraine fished the check out, crumpled up the letter, and ripped open the next.

*Your father and I played golf with the Marlowes
yesterday afternoon. It was a temperate day. A bit
windy, though.*

There were another seven letters in the stack. Her mother carried on a fairly entertaining social life, or so Lorraine had thought – how could she make it sound so utterly dreadful? Finally Lorraine just tore open each envelope, pocketed the checks, and left the letters on the bench beside her. Maybe some aspiring writer would find them and use them to write the world's most boring novel.

Lorraine planned to write her memoirs one day, but they would be *fascinating.* How could they not be? If there was one good thing about all the trials she'd been through, it was that they made it impossible for anyone to say that Lorraine's life had been dull.

She took a break from sorting, picked up the latest issue of *Vogue,* and tried to compose her face so that she'd look *alluring* and *inviting* and like a budding socialite. It was unseasonably warm for September, and Lorraine felt perfectly comfortable in her pale brown chiffon blouse and ivory flared skirt. An ivory cloche hat with a brown cloth flower rested on her short, dark bob. Lorraine would admit that her heels were a little high for running from class to class, but they looked sensational.

Besides, Lorraine didn't have class for another two hours. Plenty of time to hobble there. For the moment she sat on a bench on Columbia's campus, directly across the quad from Philosophy Hall. Magnolia trees dotted the campus, and their blossoms sailed onto the grassy sward in the light breeze. Cobbled walks crisscrossed the quad, and a fountain gently burbled in the distance.

The buildings on campus were old, but not old like Lorraine's dreadful aunt Mildred's collection of antique, rusty teapots. The buildings and statues here seemed old in a *mature* way, as if generations of knowledge had been infused into their very foundations over time. Lorraine could imagine the professors trying to gently hammer that same knowledge into the minds of their disinterested students. She watched the students now, the handsome young men in sweaters and breeches tossing a football, while others sat on picnic blankets and entertained equally attractive young ladies.

These boys weren't focused. What they *really* needed were appropriate wives who would help motivate them. Women like Lorraine.

She sighed. She had been surprised by how much she enjoyed her classes at Barnard, but she still wished she could go to school *here*. It was only just across the street, but Barnard felt miles away from Columbia's dashing young men.

Lorraine kept a hawk's eye on Philosophy Hall's arched doorway. Any moment, Marcus Eastman would walk through it, straight from his French class. After that he would head across campus to physics. Then he would be done with classes for the day, until he went off to calculus tomorrow morning.

Lorraine couldn't help but feel proud of herself. They'd only been at school a few weeks and she'd managed to memorize Marcus's entire schedule.

Most days, Lorraine was perfectly situated to bump into Marcus, to listen sympathetically to him as he talked about his difficulties in class, to offer to renew the friendship that had sustained her throughout her high school years. She was there for him, as a true-blue friend should be.

Of course, the two of them hadn't technically spoken yet. Lorraine had only seen Marcus a handful of times, and whenever he noticed her, he quickly took off in the other direction.

When Lorraine had run into Marcus at the Opera House weeks earlier, he'd given her such hope. There she'd been, heartbroken after her too-perfect bartender beau, her first true love, turned out to be an FBI agent who'd only been using her for information.

But then Marcus showed up. And he'd been *nice* to her! He even told her she looked good! He'd never done that back in Chicago. Let FBI Hank go off and solve crimes and look ruggedly handsome while doing it. Who cared? Not Lorraine! *She* belonged with someone like Marcus; that was clear. A handsome boy her own age from the same world as she.

But that notion had come crashing down after Gloria told Marcus what Lorraine had *really* been doing at the Opera House. How she'd been helping the gangster Carlito Macharelli trap Gloria and her colored fiancé. After that, Marcus had wanted nothing to do with her.

It wasn't fair. Didn't it matter that once Lorraine learned Carlito was planning to *kill* Gloria and Jerome, she'd worked with the FBI to save them? How come no one ever focused on that part? How come no one held Lorraine Dyer up as the heroine of this sordid tale? She'd been lied to, been lost and alone, and then she'd come through and saved her friends from an unsavory end.

That was the story Clara Knowles should have written up in the *Manhattanite*.

Lorraine would explain everything to Marcus in touching detail when he finally deigned to speak to her. After dating a liar like Clara Knowles for so long, Marcus *had* to understand what it was like to be misled and confused enough to make a few mistakes.

A shadow fell over the cover of *Vogue* and Lorraine looked up, her heart swelling.

But the boy standing in front of her wasn't Marcus – he was in fact the blond Adonis's polar opposite. Where Marcus was tan and muscular, Melvin Delacorte was rail thin and pale, with a dusting of freckles over his nose. It was hard to tell what color his eyes were behind his thick, black-framed glasses, only that they were small. His fiery shade of red hair looked beautiful on a girl like Gloria but was completely ridiculous on a boy of nineteen.

Today he was wearing a gray sweater vest, a rumpled button-down, and baggy breeches – but his clothing selection didn't really matter. No matter what he wore, one truth was evident: Melvin was one of the biggest killjoys Lorraine had ever met.

He was also one of the only friends she'd been able to make at college. At a Columbia-Barnard academic honors dinner early in the semester, Lorraine had been unable to stop poking

41

fun at the stuffy old professors' outfits. Melvin had been the only student sitting nearby to laugh.

Or maybe he'd just been coughing. His laugh and his cough sounded remarkably similar. But Lorraine loved to talk and Melvin loved to listen. All in all, not a bad arrangement.

Melvin slouched down next to her on the bench. He followed Lorraine's gaze past the Venetian Well Head to Philosophy Hall. 'I see you're on the watch again,' he observed in the rich, deep voice of a handsomer man.

Lorraine rolled her eyes and went back to shuffling through her mail. 'Yes, yes, you know me *so well*,' she said, bristling. But spying the name 'Eastman' on the corner of an envelope sent every other thought straight out of Lorraine's mind. Could it be a love letter? A heartfelt apology for how Marcus had been avoiding her?

Her spirits plummeted when she noted the letter was from the Eastman *family*, not Marcus.

Melvin watched her eagerly rip the letter open. 'Were you recruited for the Academic Decathlon? Our schools compete together – we could be teammates!'

'What? God, no – Melvin, just stop talking.'

Lorraine pulled the thick folded card from the envelope and opened it. Immediately her eyes were drawn to the black-and-white photograph of Marcus, his golden hair slicked back with pomade. The boy certainly could wear a suit – the pale vest, trousers, and jacket hung beautifully on him. The smile fell off Lorraine's face as she noticed the classically beautiful woman standing next to him. The girl wore the sort

42

of long, frilly deb dress Lorraine had always despised. Her delicate hand was tucked around Marcus's arm as if it belonged there, and something lovely and very, very expensive glinted on her finger.

'He's getting *married*!' Lorraine exclaimed, looking away in shock and horror.

At just that moment, the boy in question walked through the heavy black doors of Philosophy Hall. Instantly he saw her and smiled his widest grin, showing off his perfectly white, gleaming teeth.

Lorraine breathed a heavy sigh of relief. Marcus had probably sent this fake wedding invitation just to make her jealous. Now he would walk straight over to her, laugh at his elaborate joke, sweep her off her feet, and tell her all was forgiven.

She felt her face break out into a smile as she got to her feet.

'What are you doing?' Melvin asked, but he'd see soon enough.

'Why, hello there, han—'

But Marcus strode past Lorraine and Melvin and onto the quad without a second glance.

He walked straight into the arms of the striking girl from the photo, who'd been waiting behind Lorraine. How had she never noticed this girl before? Could it get any worse? Lorraine wondered.

It could: They kissed in the center of the quad. It went on longer than it should have. Lorraine and Melvin weren't the only people staring. The couple looked amazing together. The

43

girl's hair was a rich auburn that shone like mahogany in the sun. Her annoyingly stylish blue belted Patou dress set off her ivory skin beautifully. With Marcus in his casual but refined V-neck sweater and trousers, they could have been models.

Lorraine got a flash of herself and Marcus back in Chicago, when they used to be friends. When she'd hoped that *she* would be kissing him someday. When she and Gloria were still best friends. How far away that all felt now.

'Why are you standing?' Melvin asked.

After a break for air and then another kiss, the couple walked in the other direction, arm in arm. Lorraine clenched her fingernails into her palms.

'Lorraine, are you all right?' Melvin asked, and tugged at her arm.

'Perfect!' she said in a shrill voice. She slipped the photo, the invitation, and the bills to be forwarded to her father into her purse and handed her trash to Melvin. 'But, um, I have to go.'

'Do you want me to throw this away?' she heard Melvin ask from somewhere behind her. But she couldn't answer.

She marched away as fast as she could and didn't stop until she had reached her dorm room. Her feet were killing her, but at least she didn't have any stairs to climb. Her parents had made sure Lorraine got the largest room available in Brooks Hall, the newest and most luxurious dormitory at Barnard. They'd pushed for a single, but when Lorraine opened the door and saw the second, perfectly made twin bed, she was glad for her roommate.

Becky was neat as a pin and kept up with the chores, like

cleaning and whatever else one did to keep a room looking nice – Lorraine couldn't be bothered with menial tasks. The silky bedspread drooped lazily over the edge of the unmade bed on Lorraine's side of the room, and her bureau was littered with half-empty bottles of perfume, tissues covered with blotted lipstick, and heaps of tangled necklaces and earrings.

Lorraine kicked off her heels and kneeled on her bed. Above it hung a wide bulletin board cluttered with smart ads from *Vogue* and *Harper's Bazaar*. Their models wore dresses Lorraine wanted and some she already owned – she was eager to use her closet to prove that fact as soon as she convinced a friend to come over. Next to the ads was an essay from American History emblazoned with an A[++]. Melvin's braininess was rubbing off on her. She hoped that was the only thing about him that was contagious.

Or maybe Lorraine was only doing so well in school because she didn't have any parties or shopping trips or gossip sessions to occupy her free time. She'd been so confident when she'd marched out onto Lehman Lawn on the first day of orientation for the New Students' Block Party. She'd observed all the Barnard girls in their unfashionably long pastel frocks, standing stick straight and drinking lemonade. They'd probably spent their summers doing nothing more interesting than playing golf with their parents at Martha's Vineyard.

Lorraine, on the other hand, had *real* stories to tell.

But when she'd tried to join Margaret Templeton and Lillian Burnstrom, two heiresses she recognized from the society pages, in conversation, they'd pretended she wasn't even there. As

Lorraine walked away, astonished, she overheard Margaret whispering, 'That's *Lorraine Dyer*. I hear her parents basically disowned her after she got caught working in a third-rate speakeasy this summer.'

'She's the one who got Gloria Carmody arrested!' another girl announced.

The others gasped, and all turned the full power of their glares on Lorraine, the woman who'd dared to oppose their new Patron Saint of Flapperdom. Even the bespectacled, acne-ridden girls wouldn't speak to Lorraine after that.

It was like Laurelton Prep all over again, except now Lorraine didn't have Gloria to lean on.

Lorraine had planned to have her father take a picture of her in front of Brooks Hall with her newfound friends before her parents departed for Chicago the next day. But instead, she'd stood in front of the double doors alone, smiling her widest, brightest smile as her father fussed with the camera.

Now that photo hung on her corkboard, and Lorraine tacked the photograph from the invitation beside it. It was such a good picture of Marcus – a pity that shrew was there, too. Struck with an idea, Lorraine took the invitation out of her bag as well and folded the top of it like the French fan hung artfully on her wall.

She tacked the invitation right next to the photograph so they overlapped a little and she couldn't see the girl in the photograph. (What kind of name was Anastasia, anyway? Was she Russian?) Now there was just Marcus's smooth, handsome face, right next to Lorraine's. From a distance, the two of them looked like a normal, happy couple. Or maybe even just good friends, as Marcus and Lorraine had once been. Marcus's easy charm had quickly made him one of the most popular boys in Columbia's freshman class. With a friend like him, the Barnard girls would overlook Lorraine's Mafioso-ridden past in a heartbeat.

Looking at their photographs, Lorraine vowed that somehow she would get Marcus to forgive her. It wouldn't be easy. Marcus had made it clear that he didn't plan to let Lorraine explain herself any time soon. She'd have to find some other way to get into his good graces.

There was nothing Lorraine loved more than a challenge.

Chapter 5

GLORIA

Sun-dazzled, Gloria reached for the glossy issue of *Life* magazine resting on the patio table beside her. At the last moment her hand latched on to her freshly mixed dirty martini instead.

She took a sip from the crystal glass and sighed. Even her family's old mansion on Astor Street in Chicago paled in comparison to the luxury in which Forrest Hamilton lived on Long Island. A perfect turquoise pool filled the space in front of her, ringed by a white-marble-tiled patio. At the far edge of the patio, stairs led straight down to the beach of Long Island Sound, which was a deeper, more beautiful blue than the water of a pool could ever be.

To the right of Gloria's reclining lawn chair was a sandy beach, where sunbathers lay under colorful umbrellas. And behind her was a broad white pavilion with wicker tables and chairs, where Forrest's guests could grab a bit of shade after too much sun – it was unusually warm this fall. Still felt like summer. There was a bar in the pavilion, with a bartender who looked similar to but was an entirely different person from the other full-time bartender Forrest employed within his enormous villa. Gloria wouldn't make *that* mistake twice.

The girls lounging on either side of Gloria were beautiful. They were both blondes, but one, who called herself Glitz, had nearly white dandelion-fluff hair, while the hair of the girl who called herself Glamour was a burnished gold. Glitz and Glamour wore scandalous Annette Kellerman swimsuits with plunging necklines and only tiny shorts to cover their tanned legs.

Gloria *might* have felt like a prude in her modest black swimsuit with its delicate overskirt, but on the other side of Glamour, Ruby Hayworth was sunbathing in an almost identical suit – only hers was sapphire blue. What was good enough for Ruby was good enough for her, Gloria decided.

Ruby let out a heavy sigh and put down the thin script she'd been reading. 'Ugh, this musical Marty's been bugging me to read is just horrible.'

'I don't know why you don't sign on to do Forrest's musical already,' Glamour replied in her low, sultry voice. 'You'd make him the happiest man on Long Island.'

'You wouldn't have to do his *musical* to do that,' Glitz added with a suggestive waggle of her eyebrows.

All four of them laughed.

A little embarrassed, Ruby just shook her head. 'Marty says this is a very important time in my career. I have to consider all my options.' She dug through her canvas beach bag and frowned adorably. The girl probably even looked pretty when she cried. 'Drat. I left the other script in my room, and I need to let Marty know what I think by tonight.' Ruby smoothed back her dark hair, still damp from a recent dip in the pool, and laced up her bathing slippers. 'Enjoy the sun, ladies.'

49

Ruby made her way across the lawn, and Glamour and Glitz leaned close.

'I can't believe the leash that husband of hers keeps her on,' Glitz observed, her lavender-blue eyes narrowed. 'Forcing her to work on vacation! Wettest blanket I've ever met. And I've dated *politicians*,' she added dramatically. 'I really don't know what she sees in him.'

'A whole lot of green – *that's* what Ruby sees in Marty,' Glamour said. She gulped down her third gin and tonic of the morning. 'Her show needed financing and he needed a pretty dame. Bingo!'

'So she doesn't love him?' Gloria asked. 'She only married him for her career?' Gloria had only known the actress a few days but Ruby didn't strike her as the gold-digging type.

'I should do that!' Glitz called out. 'It's as good a reason as any to shackle yourself to a man, eh, Glam?'

'Sure, but it only works if you *have* a career in the first place,' Glamour replied.

'Hey!' Glitz exclaimed with a pout. 'I'm a model.'

'A model *rube*. You were in *one* magazine.'

'It sold out!'

'Only because those biddies from the Women's Christian Temperance League bought all the copies to burn those pictures of you in that sheer skirt.'

Glitz gave a delighted giggle. 'There's no such thing as bad publicity, Glam.'

Glamour straightened her red polka-dotted swimming cap and peered at Gloria. 'Maybe *you* should marry some fat cat who produces musicals. I'd suggest Forrest, but he only has eyes for Ruby. She just leads him on and he follows her around like a puppy.'

'A puppy with a diamond collar!' Glitz chimed in.

Gloria worked hard to match their smiles with one of her own. But it wasn't easy. All this talk of marriage kept turning her eyes toward her own empty left ring finger. On her release from prison, Jerome's engagement ring had been returned to Gloria. But Hank had forbidden her to wear it around Forrest.

'His lips won't be anywhere near as loose around you if he knows you're off the market,' Hank had said.

So now Gloria could wear the ring only when she went to bed at night, strung on a gold chain around her neck. Each morning she deposited the ring in the drawer of the oak vanity in her room. And each night she slipped it on before going to sleep.

After five days in Great Neck, the huge guest room had already started to feel like home. The mattress on the four-poster bed was cloud soft, and the artwork on the walls was strange and beautiful – 'By this young Spaniard named Picasso,' Forrest told her. But Gloria would've gladly gone back to the lumpy bed with its poky springs in her old Harlem apartment if it meant she could fall asleep each night in the circle of Jerome's arms.

She hadn't intended to stay longer than a day at Forrest's villa. But without even asking her permission, Forrest and the girls had sent a telegram to the prison to request that Gloria's things be sent to Great Neck. 'What do I even have this huge house for if I can't fill it with talented young things in need of a place to stay?' Forrest had remarked.

Gloria had been shocked when a huge steamer trunk arrived on Forrest's doorstep a day later. In the privacy of her room, she opened the chest to find the most resplendent dresses she'd ever seen. One silver sheath dress looked like it was woven out of moonlight, and there were high, sparkling heels to match. Another was short, black, and had a generous slit in the back. It was maddeningly sexy in its simplicity. Gloria looked at the labels and felt she was reuniting with a troupe of old girl-friends: Coco Chanel, Madeleine Vionnet, Jeanne Paquin, and the Boué Soeurs.

Along with the chest came a note in annoyingly neat hand-writing:

Here are your weapons, kid. Now go knock 'em dead.

And so here she was, until she found out whatever she could that would satiate Hank and the FBI about Forrest.

Speaking of Forrest . . . Gloria looked up as he walked across the lawn and onto the patio. Surely he must have been the best-looking Broadway producer in the business – not that she cared whether he was handsome, of course.

He wore a gray seersucker suit with a crisp white shirt. His tie was dark blue, and a white handkerchief peeked out of his pocket. His cheeks were freshly shaven. 'Good morning, ladies! I expected to find you enjoying the pool in this heat.'

Glamour rolled over onto her stomach. 'The water would ruin my tan. And you're one to talk in that heavy jacket. How about you throw on your swim trunks and join us?'

'I'd love to, but just now I'm off to the bookstore to stock my library.'

'Ugh, that big empty room is so gloomy,' Glitz observed.

'Oh, but it'll be much less gloomy once the shelves are filled!' Forrest's brown eyes glinted under his trilby hat. 'Any of you ladies care to take a break from sunbathing to come along?'

Glitz cocked her head to the side. 'That depends. Will there be drinking?'

'Only the drinking of knowledge,' Forrest answered with a smile free from irony.

'I like my knowledge with a side of schnapps,' Glitz said.

'But bringing liquor into a bookstore – that's like carrying a flask into a church!' Forrest exclaimed with a playful curve to his lips but sincerity in his eyes. 'Actually, it's worse. I'd probably do that second thing. I plan to enjoy these books for a good long time. If we pick them out zozzled, I'll probably end up with a library full of terrible books with hilarious titles.'

Gloria smiled. She'd never seen a man so excited about books. Forrest should've been a complete contradiction – a man with a serious love of literature who also had a mansion full of dissolute young things with names like Glitz and Glamour. But he managed to walk the tightrope between intellectual and playboy beautifully, and be all the more likable for it. Gloria leaped out of her lawn chair. 'I'll go! I haven't got much of a tan to work on anyway.'

Forrest offered his arm. 'Then we'll head back to the house so you can get changed.' Once they were out of earshot of the two blondes, Forrest said, 'Between you and me, I've always found pale skin far more attractive.'

Gloria blushed. 'Ruby has lovely skin,' she said quickly. 'Will she and her husband be coming along, too?'

'I wish she could – she always has some new author or poet to recommend to me.' The words tumbled out of Forrest's mouth. For all his usual self-assurance, Forrest shifted into an overeager boy whenever he spoke of Ruby. 'Like that T. S. Eliot fellow! I'd never heard of him till Ruby lent me a book of his poems. Now I've read it through about a dozen times. But Ruby's too busy reading scripts all day to come with us. With Marty looking over her shoulder, no doubt.'

Gloria frowned. Hank could send her all the sequined and gold lamé masterpieces he wanted, but it seemed that Forrest only had eyes for someone else: Ruby Hayworth.

So how exactly was Gloria going to stay out of jail?

Forrest groaned. 'Oh, not that Fitzgerald kid again! I could barely stay awake through his first book. So overrated.'

'*This Side of Paradise* wasn't really my cup of tea, either.' Gloria waved the book in her hand. 'This one is different, though. It's about flappers.' She thought of her friends in the city. What was Clara up to now? And that viper Lorraine – Gloria would be happy never to see her again.

Forrest took the copy of *The Beautiful and Damned,* opened it, and read the inside flap. 'I think you only like it because the leading lady has your name.'

Gloria laughed. 'From what I hear, her name might as well be Zelda.' The two continued down the aisles of Scribner's, commenting on leather-bound volumes they had read, wanted to read, or would never, ever read even under threat of death. 'You're one to talk about boring literature. You're buying a book of Sherlock Holmes stories!'

'What could ever be boring about the life of London's most brilliant detective?' Forrest asked.

'So predictable! I don't recall Fitzgerald ending every one of his stories with the hero emerging from a cloud of opium smoke, magically ready to save the day.'

'Mmm, that's exactly my problem with him.'

Gloria laughed again. Much as she tried to focus on getting information out of Forrest, it was hard to do anything but enjoy herself.

'I like you, Gloria,' Forrest observed, echoing her thoughts. 'It's nice to talk to a girl who knows she can use her brain for more than pairing shoes with the right dress.'

Gloria smiled. She had actually spent a considerable amount of time choosing the right pumps to go with her floral day dress. 'I like you, too, Forrest.'

And it was true: She did like Forrest. His sudden wealth might have been suspicious, but this sweet, earnest boy was a world away from the money-grubbing gangsters Gloria had tangled with for the past year.

'We have a lot in common,' Forrest went on. 'We've both taken the hard route in life.' He casually hooked his arm through hers. 'Followed our hearts no matter what – even when the people close to us sold their dreams for thirty pieces of silver.'

Gloria blinked, unsure of his meaning. 'Forrest, what do you—?'

But he had already abandoned her for another tall maple bookcase. Gloria sighed. Whenever Forrest got close to saying something the least bit personal about himself, he was always off on some new tack the very next second. Was he just easily distracted, or was there something more sinister at work? She let out another sigh and followed him.

Forrest held up a thick volume and handed it to Gloria. 'Now *I* have a book for *you*,' he said triumphantly.

A Passage to India, the cover read at the top, and, below, *E. M. Forster,* in red against an off-white background.

Gloria turned it over in her hands, frowning. 'I'm not really much for traveling narratives . . .'

'It's not that at all, though! It's all about the terrible way the British have been treating the Indians ever since they took over the country.'

'Oh! Well, I guess that could be interesting.'

'Forster's got real courage,' Forrest explained, leading her farther down the aisle. 'While Fitzgerald spins his dizzy parties, this man writes about what really matters. He's willing to tackle the bigotry and ugliness in other parts of the world.'

She gave a grim chuckle, thinking of Jerome, how people

glared at him on the street. Of the way they'd had to sneak around to live together. 'A lot of that goes on right here in America. Too bad no one's writing about *that*.'

Gloria glanced at the floor, her heartbeat quickening. She hadn't meant to sound so bitter.

But when Forrest's eyes flicked toward her, they were full of sympathy. 'You're right. Maybe that writer cousin of yours could write a book about you and Jerome Johnson.'

Gloria raised her eyebrows and felt her stomach twitter – hearing Jerome's name come out of Forrest's mouth seemed wrong. 'When we met I got the feeling you didn't know much about my case.'

'I didn't. But I've read up on you. And I think what you've done is inspiring. I'm sure a lot of people wish they could be as brave as you.' He stared right at her for a moment, as if about to say something, then looked away. 'How is your piano player, by the way? He's welcome to post letters to you here, I hope you know.'

Gloria had never heard someone with Forrest's skin color sound so open to the idea of her relationship with Jerome. She knew Hank would want her to say she'd broken things off with Jerome – so Forrest would think she was available – but she couldn't help telling the truth. 'I haven't heard from him in nearly two weeks.' She exhaled slowly. 'I'm so worried about him.'

Forrest patted her shoulder. 'Oh, Gloria, I'm sorry.'

'I know it's not that long, really, but—'

'Are you kidding? I bet he used to write you every day. I

know I would if I had a girl like you.' He paused and scratched his chin. 'It must have been hard for him to see you behind bars. Maybe that's why you haven't heard from him recently.'

'Jerome wasn't allowed to visit me in jail, and neither was his sister, Vera.'

'You're close with Jerome's sister?'

'We didn't exactly get along at first. But when she got back to Chicago, she wrote to apologize for how wrong she'd been about me. And then I wrote her back, and she wrote me back, and now we've got a big stack of letters between us. Vera's a wonderful girl, once you get past that top layer of sass.'

'Oh, I remember Vera from the articles! She ran all over New York with that trumpet player looking for the two of you.'

'And now she's going to marry him.' Gloria smiled a little. As hard as the summer had been, Vera and Evan's engagement had been a happy result of it all. 'You paid close attention to those stories, didn't you?'

'It wasn't hard. That Clara Knowles has got some serious wit. You must be proud, huh? Not even twenty and she's already got a serious writing career going.'

'It's not that simple,' Gloria began.

And before she knew it, she was laying out the ups and downs of Clara's life – how she'd been sent to live with Gloria and found true love with Marcus, and then how she'd later lied to him and broken both their hearts. Gloria kept expecting Forrest to grow bored with her stories, but he didn't; he asked questions and seemed to understand just how painful it had been to have two of her closest friends in the world break up and know there was nothing she could do to bring them back together. 'They're tailor made for each other,' Gloria said.

'Sounds like it,' Forrest said with real sympathy.

The more she talked and the longer he listened, the clearer it became to Gloria that Forrest was no villain, no matter what Hank and the FBI believed.

Until Gloria had met Jerome, she'd always been taught that women were meant to be seen and not heard in the presence of men. The way Forrest admired Clara's writing reminded her of how Jerome had encouraged Gloria's singing career. Like Jerome, Forrest seemed convinced that with intelligence and talent, a girl's dreams could take her wherever she cared to go.

'Now Marcus says he's in love with this new girl,' Gloria finished. 'But I'm afraid he's jumping into this marriage too fast.'

'That *is* fast,' Forrest agreed as they approached the cashier at the front of the bookstore. 'But when you get your heart broken . . . it's tough, trying to figure out how you're supposed to put it back together. I think everybody makes mistakes when it comes to that,' he added a little wistfully.

'Like you?' she replied without thinking. 'Sorry, you just sounded like you were speaking from experience. Want to tell me about it? I've been talking so long already.'

Forrest looked at his expensive gold watch. 'Another time, Gloria. We've got to get a wiggle on. But first . . .' He moved to a table with several volumes laid on top. He picked up a book and dropped it into the basket he'd been carrying. Then he walked toward the cashier and took his place in the long line of customers.

Gloria followed. 'What's that last book?'

'That's the book I'm buying for you.'

'Oh, you don't have to. I'm already planning to steal *A Passage to India*.'

He laughed. 'And you're free to borrow it. But I wanted to buy you one to keep.' He pulled the book out of his basket and handed it to her. 'It only just came out, but people are already saying it should snag the Pulitzer for Edna Ferber.'

'*So Big*,' Gloria read on the cover. 'I hope that's not some kind of comment on my looks.'

'God, no, you're too skinny as it is. See, the book's about a girl – a teacher – named Selina. Everyone else thinks getting rich should be the only goal in life, but Selina teaches her kids to follow their dreams.' Forrest paused. 'She reminds me a lot of you.'

Gloria's cheeks flamed. 'Thanks,' she managed to choke out.

When they reached the cashier, Forrest began stacking book after book on the counter. Lastly he slapped down *The Beautiful and Damned*. Gloria was pleased to see he hadn't put it back as she'd thought he would. 'Don't get too excited, Gloria,' Forrest said when he noticed her expression. 'I'm buying this for Ruby. I want her to star in *Moonshine Melody*. I hope this wins her over.'

Gloria watched Forrest's face as he gazed at the book. His features lit up – with hope or love or maybe just the thought of

Ruby. She suspected that Forrest wanted to win more than just Ruby's name on a contract.

He nodded at the elderly cashier and gestured at the books on the counter. 'Now, we'll take all of these, and then I wanted to also order fifty yards of books, chosen by your manager. I spoke to him the other day, and he said he'd fill my library. I don't have time to pick and choose all of the books to fill the shelves. I'll pay on delivery.'

'Of course, sir,' the cashier replied.

Gloria studied Forrest for a moment and decided she liked him. He seemed kind – a gentleman – and was a patron of the arts, which she admired. But also he seemed *real,* as though maybe he, too, knew the struggles of life and love not just from books, but from personal experience.

It was going to be such a shame when she turned him over to the FBI.

Chapter 6

CLARA

'You wouldn't believe it from how she looks in her films, but she's a tiny little thing,' Parker explained, swilling his martini. 'Barely five feet tall.'

'Really?' Clara asked with more interest than she felt.

'Really! But the woman has presence, all right. She may be small, but Gloria Swanson fills every room she enters with that wondrous charisma of hers.'

Why did Parker think his stories needed to be dotted with celebrities to be interesting? It was pathetic. 'Mmm. Was she wearing her peacock feathers when you met her?'

'Ostrich, actually.'

Clara pasted a smile on her face. When she'd first come to New York what felt like a lifetime ago, Parker's association with one of Clara's fashion idols would've earned him at least a dozen points on the potential-beau scale. *He's an absolute sheik*, ex-Clara would have told her girlfriends at home. *He dresses well, he took me to a swanky spot, and he even knows Gloria Swanson.*

But now Clara was seeing things with clearer eyes: So he'd interviewed a celebrity; that was part of his job, wasn't it? What was the big fuss? In the end celebrities were just people like everyone else.

'She'll look fantastic on this month's cover, don't you think?'

he asked, but didn't wait for Clara's response. 'We'll have our highest sales to date, I'm willing to bet.' Parker went on and on, happy to bask in the glow of his own success.

Clara looked out at the other diners. The Colony was Parker's favorite restaurant. It was a lovely place in an understated way – silver sconces on the white wood-paneled walls, ivory pillars, crystal chandeliers hanging from the ceiling. White cloths covered the tables, and vases of poppies stood in the center of each. A person wouldn't even know that the Prohibition amendment had been passed in a spot like this. The restaurant counted too many government officials among its regulars to ever have to worry about a gin bust.

But people didn't come to the Colony for the décor or the booze – they came for the stars. Clara had already spotted two Vanderbilts and three senators. Louise Brooks, the silent-film actress, demurely sipped a glass of amber liquid at a corner table, the ends of her short, dark bob flawless against her porcelain cheeks.

Perhaps the banquette getting the most looks was that of Babe Ruth, the famed baseball player and unofficial King of New York. The big man looked as at home in a suit as he did in his Yankees uniform. He had his arm around the beautiful young girl sitting beside him – a girl who was definitely *not* his wife.

Clara had wanted to sit in one of the upholstered banquettes in the back, but Parker had been quick to request the table by the window – where all the patrons couldn't help but see them on walking through the restaurant's double doors.

For what seemed like the thousandth time that evening, someone walked over to the table. 'Parker, old boy! How are you?' The man speaking was young and handsome, with a doe-eyed girl on his arm. The girl was far too young to be wearing so many diamonds.

Parker sprang from his seat. 'Robert Paddington! Clara, this is an old college buddy of mine, plays the Wall Street game now. Robert, you'll be pleased to meet Clara Knowles. Remember all the stories we used to hear about her?'

Robert reached over to kiss Clara's hand. 'The Queen of the Shebas, of course! Looking as beautiful as the stories say.'

'Thank you.' Her sleeveless black silk crepe evening dress had bands of Oriental-patterned gold lamé and a two-tiered hem. The neckline was respectably high, but wide armholes gave just the right flash of skin whenever Clara moved to lift her martini.

'That's right! She and I are together now,' Parker said, puffing his chest out proudly. First a degree from Columbia, then a career as a successful magazine editor, then a famous flapper for a girlfriend: all stepping-stones to becoming the rich and interesting man that Parker so longed to be.

'We *work* together,' Clara corrected. A few fancy dinners – most of which were spent discussing work – did not make the two of them a couple, not in her book.

While Parker made small talk with Robert and his lady friend, Clara's thoughts drifted back to a dinner date nowhere near as sophisticated as this one. It had been a week after Clara had arrived in New York. She and Marcus had lounged on the

East River ferry, quietly baking underneath the afternoon sun.

'Now you can proudly tell your friends that you've been inside the Statue of Liberty!' Marcus had exclaimed with an arm slung over her shoulder. 'Explored her every nook and cranny. Compromised her virtue by climbing—'

'Marcus!' Clara swatted him and laughed. She peered out at the aquamarine statue, which was slowly becoming smaller and smaller. 'I like it much more at a distance. Up close it's just stairs, stairs, and more stairs.'

'With a fantastic view at the top, though, you have to admit.'

'And a fantastically hot sun pounding down on us,' Clara replied, tired and cranky. While very fashionable, cloche hats did next to nothing to protect a girl against sunburn. 'Be honest – am I red all over?'

Marcus turned to her, put his hands on her shoulders, and surveyed her. 'Yes. Red as a ripe tomato.' He kissed one of her cheeks lightly with his velvet-soft lips. 'You are quite possibly the most hideous sight I've ever seen.' He kissed her other cheek. 'You should be glad there are no children on this boat. Their screams would be deafening! The horror!'

'You're one to talk,' Clara said, and flicked his red nose.

'Ouch!'

'You look like a dipsomaniac. Or like you have a fever.' Sunburned Marcus might have been even more adorable than Regular Marcus.

'Just the fever of my love for you, darling,' he replied with a grin. Then he gave her a kiss that made her forget all about her sunburn.

When they reached shore, they were too tired to journey back to Brooklyn Heights to look for a proper restaurant. 'We probably shouldn't expose you to respectable society, as a courtesy,' Marcus said.

So they found a dingy joint near the Fulton Ferry Landing, where they had a dinner of greasy burgers, a bucket of fries, and a shared chocolate milk shake.

The food was delicious in the way only cheap, greasy food could be. Through the restaurant's smudged windows, they watched the sun set behind the Manhattan skyline and the way the streetlights glinted off the water. Afterward they walked across the Brooklyn Bridge, and when they reached the first of the arches, Marcus kissed her with only the moon and river as an audience.

The entire date had cost about as much as Clara's appetizer at the Colony. It had been one of the best dates Clara had ever had – magical exactly because it was so ordinary.

Now, Clara peered across the table at handsome, tedious Parker, who was rehashing the Gloria Swanson story for his college buddy. Unlike Parker, Marcus couldn't have cared less about movie stars or celebrities or Clara's old, raucous life. He only wanted to be with her because of *her*: the person Clara hadn't even been sure was actually there beneath all the glitter. Marcus had showed her that she was still real and interesting once all the witty double-talk and sideways glances were stripped away.

And she had let him go. Now he was marrying someone else.

Parker's friends finally left. 'I'm about finished with my pheasant – how about you?'

Clara nodded. 'Yes, it was delicious.'

'Shall I order you another martini before we head out?' He raised his glass to her. 'They're the very best in the city.'

Clara drained the last sip of her drink. 'Are they, now? They're a little cloudy for my taste, really.'

He hiked an eyebrow and grinned. Parker, it seemed, was the sort of man who loved a dissatisfied woman. Clara had found that young men who came to early, large success with comparatively little struggle usually did. 'Hmm. Well, I just got a silver-plated shaker and haven't had the chance to test it out yet. Shall we try to give the Colony a run for its money?'

Just a few moments ago Clara had been eagerly awaiting the end of the date. But the image of Marcus and his perfect little fiancée popped up in her mind. The Marcus who'd kissed her sunburned cheeks was lost to her now. Clara could be heart-broken alone, or she could have some company. Even if that company *was* Parker.

'All right,' she said. 'But there will be no shaking. I'm a girl who likes her martinis stirred.'

Clara had thought the view from Parker's office was good, but the view from his apartment put it to shame.

Through the many floor-to-ceiling windows in Parker's living room Clara could see the wide expanse of Central Park and the lights of the city floating around it. The room was filled with oak bookcases, and framed articles hung on the walls. A long leather couch curved in an L-shape across a Persian rug, and the dimmed lighting gave everything a lush, classy feel. Parker was a man with real taste. There was no question about that.

'Gorgeous, isn't it?' Parker stood uncomfortably close to her in front of the window, his arm pressing against hers. 'I had a bidding war with Richard Whitney from the New York Stock Exchange over this place, you know. He put up some real cabbage, but I won in the end. I couldn't lose out on this view.'

God, did he ever stop bragging? 'Yeah, it's jake,' she mumbled, bored.

'So, how's that cousin of yours doing since we sprang her from the big house?'

Clara shrugged and moved over to put some distance between them. 'She's out of town, so I haven't heard much from her.' Just a postcard from Long Island: *I'll be out of the city for a while – can't really say why – but I'm doing fine and I miss you!* 'She's taking the train into the city for a day week after next and we have plans to get lunch – I'll give you an update then.'

'Just a day? What for?'

'She has a dress fitting for this wedding she's in,' Clara replied. She hoped Parker didn't ask her *whose* wedding. Talking to Parker about Marcus was the last thing she wanted to do right now.

'Oh, the Eastman wedding?' Parker asked, twisting something in Clara's chest. 'How is that old beau of yours?'

'I wouldn't know,' Clara said curtly.

'The sap's probably busy flunking his way out of Columbia. Family money can only take you so far – unless he hires someone else to sit his exams for him.'

Clara scowled. Marcus was one of the cleverest people she knew. When they'd been together she'd loved nothing more than wandering through the Brooklyn Museum with him and listening to his commentary.

On one visit they'd stopped in front of a painting of a worried-looking oarsman in a top hat, rowing down a river. 'I wonder what he's thinking about,' Clara had said.

'Well, that's obvious,' Marcus replied. 'It's windy, and he's wishing he could hold his top hat on his head to keep it from flying off. But he needs both arms for rowing! Poor man. That's why I could never be an oarsman – I'm nothing without *my* top hat.'

And yet in front of a painting by Frederick Childe Hassam of New York in winter, Marcus had been serious. 'We'll have to come back and look at this again once it's snowing outside. We'll be so tempted to complain about the cold and chill that we'll forget how lucky we are to be here for it. But look at it! New York's at its best covered in snow. Sometimes you need paintings to remind you to enjoy life's beauty, you know?'

But Clara and Marcus hadn't even made it through the summer. If Marcus went back to look at that Hassam painting during the winter, he'd be doing it with his wife.

'Shouldn't we be drinking martinis about now?' Clara

needed some booze to flush Marcus's handsome face from her mind.

'Let me just chill the glasses.' Parker leaned in for a kiss, but she turned her head so he caught her cheek instead. It might have been a mistake to come here. She and Parker had never kissed, and Clara was beginning to think that she didn't want that to change.

While Parker was off in the kitchen, Clara crossed into the wood-paneled study. She was surprised at the towers of old letters, papers, and invitations heaped over the oak surface of the desk. Parker was fastidiously neat in the office – it was nice to see a bit of disorder in his sleek, polished life. With barely a scruple she picked up one of the smaller piles and shuffled through it.

She paused when she reached an already-ripped-open envelope with an invitation lying on top.

Celebrate the theater, art, love, and life!
Forrest Hamilton invites
Parker Richards and Clara Knowles
to join him for a night of revelry
at 8:00 p.m.
on September 13, 1924
at 6 Shorecliff Place, Great Neck, Long Island

Clara picked up the envelope and saw that it was dated August 5 – back when Clara had still responded to Parker's each and every dinner invitation with a resounding no. She clenched the invitation in a tight grip and fought the urge to tear it into pieces. Parker had been bragging to this Forrest character and Lord knew who else that he had managed to bag the Queen of the Flappers.

Clara had known that her editor was arrogant and self-satisfied, but this was a whole other level. Who else had Parker told about this 'relationship' of theirs? And what had he said? He must've made things out to be pretty serious between them if someone was putting *both* their names on a party invitation.

'Clara,' Parker called from the living room. 'Where did you disappear to?'

She took a few deep breaths, then smoothed a mask of cheeky flirtation over her displeasure. She sauntered back into the living room. 'You didn't offer me a tour, so I had to give myself one.'

Parker was standing behind the expansive oak bar against the wall. He'd laid his navy blazer over one of the leather-upholstered barstools and stood in just his trousers and a silky burgundy shirt. Parker's dark brows were drawn in concentration over his pale green eyes. The martini shaker stood on the bar with its lid off, next to a bowl of ice and two unmarked bottles. He lifted one of the bottles and put it down, then lifted the other.

Clara was amused by his floundering. 'Parker Richards. You don't know how to make a martini, do you?'

He smiled back. 'But I'm *very* good at ordering them.'

She joined him behind the bar and picked up the shaker.

71

'You do realize this makes me more of a man than you are.'

'You look remarkably good in that dress, then, considering.'

Showing Parker how to mix martinis might have been fun if Clara hadn't been consumed by the urge to throw her drink in his pompous face once she was finished. And once he was soaked in gin and vermouth, Clara would berate Parker for his idiotic presumptions and the lies he'd spread about the nature of their relationship. She would tell him that she hardly even liked him – and that she could never be even a fraction as in love with him as he was with himself.

But instead, she showed him how adding a dash of orange bitters made all the difference to a martini. And when he mentioned Forrest's party on Saturday, Clara feigned complete ignorance.

As satisfying as it would be to get her revenge now, Clara couldn't forget the fact that Parker *was* her boss. Throwing a drink in his face would definitely be grounds for dismissal. Without the income from her column, Clara would barely be able to get by. Not to mention the fact that if Parker fired her, her writing career would be over practically before it had begun.

So she'd have to be crafty about it. She'd go to this Great Neck party. She'd don her flapper best and flutter her lashes at all Parker's rich, influential friends.

But soon enough, Parker would wish he'd never met Clara. Much less claimed to date her.

Chapter 7

LORRAINE

'You make the best coffee in New York, Becks,' Lorraine remarked, rising from her bed to accept the steaming mug from her roommate. 'Or at least, you make the best coffee in this dormitory.'

Becky tucked her yellow curls behind her ears and smiled. She sat on her own bed, neatly settled her pink pleated skirt over her legs, and took a sip from her own mug. 'Thank you. I'll have to bake my shortbread to go with it next time.'

'Ha! Shortbread!' Lorraine exclaimed, slapping her knee. 'You and your jokes.'

Becky raised an eyebrow. 'I'm being serious, though, I absolutely *love*—'

'Okay, okay,' Lorraine said, cutting Becky off. 'Enough with the jokes, I might throw up from laughing so much.'

Lorraine had expected the worst when she'd met her blonde roommate nearly a month earlier. She wasn't a beauty – certainly not an exotic one like Lorraine – but her dimples and tiny nose were nearly head-cheerleader adorable. Lorraine had been sure Becky would reject her modern ways and innovative fashion sense just the way the debs in Chicago had. But Becky turned out to be absolutely hilarious. Like those shortbread jokes – hysterical!

Becky was committed, too – she covered every surface on her side of the room with lace doilies and owned a whopping *five* aprons. Someone who didn't know her as well as Lorraine would think Becky actually liked all this matronly hooey. But the rumors of Lorraine's mob past that caused other Barnard girls to turn up their noses didn't seem to faze Becky one bit. So Becky couldn't possibly be a real Mrs. Grundy – she was just an amazing comedienne.

'You know what would go even better with this coffee than shortbread?' Lorraine looked through the open window at the quad, where a group of girls lounged on a picnic blanket. They were giggling so loudly that they had to be sneaking sips from a flask. Either that or they were crazy people, and a respectable institution like Barnard didn't accept crazy people. 'A shot of brandy, maybe two.'

Becky rolled her brown eyes. 'Lorraine, you know we can't risk getting caught drinking in the dormitory.'

Lorraine set her mug on her cluttered end table and lay back on the floral bedspread. 'I can't help it! It's Saturday – everyone knows this is a day for drinking!'

'It's Saturday *morning*.'

'Still. If those mob rumors killed any hope I had for a social life, then this Drought is dancing on its grave.' Lorraine hadn't frequented a gin joint since school started, though not for a lack of trying. All the police in New York knew Lorraine as a shady character, while speakeasy proprietors thought she was a rat. Most of them had her picture on the wall, reminding the burly men who guarded the doors *not* to let her in – which was so tragically unfair, seeing as how it wasn't even a flattering picture.

Lorraine had initially named the dry spell 'The Great Drought of 1924.' But that was kind of a mouthful, especially considering how often she complained about it. This unfortunate period could go back to its original name when she wrote her memoirs.

Lorraine had hoped her summer spent managing the Opera House would *improve* her popularity at Barnard. 'Hey, look!' everyone would exclaim. 'There goes the dame who helped the bureau catch those mobsters! I knew she was brave, but I never expected her to be beautiful, too!' But that lying phony Clara Knowles had destroyed Lorraine's chances. Thanks to the not-so-flattering articles Clara wrote for the *Manhattanite,* the popular girls at Barnard wanted nothing to do with Lorraine. And why? Because Lorraine had wanted revenge against everyone's new favorite flapper, Gloria Carmody.

What a joke. If anyone would listen, Lorraine would explain that *she* was the flapper queen. Gloria hadn't even bobbed her hair until Lorraine made her! Gloria hadn't known how to dance anything other than a boring old box step! Gloria had worn dresses that went down to her ankles! Until Lorraine stepped in and saved her. But now people acted like Gloria was some kind of . . . hero. It was enough to make a girl want to punch someone.

'I think taking some time away from booze has been good for you,' Becky observed. 'You're so far ahead on all our coursework and reading – you even managed to finish *Paradise Lost* early, isn't that right?'

Lorraine nodded. 'I wish I'd paradise *lost* my copy of it,' she muttered, waiting for Becky to laugh. When she didn't, it only made Lorraine want a drink even more. 'Maybe then I'd have had an excuse not to read all ten million pages of it.'

'You've got to admit sobriety has given you a lot more free time.'

'Yeah, *too much* free time.' Lorraine picked up a white woven pillow and tossed it onto her roommate's bed. 'I'm knitting, Becks. *Knitting*.'

The truth was that Lorraine was actually very good at school – there had always been so many distractions, though, and why study biology in a textbook when you could get up close and personal with an actual boy? Sadly, Lorraine had more than enough time on her hands these days to excel academically. Oh, how she wished she could change that!

' "They say a clean conscience makes a soft pillow, but this one suits me fine",' Becky read from the embroidery on the pillow and giggled. 'That's funny, Raine!'

'It would be funnier if we were drunk,' Lorraine replied. 'Have you heard about any parties or anything? Just because we have all the same classes doesn't mean you have to be my warden, you know.'

Becky gave her a long, hard look. 'Well, it *is* the weekend.' A slow smile appeared on her face. 'And since you're persona non grata in the city, why not come out with me to Long Island?'

'It sounds *long*. As in *and boring*.'

'Only if you go to the wrong parties. The real shoe spinners are on the estates out there, and tonight there's a big to-do down in Great Neck. You heard of a fellow called Forrest Hamilton?'

Lorraine caught her reflection in the mirror and fluffed her bob. 'The Broadway producer? Sure.' The society pages were thick these days with photos of and stories about the handsome young entrepreneur.

'Well, the party's at his house.'

Lorraine raised her eyebrows. 'And *you're* invited? Why did he invite *you*?' Sure, Becky had a more thriving social life than Lorraine's, but study groups and coffee klatches didn't count, did they? Who would've expected Becky to have such an impressive acquaintance? 'Becks, you've been holding out on me!'

Becky laughed. 'Not exactly. My friend Dorothy's brother starred in *Bug-Eyed Betty,* Forrest's first show, and he was able to snag us invitations. Dorothy says it's going to be the biggest bash since Sodom and Gomorrah got burned up.'

Raine leaped from her bed to hug Becky, nearly spilling coffee all over her roommate's pristine bedspread. Finally, a *real* night out! 'Thank you, thank you, thank you! You have no idea the public service you're doing.' She sat down beside Becky. 'Without you I probably would've been stuck studying flash cards with Melvin.'

'Oh, right, your friend from Columbia. You should invite him along! He's cute.'

Lorraine almost choked on her coffee. 'Seriously, Becks, you should go down to the Ziegfeld and try out your comedy act there. That stuff is gold! You and Eddie Cantor will be best pals in no time.'

Becky crossed her arms and pouted. 'I'm being serious! Maybe he's not a big six or anything, but you've got to admit Melvin's got a handsome face.'

'You can't even see his face behind those enormous glasses,' Lorrain muttered. She tried to imagine Melvin wandering among the glittering young things in his bow tie and sweater vest. 'Trust me. He'll be much happier with the flash cards.'

Besides, she wouldn't want to be seen with Melvin if Marcus happened to be at the party. Not that she was still thinking about him . . . *that* much.

'He has a car, though, doesn't he? Dorothy and I were planning to take the train out, but it would be so much more stylish if we drove. Plus we might need someone to get us home safely if we get too tight,' Becky said.

'Good point.' Always thinking, that Becky! No matter how sweet and dopey she might look, the girl had some real smarts underneath all those curls.

'It'll be such fun!' Becky exclaimed, and her small lips stretched into a gleeful smile. She clapped her dainty little hands. 'We'll dance the Collegiate Shag and show those starched shirts how to cut a rug.'

Lorraine narrowed her eyes. She'd once prided herself on knowing all the hottest new dances, but that had been in the pre-Drought days. 'How does that one go again?'

Becky stuck out her lip and blew her bangs off her forehead. 'Honestly, Lorraine, how can you have worked in a club and not learned it?'

She popped up from her bed and took Lorraine's hand

to pull her up as well. She raised her left arm. 'Okay, you need to hold your right arm so your elbow is touching my left elbow.'

Lorraine did so but felt awkward. 'Are you sure? That's a lot higher than couples usually hold their arms . . .'

'Mmm-hmm – that way your arms don't get in the way of all the hopping around in the dance.' Becky did a zippy combination of kicks and hops on her own and put all doubt out of Lorraine's mind. Becky was a surprisingly good dancer, and Lorraine couldn't wait to show the bouncy dance off on the floor.

She put one hand on Becky's shoulder and held her other hand. Then she began to follow her roommate through the steps.

'Well, no, you kick your legs *behind* you when we're close like this, Raine,' Becky said when Lorraine whacked her in the shin. 'Let's try again.'

They pulled apart and held hands, and now Becky said she was allowed to kick forward. Becky spun her around and Lorraine nearly ran straight into her. 'Maybe we should go slower . . .'

Lorraine continued dancing without Becky, swinging her legs back and forth. 'No, I think I'm catching on just fine!'

'Well, that's *better,*' Becky said. 'What you need to remember is . . .' Her eyes fixed on something behind Lorraine. She gave a low whistle. 'Who's the Handsome Dan? Does he go to Columbia? I feel like I've seen him around.'

Lorraine followed her roommate's eyes to the photo of

Marcus tacked to the bulletin board above her bed. 'Oh, that's Marcus Eastman.' She paused. How to explain Marcus Eastman to Becky? How did Lorraine even explain Marcus to herself? 'He's an old . . . friend. A *very close* friend.' She stopped again. Had they ever been more than friends? Lorraine had certainly wanted them to be. And Becky didn't know one way or the other, did she? 'We have *a lot* of history together,' she added. Would it be too much to wink?

Becky scanned the wedding invitation and sighed. 'Wow, the *Plaza*? Did every wedding invite have a photograph? That's rich business. This swell must have a lot of dough.'

'Mmm, no extravagance is too extravagant for old Lillian and George,' Lorraine said, as though she and the Eastmans were particularly close. 'Even their servants are dipped in gold.'

Becky pulled the photo down and examined it. A wrinkle appeared between her pale brows. 'What is he doing with Deirdre Van Doren? She's a total gold digger. She tried to get Francis Chase to marry her, but only for his money. He's none too sharp, but even he got smart to her ways and got rid of her.'

Lorraine's ears pricked up. Deirdre Van Doren – who was that? 'But that's not her name.' Lorraine unfolded the invitation. 'See? Her name's Anastasia Rijn.' She cocked her head. 'Do you think you're supposed to pronounce the *j*?'

Becky let out a tiny cough. 'I think you can pronounce it however you want because that's not her name. I'll bet you dollars to doughnuts that this girl is Deirdre Van Doren.' Becky glanced down at the silver watch wound around her wrist. 'Well, anyway, we should get going in a few hours and I still need to pick up my dress from the tailor. Don't forget to invite Melvin!'

As Becky scurried out the door, Lorraine looked back at the invitation in her hands. What in the world was Marcus getting himself into?

Oh, how Lorraine had missed slipping into the perfect party dress!

Her fingers hungrily climbed over the gold lamé, deep green satin, pale rose silk chiffon, sparkling silver sequins, and fluffy black feathers that lived inside her closet . . .

In the end she pulled out a fire-engine-red number covered entirely in tiers of fringe. The bodice dipped into a low V in the front and back, and the skirt barely reached her knees. It was one of the more scandalous dresses Lorraine owned and was perfect for her brief return to the wild life she'd missed so much these past weeks.

She barely recognized the raven-haired, oxblood-lipped, sophisticated flapper who greeted her in the mirror. She loved the way the light caught her dangling diamond earrings, how her bob curved against her cheek and softened the sharp angles of her face. Lorraine still had it after a few weeks of forced retirement. She could hardly wait to see the reactions of the boys at the party.

Becky was adorable in a vanilla silk chiffon dress. Rhinestones dripped along the dress's neckline and dropped waist. Ho hum! Her roommate was cute, but she was certainly not the sultry vixen Lorraine saw when she looked at herself in the mirror. Becky would get all the dull, wholesome suitors, while the more intriguing boys would be entranced by Lorraine's irresistible mystique.

Or that was the plan, anyway.

The two girls stood in front of the wide mirror to put the finishing touches on their makeup, and Becky glanced at Lorraine. 'I can't wait!' Becky said, settling a pearl headband over her short hair. 'Do you have some pearl earrings to go with this?'

'Top right drawer of my desk.'

Becky opened the drawer and began to search through it. 'You should really try to organize your things better, Raine. How do you ever find anything?' She pulled a pair of antique opera glasses out of the drawer. 'And what on earth are these for?'

Lorraine laughed. 'My parents practically forced them on me, along with their season tickets to the Met. I never *could* understand why people get so excited about watching a boring musical.'

'Ah, here they are,' Becky said, holding a pair of pearl studs triumphantly. 'I hope we find some fellows with shiny hair tonight. How about you, Raine? What do you like most in a man?'

'A pulse,' Lorraine answered, making Becky laugh.

But it was true. After weeks of no one but Melvin for male company (and he barely counted), any of the upper-class party guests would do for a bit of necking. Besides, Forrest

Hamilton was a rich, handsome man. It stood to reason that his friends would be rich and handsome as well. For a second, she thought of Hank – how he'd kissed her underneath the overturned boat in Central Park, told her she was beautiful.

But that had all been one big lie.

Lorraine glanced at the photo invitation on the bulletin board one more time. If what Becky said was true, Marcus couldn't know his fiancée very well. Maybe *this* was how she would get him to forgive her. If she saved Marcus from a sham marriage, he'd be so grateful he'd *have* to be her friend again, right?

Lorraine missed the days she, Gloria, and Marcus used to spend walking through Astor Square Park or lounging around the Carmody mansion, gossiping and joking. She might never get Gloria back, but there was still hope for her and Marcus.

And once the Barnard girls and Columbia boys saw her palling around with Marcus, they would want – nay, *beg* to be her friend!

She would find out the dirt on this Anastasia woman as soon as she got back to New York. But now was the time for fun, at long last.

'Are you ready to go, Raine?' Becky asked.

Lorraine snapped her black beaded purse shut. 'Ready?' she asked with a smile. 'I think the better question would be: Is this party ready for *me*?'

Chapter 8

GLORIA

Gloria could feel sweet jazz pulsing through the walls.

She leaned against one of the many maple bookcases in Forrest Hamilton's library, listening to the sounds of the party next door. She'd felt so glamorous when she'd left the guest room twenty minutes earlier, outfitted in her favorite of all the dresses Hank had sent: a Boué Soeurs dress of the deepest pink, which brought out the rosiness in her complexion. Purple beading ran in vertical stripes down the length of the dress, and its midsection was covered with white beaded flowers. She wore a simple white beaded headdress and pink velvet heels by Pietro Yantorny.

But standing across from Ruby and Forrest, Gloria felt like an ugly duckling. Ruby looked heart-stoppingly beautiful in a flesh-colored cotton tulle evening dress with a fishtail train and silver beading. A rhinestone evening cap covered most of her hair – only a few dark, wavy tendrils framed her delicate face. Forrest was dapper in a tuxedo. His waistcoat and bow tie were just a shade darker than his white shirt, and a red rose was pinned to his lapel.

Forrest touched Ruby's hand lightly, letting his fingers linger there. 'Goodness, you're shaking! I would've thought singing onstage would be old hat for you by now.'

Ruby smiled back, and her dark eyes positively glowed. Gloria was beginning to wish she hadn't accompanied Ruby 'backstage.' Ruby wouldn't have to sing for another hour – she'd go on between the Blue Rhythm Orchestra and the famous singer Paul Solomon. Forrest certainly had quite the lineup for his party.

'I still always get nervous,' Ruby confessed. 'It's what I love most about performing – the frightening thrill of it all.' A flush crept up Ruby's neck. Forrest still hadn't removed his hand from hers. Now it was clear: Forrest's feelings for Ruby weren't as unrequited as Gloria had previously thought.

Ruby suddenly tore her eyes from the young millionaire. 'Don't you agree, Gloria?'

'Considering I've only ever worked for gangsters, I'm looking forward to a far *less* frightening singing career from now on,' Gloria joked. She waited for a laugh, or even a chuckle, but got none. Forrest and Ruby were back to gazing at each other with their matching, nearly black eyes.

Watching those two stare at each other twisted something in Gloria's chest.

She thought of falling in love with Jerome while he gave her vocal lessons back at the Green Mill in Chicago. She could still feel his hand, firm and strong, right beneath her rib cage. He'd been showing her where her diaphragm was, but Gloria hadn't been able to focus on anything but his hand and the way it, the way *he,* made her feel. Gloria could see that the same sort of love was blossoming between Forrest and Ruby.

Too bad Ruby was already married.

'Ruby?' Marty called out, bursting through the library's side door. There was a brief thunderclap of chatter and laughter from the party guests next door before the door slammed closed. In a tweed suit nowhere near formal enough, Marty looked dull and cheap and tacky.

'Yes?' Ruby said, moving a few inches away from Forrest.

Marty's cheeks were red, his forehead scrunched up. 'What's this I hear about you singing tonight?'

'I asked her to,' Forrest responded quickly. He made an attempt at his usual charming laugh, but it sounded hollow. 'It seems a crime to have Ruby Hayworth here and *not* have her sing, doesn't it?'

Marty glared at the taller, younger man. 'You think we give the milk away for free? This is a Broadway star you're talking about! Ruby doesn't wail without a contract.'

Ruby turned to her husband, eyes wide in dismay. 'Marty, what's one song?'

'You gonna pay those colored boys out there a fee but let *my wife* go on free of charge? I don't think so.' Marty seized her arm with his pudgy hand. 'She's a *professional*. Come on, Ruby.'

She gave Forrest a helpless look as Marty dragged her out the door.

For a moment Forrest looked absolutely crestfallen – his dark eyes were enormous, as though he couldn't quite believe what had just happened. Then his brows lowered, his full lips leveled into a straight line, and he clenched his fists at his sides. But he remained silent.

Once they were gone, Forrest smoothed back his brown hair and took a deep breath. He gave Gloria a shadow of his usual grin. 'Good thing I had the sense to invite more than one canary to this party.'

Gloria's mouth fell open. 'You can't mean—'

He laughed, and his disappointment seemed to vanish. How strange, Gloria thought, to seem so downtrodden one second and happy-go-lucky the next.

'You were just saying yesterday how eager you are to get back to your singing career!' Forrest said. 'Do you have any idea how many producers and club owners there are out there? You couldn't ask for a better showcase than this party!'

'But I'm not ready, I haven't prepared—'

'Don't worry!' Forrest put a calming hand on her shoulder. 'Just sing whatever you want. This is one of the best bands you've ever been with – I guarantee it – and they'll pick up what you throw them and run with it.'

The mention of a band made Gloria think of the last time she'd seen Jerome, how handsome he'd looked sitting at the Opera House's piano in his gray suit and crimson tie. Gloria didn't care who was in this band – if Jerome wasn't in it, no way would it be the best she'd ever worked with. The nervousness she'd felt a moment earlier paled in comparison to the worry that clenched at her stomach. Hank had promised to find Jerome but hadn't turned up any information yet.

Yet here Gloria was, living an easy life of luxury with a man she was supposed to be investigating. What if she couldn't dig up any dirt on Forrest – would Hank send her right back to jail? Would he stop looking for Jerome?

Misreading the worry on her face, Forrest added, 'Baby doll, everyone here knows who you are! And they're on your side! How about you come out to the party with me and see?'

There had to be a way out of this . . . except Gloria realized she didn't want a way out. She wanted to sing. That was about all she *could* be certain of in this strange new world.

And she couldn't afford to make Forrest unhappy. His trust was the only bargaining chip she'd managed to gain during her stay at his villa.

'You go on,' she said. 'I've gotta go fix my munitions if I'm going onstage.'

'That's my girl.' Forrest put a gentle hand on her arm. 'Really, thank you for stepping in, Glo.'

Forrest's touch gave her chills. 'Erm, of course,' she mumbled as he left.

Gloria sighed and thought of Jerome again, how long it had been since she'd felt so much as his hand on her arm. She would keep fighting for her freedom so the two of them could finally be together.

Quickly, she ran upstairs, into the bedroom Forrest had said she could use as long as she wanted. It reminded her of her room back in Chicago: truly lavish. A four-poster bed with its burgundy hangings stood next to a large window with a glorious view of the front lawn. A huge oak vanity took up most of one wall.

She crossed to the vanity and grabbed a tube of lipstick. That wasn't the real reason she was here, though.

Her ring.

She wasn't supposed to wear her engagement ring – Hank's orders – but after watching Forrest and Ruby, she was missing Jerome more than ever. Surely she could hide the ring under her dress. Would it be so wrong to keep it close by, to remind herself of why she was doing all this? Besides, Forrest already knew about Jerome, and he didn't care.

Gloria opened the drawer and pulled out a long white silk glove. She removed the chain from inside the glove, where she always kept it, and felt instantly calmer with the ring in her hands. To think how she would've mocked the ring's tiny diamond and its simple gold band back in Chicago! Now it was the most beautiful thing she had ever seen – its sparkle outshone the sequins on her dress and all the resplendent guests downstairs.

Gloria fastened the ring around her neck and hid it beneath her dress. The gold chain was definitely visible in the mirror, but it actually looked pretty nice with the rest of her outfit. Hopefully none of the guests would ask to see it – she wouldn't want to explain why she was hiding an engagement ring. And even in these progressive circles, where having an exonerated criminal perform was a novelty, folks would be much less welcoming if they knew she was still involved with Jerome Johnson.

With one more sweep of rouge against her cheekbones, Gloria walked into the hallway. At the end of the hall were the double doors to Forrest's bedroom suite – she felt drawn to them like a magnet. Forrest was busy with his guests; no way would he show up now. Maybe Forrest himself wouldn't admit anything to Gloria about the source of his wealth. But who knew what Gloria might find in Forrest's *bedroom*? A closet full of cash? Stacks of correspondence with nefarious mobsters? Her feet led her closer, past the gilded framed paintings, her heels padding softly on the plush carpet.

Finally she reached the heavy wooden doors.

She reached out her hand, her fingers touching the cool glass knob. One twist and she would be inside. Names flashed through her mind: Hank, Jerome. If anyone caught her she could just say she was searching for a lost earring. Was there any good reason to think it would be in Forrest's room? No.

But sometimes a girl didn't need a good reason.

Gloria turned the knob, but the door wouldn't budge. Locked. Her heart sank. She tried again, but no luck. How silly to think he'd have left it unlocked.

Then Gloria pivoted and found herself staring into a pair of cold gray eyes.

She gasped. The man was about her father's age, dressed well in a charcoal-gray suit and a scarlet bow tie. He had burly arms and a prominent scar that ran diagonally from the right side of his nose, across the bridge, and up to his left eyebrow. A thick gray mustache sat atop his upper lip, while his head was completely bald, and his eyes were only a bluish shade darker than white.

'What are you doing?' he growled.

Gloria hid her hands behind her back, not wanting the man to see them shaking. Why did he seem so familiar?

'I – um—'

'Speak up,' the man said, coming closer.

Then it hit her: She recognized him from a photograph in Hank's file on Forrest. His name was Pembroke, and he worked for Forrest as some sort of servant.

'Pembroke!' she cried out.

He seemed surprised that she knew his name. 'Yes?'

'I'm . . . late! To perform!' She rushed past him without waiting for a response, without looking back, even though she could feel Pembroke's eyes on her. Watching.

The grand room was far more crowded than it had been before. The party had truly started.

The red-carpeted staircase curved down to the marble floor. Skylights lined the arched ceiling on either side of the room, and chandeliers dripping with crystals hung between them. At each corner stood thick ivory columns. At least two or three men and women stood around each column, kissing, laughing, smoking, or just leaning back and taking a rest from dancing. On any available surface sat delicate ivory vases filled with roses – red, white, and even some that had been dyed black. White-coated waiters moved through the crowd with silver platters of crab-stuffed mushrooms and cucumber-watercress sandwiches held high.

On the left was a stage with a heavy gold velvet curtain and matching golden wood floor. Just in front of that spread a wide dance floor, where bobbed women and men in top hats hopped and kicked at a dizzying pace. These dancers were scary good – probably due to the fact that many of them danced on Broadway for a living.

Groups of Forrest's well-dressed friends gathered around various paintings on the walls, pointing with long ciga-rette holders as they carried on spirited discussions about the significance of each work. They seemed more intelligent and refined than anyone Gloria had met in New York or Chicago. Maybe it was because they were older, or because they had the artistic sensibilities that came with a life in the theater.

Before Gloria even stepped onto the marble floor, a group of party guests had gathered around her. 'Gloria Carmody!' a tall, handsome man exclaimed. He had slicked-back hair and couldn't be older than thirty. He wore a red scarf looped over his formal suit, a personal touch that would've looked ridiculous on anyone else. 'The singing jailbird! I heard you were from Chicago.' He extended his hand. 'Charles LeMaire. I *so* love meeting other Chi-town natives, especially when their stories are as fascinating as yours!'

'Thank you,' Gloria said, shaking his hand. 'What do you do?'

'I'm a costume designer.' He gestured toward the two girls standing beside him. 'This is Mara Livingston and Lisa Burrows – they have to wear getups made entirely of feathers in the Follies if I tell them to.'

'He *does* and I *did*,' Lisa said. 'Very itchy.' Her bob was an even deeper red than Gloria's. She was dressed in a lime-green satin dress that seemed tame until she turned and Gloria saw that it was backless.

'At least *you* didn't perform in the Heavenly Goddess number,' Mara replied. She had light brown hair that looked blonde in the right light and wore a black silk lace evening dress with an elaborate beaded pinwheel pattern. 'I'm still picking the glitter out of my hair, and we performed the number three weeks ago!'

'The Follies? As in the Ziegfeld Follies?' Gloria had to stop herself from squealing. The costume designer for the Follies knew who she was?

Charles nodded. 'So I hear from Forrest that you're going to perform for us. What are you planning to sing? I can't wait to finally hear that bluesy voice of yours.'

'"I Ain't Got Nobody",' Gloria replied. 'Do you know it?'

'You certainly can't go wrong with Marion Harris,' a woman's deep voice said. She was in her early forties and wore a tasteful peach-colored dress with a wide skirt, and she hung on the arm of a distinguished-looking man with thinning dark hair. 'I interviewed her once for the *Sun* and she was an absolute doll.' The woman extended her hand. 'Marie Mattingly Meloney.'

'It's a pleasure to meet you. And you write for the *Sun*?'

'Not anymore – it wasn't much fun once Willie wasn't editor anymore,' Marie said, squeezing the man's arm. 'Now I'm editor of the *Delineator* magazine.'

A *female* magazine editor! It made Gloria wish Clara were here so she could introduce her.

She couldn't help it: Excitement tingled in her stomach. Not only did these people know who she was, but they were excited to hear her sing! It was what Gloria had always dreamed of.

Gloria started when she felt a hand on her shoulder. She whipped around to find Forrest standing beside a thin black man with a receding hairline and a kind smile. 'There you are!' Forrest exclaimed. 'I was planning to introduce you around, but it looks like you've already found the cream of the crop for yourself.'

'You flatter us, Forrest,' Charles said. 'But please – don't stop.'

Forrest chuckled. 'No, really – I'm not even sure how the rest of these rascals got in here,' he said, his eyes twinkling. 'I'll have to have a talk with my butler.' While the others laughed, Forrest tugged on Gloria's arm to pull her closer. 'Are you ready to wail up there, kid?'

Gloria hadn't even noticed that the orchestra had stopped playing. But now that she did, the party seemed distinctly less lively and romantic without it. She gave Forrest a confident smile. 'If there's one thing I'm *always* ready to do, it's sing.'

'Now, that's an attitude I like to see,' the thin man beside Forrest said. He shook Gloria's hand. 'I'm Bernard, the band leader. My boys and I will take good care of you up there, I promise.'

Once Gloria and Bernard had discussed the song – a tune he and his band knew well – Forrest nodded to them both. 'Okay, Bernie, you come onstage with me. Gloria, you wait until I introduce you.'

'Good luck!' her new acquaintances whispered as Forrest and Bernard climbed the steps on the left side of the stage.

Bernard picked up his conductor's baton and stood in front of the orchestra. The men set their drinks on the stage and picked up their instruments. Forrest approached the microphone and the crowd's roar hushed to a dull murmur.

'I hope you're all having a fantastic evening!' Forrest called. 'And let's have another round of applause for the Blue Rhythm Orchestra!' The room filled with hoots and whistles.

'Now, I know many of you may have heard that the beautiful and talented Ruby Hayworth would be singing tonight. But I have, with no offense to Ruby, an even more enticing treat for you all.

'Some of you've already had the pleasure of meeting one of my most honored guests. For those of you who live under a rock and don't know her story, she's a woman who was wrongly imprisoned after shooting a gangster to save the life of the man she loved. She also happens to be a very talented singer. She'd like to celebrate her recent release from the big house by gracing us with a song! So without further ado, may I introduce the Diva of the Downtrodden, the Songbird of the Wrongfully Accused – performing under her own name at long last – Gloria Carmody!'

The crowd exploded into applause. Gloria took one last deep breath and made her way through the crowd to the stage stairs. Then she took her place at center stage. Her heart was hammering in her chest – this was by far the largest group she'd ever sung in front of. But Ruby was right. The frightening thrill of it was what made singing so exhilarating.

The music began to swell, and even though a million thoughts were running through her mind – thoughts about Jerome, Forrest and Ruby, Hank – there was nothing she could do now except what she'd been born to do.

Sing.

Chapter 9

CLARA

Clara wanted to slap that smug grin right off Parker's face.

She didn't know what bothered her more – Parker's constant bragging and self-congratulation, or how every guest but her at Forrest Hamilton's party seemed completely bewitched by him.

'She said I could come see her in Los Angeles whenever I happen to be in town,' Parker explained to his friends.

Two men and three women scrunched together on a dusky red davenport. The group had left the main room of the party and were holed up in one of the studies, where it was quieter. The men grinned in awe at Parker's story, while the girls all sought desperately to meet Parker's jade eyes. When Parker wasn't looking, these women fluffed their bobs and checked their makeup in the mirror on the wall. They were trying to be subtle and they were failing miserably.

Parker and Clara stood across from the group; Parker had explained the oh-so-impressive ways in which he'd met each of these flat tires, but Clara hadn't really been listening. So far this evening had been a total waste of Clara's favorite dark blue Chanel evening dress.

Now Parker pulled Clara's arm tighter around his own. 'But I guess I won't be doing that anytime soon. Not now that I've got this knockout by my side.'

Clara smiled and dug her red fingernails into his arm. Hopefully he could feel it through his linen suit.

'Aw, come on, it's Madge Bellamy!' a handsome swell in white exclaimed. Clara had already forgotten his name. 'I think Clara would understand.'

'He's absolutely right,' Clara said. 'You go off to Hollywood to wine and dine the pretty little actress. Meanwhile, I'll take over the *Manhattanite* and turn it into something actually worth reading.'

Parker laughed with the others, but Clara could see annoyance in his eyes. 'I discovered her and taught Clara everything she knows, I'm happy to confess.'

'You've always had an eye for talent, Parker,' said a brunette beauty in a sparkling sheath, fluttering her lashes.

Parker's cigarette dangled elegantly between his fingers and his green eyes lit up with interest as the brunette began to tell a story about running into Charlie Chaplin at the 21 Club. Parker looked like he was posing for a photograph, just like everyone else at Forrest Hamilton's party.

Clara had been hoping to find more stimulating conversation, but alas – she hadn't. She'd left the dance floor when she saw a girl in an orange beaded dress dance the treacherously fast quick-time fox-trot with a man in a blue suit. Their moves were perfect, without even the hint of a stumble, their faces etched with the self-satisfied, determined smiles of people eager to impress.

It had annoyed her.

Everyone at this party was trying so hard to prove how

wonderful and interesting they were. These flappers and swells were supposed to be the most fun-loving people in the world. But what time was there for fun when a person had to put so much effort into having it?

'You know, Hamilton's a Broadway producer!' Parker's oh-so-admiring brunette friend exclaimed, startling Clara out of her reverie. 'Harold and I have invested in his new show, *Moonshine Melody*.'

The much-older man sitting beside her nodded. 'No one liked *The Cat's Meow*, but a man this young with so much money – this Forrest Hamilton must have some idea what he's doing.'

'Mmm, because if he's got money, he must be talented!' Clara said. No one but Parker caught her sarcastic tone. 'It's not like anyone ever made a dishonest dollar in show business. Like Parker here!' she continued. 'He makes his living trying to guess which starlet might have an affair next and which ones are married to crooks.'

The mood of the group grew a bit sour. Parker loosened his collar and narrowed his eyes at Clara. 'If you'll excuse us,' he said.

He grabbed Clara's wrist and steered her out of the room and down the hallway, back to where the party was in full swing. She could hear the faint sounds of someone, a girl with a pretty voice, singing with the band. 'What has gotten into you?' Parker asked in a hushed voice.

Clara backed up. Was he serious? 'What's gotten into *me*? What about you? Where do you think you got the right to call me *your* Clara?'

He raised his eyebrows. 'We've been together for weeks now—'

'No! No, we have not,' Clara said. It had been a stupid idea to come here with Parker. She hadn't been able to get up the courage to embarrass him in front of his friends. And anyway, what good would it have done? It probably would've just gotten Clara fired. Bursting in and making a scene without thinking of the consequences – that was more horrid Lorraine Dyer's style. Clara just needed to put an end to this . . . whatever it was Parker thought was going on between them, once and for all. No matter the consequences.

'We've gone to dinner *twice,*' Clara went on, seething. 'Where do you get off bragging to everyone in New York that you and I are an item – ugh! I have half a mind to slap you across the face.' She raised her clutch as though to strike him.

Parker ducked, then opened his mouth and closed it, at a loss for what to say.

'You don't care about me – all you care about is yourself. I'm just one more trophy on your way to the top!'

Parker's cheeks reddened. 'Clara, lower your voice.'

'I've got a better idea.'

Clara whipped around and walked away without looking back. She could faintly hear Parker call her name, but she quickly let herself get lost in the crowd.

And ran straight into a girl in a red dress, sloshing half the girl's martini onto the marble floor.

'I'm so sor—' Clara began. But as she took in the girl's dark brown bob, wide hazel eyes, and too-smoky eye makeup, the words died on her lips. 'You have *got* to be kidding me.'

Lorraine latched on to Clara's arm with her free hand. 'Why, Clara Knowles! I'm so glad you're here!' Lorraine said with a slightly desperate smile. A diminutive blonde in a white dress who looked way too nice and normal to be friends with Lorraine stood beside her. 'We need to talk.'

'I have nothing to say to you,' Clara snapped, yanking her arm away. 'And don't ever touch me again.'

A very tiny part of Clara wanted to know what Lorraine Dyer was doing here. But she couldn't imagine a person she wanted to see – or chat with – less. Lorraine was just one more reminder of Chicago. Of Marcus. And Clara couldn't bear to think about her ex-boyfriend just now. *Don't cry,* she told herself.

Clara whipped her head around, trying to find an escape route, when a tall redheaded boy with thick-framed glasses appeared and blocked her in.

'Raine, I've been looking all over for you. You said you and Becky were just going to get drinks!' His brown suit hung baggy on his thin frame. He might have been cute, but the oversized glasses made it nearly impossible to tell.

'It was crowded at the bar,' the blonde girl – Becky – said dreamily, 'but I think I saw Rudolph Valentino!'

Lorraine ignored them. 'Clara, I'm not playing any games this time.' She waved a hand in the air. 'I've turned over a new leaf! A whole *tree* of new leaves! I haven't had a drink in eight weeks!'

Clara pointed to the half-empty martini glass in Lorraine's hand.

Lorraine's face twisted. 'Other than this one!'

'She's telling the truth,' Becky said. 'She's been sober as a nun.'

Clara groaned. 'I don't care whether you're drier than the Gobi; I don't want to have anything to do with you.' She shoved past them.

As she walked away, she half recognized a few faces from the Manhattan party scene: a handsome man wearing a top hat, a blonde in shimmering gold lamé. What were their names? Maybe she could convince one of them to give her a ride home . . .

'This isn't about me!' Clara heard Lorraine call out from behind her. 'It's about Marcus!'

Clara stopped dead in her tracks.

Marcus. She couldn't escape him for even a few minutes, could she? They were no longer together, he was about to marry someone else, yet even now hearing his name gave her chills. It called him up where he was always lurking at the surface of her memory, and suddenly it was as if he were standing right next to her, looking dapper and slightly amused, one blond eyebrow raised, a smile quirking the corners of his lips, just before kissing her ever so lightly at the nape of her neck.

'He's in mortal danger!' Lorraine yelled, causing several guests to glance over.

Before Clara even realized what she was doing, she marched her patent-leather heels right back to Lorraine. She crossed her arms and looked up at the taller girl. 'Mortal danger? Really, Lorraine? Start talking. This had better be good.'

As soon as Lorraine opened her in-desperate-need-of-blotting mouth to speak, she froze with her eyes fixed on the stage. Ruby was still singing – she was absolutely killing it. Clara had never seen the Broadway star's hit show, but her voice definitely sounded familiar. Lorraine's mouth continued to hang open. 'Oh my God,' she finally said.

Clara whipped around to face the stage. And she saw that the singer wasn't Ruby Hayworth at all. It was Gloria.

'Seriously?' Clara said. 'You have got to be kidding me.'

Chapter 10

LORRAINE

Lorraine always thought that if heartbreak were a sound, it would be like shattering glass or the angry screech of a halting train. But Gloria Carmody's voice was pure heartbreak, all right, and it sounded *fantastic*.

Her old friend looked beyond beautiful. Gloria's short, flame-red hair waved softly around her doll-like face like some kind of halo. She'd gained some of her weight back since her stint at the Opera House, but those sharp cheekbones and that world-weary depth in her big, pale eyes were here to stay. Her dress was pink, as it had been the night of her first and only performance at the Opera House. But *that* dress had been pale pink – just a rosy shade darker than white. Lorraine remembered thinking how well the color would've suited the blushing ingenue Gloria had once been. *This* dress was a deep, sultry pink that suited the full-blown diva Gloria had become. This Gloria knew men, life, and love – and she knew how to make the audience feel all she'd been through with a flash of her emerald eyes. She wasn't the by-the-book deb Lorraine had grown up with, but she wasn't the beaten-down, desperate woman who'd walked in to audition at the Opera House, either.

No, the Gloria who held her hand to her chest, closed her eyes, and wailed onstage was someone else altogether.

I ain't got nobody,
And nobody cares for me
That's why I'm sad and lonely,
Say, won't you just take a chance with me?
'Cause I'll sing sweet love songs all the time
If you will be a pal of mine
'Cause I ain't got nobody,
And nobody cares for me.

Through everything, Gloria had never completely lost her adorably naïve innocence, that hopeful fire that had allowed her to march into a love affair with a black man without looking back. Now Gloria's innocence had just been bruised. The audience could see it in the way Gloria sometimes hugged herself as she sang, the faraway look she got in her eyes. But that vulnerability made her even more fetching and compelling. Gloria Carmody didn't just sing the blues – she lived them; she was their very essence.

As Gloria wailed on about her sorrow and loneliness, it made Lorraine wonder where Jerome Johnson was. Gloria was so convincing when she sang about her broken heart. Had something gone wrong between her and her fiancé?

As soon as Gloria finished singing, the room exploded into deafening applause. Before Gloria had come onstage, small groups had been convening around the furniture scattered throughout the room – playing cards on the wooden coffee tables, sitting in cushioned chairs around the dark fireplace, lounging on the long couches and davenports that stood near the ivory walls. Now those cards lay forgotten on deserted tables, and several guests had dragged their chairs and couches closer to the stage and dance floor. Lorraine could barely see Gloria over the heads of the scores of men who'd risen from their seats. Everyone in the large room had leaped to their feet with such enthusiasm that more than one flute of champagne had tumbled to the floor.

The guests chanted 'Encore, encore' until Gloria whispered to the band, taking the mike for a second time.

Clara's silver bangle slipped down to her elbow as she brushed away tears. 'I keep thinking she can't get any better, and then she goes and does something like that.' In her amazement at Gloria's performance, she seemed to Lorraine to have forgotten how angry she'd been a few minutes earlier.

Which meant Lorraine needed to tell Clara about Marcus *now*.

The bald piano player banged out a short, upbeat introduction, his shoulders rocking. This was the orchestra that had been playing all night, but they had found a new energy with Gloria onstage. She turned to give the musicians a dazzling smile before she launched into a faster tune.

> *There ain't nothin' I can do or nothin' I can say*
> *That folks don't criticize me*
> *But I'm going to do just as I want to anyway*
> *And don't care if they all despise me.*

Many of the guests abandoned their chairs and couches for the dance floor, shaking and shimmying all over the place. Lorraine gulped down the rest of her second martini before someone's jabbing elbow could knock it out of her hands. She'd already sacrificed half a drink on her night of freedom – she wasn't going to let any more good booze go to waste.

'*That's* Gloria Carmody?' Becky asked, her brown eyes full of awe. 'The way you described her, I expected her to be less . . . just *less,* I think.'

'Yeah, gosh, isn't she amazing?' Melvin exclaimed with a goofy smile.

No one, not even Lorraine's best friends at school, could help falling head over heels in love with Gloria Carmody. Didn't they remember the way she had abandoned Lorraine, how she had believed Lorraine would tell Gloria's then fiancé Bastian about her affair with Jerome back in Chicago?

'She's okay, I guess,' Lorraine replied, fuming.

Melvin shook his head. 'Don't worry, Raine, I still think you're prettier.' Lorraine brightened a little at that.

She felt that oh-so-familiar twinge of jealousy when she looked at Gloria's glamorous cousin. Tonight Clara wore a red-carpet-worthy dress of sapphire tulle. The torso was decorated with Egyptian motifs made of iridescent sequins, and the semisheer skirt fell to her knees. Her blond bob was swept off to the side and pinned back with a blue-feathered hairpin.

Lorraine pushed her envy away. It would be one *huge* understatement to say that she and Clara had had their differences in the past. But if Raine was going to save Marcus, she'd need Clara's help. When she had spied Clara from the bar she'd known it was a sign. She and Clara were meant to drag Marcus away from that gold-digging roundheel.

Now she just had to convince Clara of that.

Lorraine tugged on her arm. Clara frowned. 'Not now, Lorraine – Gloria's still singing.'

'This is important!' Lorraine insisted. 'Come on!'

Reluctantly, Clara allowed herself to be led between twisting and turning couples and under the waiters' silver serving platters. But her narrowed blue-gray eyes showed that she didn't like it one bit.

Lorraine smiled while she marched through the crowd with Clara. No one whispered behind their hands as Lorraine passed or cut angry glares in her direction. They didn't notice her at all! Once upon a time Lorraine had loved being the center of attention. But now it felt so nice to be free of the shady reputation that clung to her like some kind of disease in the city. Here the only looks she got were from the women who admired her dress and the men who admired everything else.

This was what Lorraine hoped it would be like at Barnard, once she'd secured Marcus's friendship and the popularity that would come with it.

Finally, Lorraine followed a white-suited man with coffee-and-cream skin through a swinging white door into a bustling kitchen. It didn't seem like the kind of kitchen that would be in a person's home: Several men assembled cucumber sandwiches and shrimp cocktails on a wide steel table while others squirted delicate twists of whipped cream onto decadent miniature chocolate cakes to prepare for the dessert course later on.

The men were all black and acted as though Lorraine and

Clara were invisible. They didn't even look up when Melvin shuffled through the door a few moments after Clara and Lorraine, dusting the remains of a deviled egg off his coat.

'Scram, Melvin, this is a private conversation!' Lorraine yelled at him.

'But I don't know anyone else here—'

'Can't you socialize for once in your life instead of just mooning after me all the time?' Lorraine glanced at Clara to find her scowling. Was she actually getting angry on Melvin's behalf? 'You can talk to Becky,' Lorraine said more gently. She looked behind Melvin, confused. 'Where *is* Becky?'

'She wouldn't come in – she said we probably shouldn't be in the kitchen.'

Lorraine chuckled. Shouldn't be in the kitchen! Becky and her jokes. 'That girl is hilarious.'

'So out with it,' Clara said impatiently. 'Marcus? In mortal danger?'

'I know you're still in love with him,' Lorraine said, hoping to see a crack in Clara's cool mask.

'I'm over him,' Clara replied. 'Completely. Besides, he's getting married.' She watched Lorraine's face. 'As if you didn't know! Don't tell me that you're trying to destroy him, too? Haven't you ruined enough lives?'

'No, no!' Lorraine exclaimed. 'Becky, the blonde girl out there – she's my roommate at Barnard. I'm enrolled at Barnard now, did you know? It's a—'

'College, Raine; we all know,' Clara said, rolling her eyes.

108

'Anyway, Becky says that the woman Marcus is marrying isn't really who she says she is. She's little better than a common criminal. A grifter! A cheat! A liar! A . . .' Lorraine paused and tried to think of more insults.

'Hmm . . . that sounds an awful lot like you.'

Lorraine waved her hand in the air, then paused to pick up a mini quiche from one of the nearby platters. 'The *old* me, maybe.' She popped the hors d'oeuvre into her mouth. 'But that was so a-month-and-a-half ago. I told you, I've got new leaves!'

'Yes, yes, you're an absolute *tree,* Raine,' Clara said with a sigh. 'Go on.'

'This girl, she's bad news. She's only marrying him for his money!'

Clara dug through her sequined clutch. She withdrew a cigarette from a silver case. 'So what am I supposed to do? Break them up?'

'Yes! Basically. That's what I would do.'

'Lorraine,' Clara said darkly, '*no one* does the things you do. Because the things you do are stupid. And selfish. And thoughtless. And mean.'

'No, they're not! I think about them a lot!'

'Marcus is happy – doesn't that matter to you at all? Is the happiness of other people so repulsive to you?'

'You're not listening to me, Clara! This woman is a snake! She's absolutely reptilian!'

'*You* listen to *me*: I am not going to ruin his life. And neither are you. Try being a friend for once.' She turned and stormed toward the kitchen door.

'You think he's happy?' Lorraine called at Clara's sparkling back, making her halt. 'Who gets engaged five weeks after breaking up with the love of his life? That's not the act of a happy person, no sirree.'

Clara turned, blinking. Lorraine thought she saw a hint of something in the girl's eyes – longing, perhaps?

Suddenly, a handsome swell with dark, wavy hair and brilliant green eyes poked his head in. He looked familiar from the Opera House – was he a gangster? No, after a few moments Lorraine remembered that he was Clara's editor at the *Manhattanite* . . . Parker Richards. Not only did Clara have a glamorous job writing for one of the city's hottest magazines, but she got to stare at this man's gorgeous mug all day at the office. Some girls had all the luck.

'Clara, there you are! I've been looking all over for you,' he said. 'You're missing a great show out there.'

'Well, you're missing a pathetic show in here,' Clara replied. She glanced from Parker to Lorraine. 'Huh, would you look at that? My two least favorite people in one place. I'll take that as my cue to leave.' Then she marched back out to the party, nearly mowing Parker over, and the door swung closed behind her.

Lorraine swallowed hard. How was she supposed to help Marcus now? She wanted to have new leaves, she really did. But already her plan had gotten all fouled up, just like all her plans did.

'That didn't go so well,' Melvin observed. 'What did you do to her to make her hate you so much?'

Lorraine bit her bottom lip. It seemed that Clara really *did* hate her. And deep down, Lorraine couldn't blame her. She couldn't blame Gloria, Marcus, her parents, or anyone else. She was a life ruiner, just like Clara had said. There was nothing she could do to fix it.

'Oh, please,' she said, her voice breaking. 'I don't want to talk about it.'

Melvin pulled her into his skinny arms, and she felt so pathetic that tears pricked at her eyes. She cried against his tweed jacket while he patted her hair. 'There, there, Raine. It'll be all right.'

As she clung to him, Lorraine realized he smelled really nice. Not of cologne, like the other boys, but of the comforting scent of soap and clean laundry. His arms felt stronger around her than she'd expected. Maybe lifting all those heavy books had given him a bit of muscle.

Lorraine pulled away a little and looked up at him. Melvin wasn't so unattractive, really. He had a fine, straight nose and a cleft in his chin that she'd never taken the time to notice. He didn't have too many freckles, just a few – and they were sort of cute. Plus Melvin had always been so nice to her. Unlike Hank, he didn't have any ulterior motives.

'I wonder what you'd look like without your glasses,' Raine said, her voice light and feathery.

Melvin kept one arm around her and raised the other to take his glasses off.

His eyes immediately crossed, and any hint of romance Lorraine might have felt was whisked away.

'Oh God, put those back on right this instant!' she ordered.

He slid the glasses back onto the bridge of his nose, then put his hands in his pockets and gave her a bashful smile. 'Yeah, they really do something for my face.'

Lorraine nodded. 'They hide it. But enough of this.' She dragged her fingertips under her eyes to remove any black tracks of mascara and turned toward the door to walk back out to the party. Lorraine had come here to have a good time; she wasn't going to let Clara Knowles or Melvin and his disconcertingly small eyes keep her from doing just that.

She thought about her sorry life at Barnard and how much it would be improved if Marcus introduced her to his friends, if the other girls saw that she was popular and fun and a good person – whatever that meant. Was it just a silly dream? She didn't think so. Even the worst sinner could be redeemed, if only she found the right task to prove her worth.

'If Clara won't help Marcus,' she announced, 'I'm going to have to do it myself.'

Chapter 11

GLORIA

Gloria loved the Long Island Sound.

Especially when she was looking at it from the deck of a yacht.

The *Sabrina,* Forrest's yacht, represented the highest standard of luxury – just like everything else Forrest owned. It was a long, pearly white affair with a shining wooden deck.

Gloria had been walking along the steel railing until she'd stopped to take in the view. To her left, Forrest's other house-guests were lounging on cushioned chairs on the foredeck. All afternoon the gin had been flowing as freely as Ma Rainey's voice pouring out of the gramophone on deck.

Forrest appeared next to her at the boat's railing. He'd abandoned his pale blue seersucker jacket and wore only the matching waistcoat, a white shirt, and a dark blue tie.

'I was wondering where you disappeared to,' he said with one of his entrancing smiles. He offered Gloria a flute of champagne. His fingers grazed hers when she accepted it. 'You look like you're having thoughts far too deep for this little soiree.'

Gloria could hear Glitz's and Glamour's raucous laughter wafting from the foredeck. Those girls sure could turn life into a party wherever they went. 'Well, your boat gives such a glorious view of the Sound. It seemed a shame not to spend a few minutes looking at it.'

'Mmm, absolutely beautiful,' Forrest agreed. But when

Gloria turned to him, he wasn't looking at the sea. He was looking at her. 'It seems you and I are a matching set this evening. Though the color suits you far better.'

Her Babani dress *was* nearly the same shade of blue as his suit. Gloria ran her finger quickly across Forrest's cheek. 'You're just not wearing enough rouge.'

He laughed, but he didn't stop looking at her. Even though Gloria liked joking around with him, she knew what his look meant. He was interested.

But why would he look at her like that? Wasn't he carrying a torch for Ruby? Besides, *she* wasn't interested in *him*. She had Jerome.

Wherever he was.

Forrest withdrew a tortoiseshell cigar case from his trouser pocket. He opened the case and offered it to Gloria. 'We'd practically be twins if you took one of these.'

'Smoke a cigar? That wouldn't be very ladylike.'

'Well, then, it would suit you. You're a hell of a lot more fun than a proper *lady* could ever be.'

Gloria smiled back and accepted a cigar. While Forrest lit it for her, he leaned in far closer than necessary and placed his hand on the small of her back.

She shook off his hand and puffed on the cigar, pointing to the case. If Forrest was going to flirt with her, she might as well use it to her advantage and dig up some dirt. 'That's gorgeous. Must have set you back a pretty penny.'

'Seemed like a good investment, considering how often I smoke these things.'

'Beautiful little yacht you've got, too,' Gloria went on, motioning around her. 'For such a young man, you're able to afford quite a number of beautiful things.'

Forrest tilted his head. The late-afternoon sun reflected off his cheeks, making his skin look warm, tanner than it already was. 'I think the company I keep is much better to look at than anything I could possibly buy.'

But Gloria wasn't going to let him worm away from her questions again. 'Really, Forrest. You know everything about me already. It isn't fair that I know so little about you.' She paused, inhaling. 'How did a fellow like you come into so much dough? I'd love to know so . . . you know, maybe some of your secrets could rub off on me. If you haven't noticed, I'm not exactly rolling in it these days.'

Forrest smoked silently for a moment, and Gloria thought they'd hit yet another dead end. In the few days since Forrest's party, she hadn't found a spare moment alone to make another attempt at searching his bedroom or any other room in his huge house. There was always a new club in the Hamptons to visit, or a drunken picnic to be had on the Village Green, or Glam and Glitz waking her up at two in the morning for a late-night stroll on the beach. At this rate, she'd never get the information she needed to hold up her end of the bargain with Hank.

But after a waiter collected their empty champagne flutes, Forrest leaned his elbows on the railing beside her. 'You're right, Glo. I've become pretty fond of you, you know. You're smart and brave, and now we all know you've got real talent. And here you must think I'm barely more than a stranger. I'm afraid my story's nowhere near as interesting as yours, though.' He sucked in a breath. 'My father . . . died, and left me a large inheritance.'

'I'm sorry,' Gloria said, an immediate reaction to hearing such news. She placed a hand on Forrest's shoulder.

Forrest waved off her concern. 'That's all right. It's my lot in life, I suppose. Anyhow, that's how I got my money, Gloria. No secrets to share. No stock tips. Things . . . weren't going well for me, but Pop's fortune gave me new hope. I decided to let my heart dictate how I spent my money – that's why I'm here.'

'So you can be close to Broadway?'

Forrest gave a little nod. 'There's been a lot of sadness in my life. Theater makes me happy. Besides, artsy folks are always such a hoot. They make me laugh like nobody else. Now that I've got some money, I've got another shot at happiness.'

'You think producing Broadway shows will make you happy?'

'With the right talent.'

'With Ruby, you mean?'

'I was actually talking about *you*.'

Gloria withdrew her hand from Forrest's shoulder so she could place it over her heart, which was beating so rapidly she thought it might burst. A real Broadway producer wanted to work with her?

He smiled. 'You blew the roof off my villa Saturday night, you really did.' He moved a little closer on the railing. Gloria could smell the salt in the water, and the movement of the yacht was making her seasick. 'You know, doll, with the right role I bet I could make you a star.'

Gloria closed her eyes when she heard the word *star*.

Broadway. No more singing for drunken men who focused more on her body than her voice, no more frightening mobster bosses. She'd spend each afternoon and evening in a gilded theater full of well-dressed patrons who paid very well for the privilege to watch her perform.

Then she opened her eyes. Her stomach felt like it was being attacked by angry butterflies. People would be paying to watch her perform. And not just the cost of some gin at a nightclub. Tickets were expensive. What if she was bad, and they wanted their money back? What then? 'I don't really have any experience.'

'Well, how else do you think you get it, Glo?' He noticed when she dropped the butt of her cigar into the water. 'So, what'd you think of your first cigar?'

'I liked it – very spicy. I should be unladylike more often.'

'Who says it has to end with a cigar? I have an idea!'

Without another word Forrest grabbed her hand and led her to the aft of the yacht. They climbed the short flight of stairs to the bridge deck. From there Gloria could look down and see Ruby, Marty, Glitz, and Glamour lying on their reclining deck chairs. Ruby read, Marty slept, and Glitz and Glamour pelted each other with cocktail olives. Glamour saw Gloria and Forrest and waved, using her other hand to overturn the entire jar of olives on Glitz's head.

Gloria was sure Ruby noticed her – and Forrest as well – but the actress didn't do anything more than purse her lips and return to her script.

Looking beyond Forrest's houseguests, Gloria watched the bow cut into the deep-blue water like a knife. It was wonderful being so high up on the yacht – it made her feel like she was flying.

On the bridge deck, a man in a blue jacket with gold buttons and white trousers stood at the helm with both hands on the wooden steering wheel. He nodded at Forrest. 'Afternoon, sir.'

'Good afternoon, Otto! I'd like you to meet the best singer in Chicago, New York, Long Island, and just about anywhere else she decides to grace with her presence: Gloria Carmody. Gloria, this is our captain, Otto Pendergast.'

'Pleasure to meet you, Miss Carmody,' Otto said with a nod to Gloria. 'I hear you were a real hit at Mr. Hamilton's party Saturday evening.'

'She is one talented girl,' Forrest agreed. 'You know what else she can do? She can steer a yacht!'

'What? No, I can't!' Gloria exclaimed, laughing.

Forrest gave her a look of mock surprise. 'You *can't*? Well, that simply won't do. I'm afraid I'll have to take it from here, Otto.' He tapped the captain on the shoulder. 'This is something of an emergency, as you can see. A singer who can't drive a yacht! I've never heard of such madness.' Forrest took the wheel and Otto walked down the steps to the lower deck, leaving them alone. 'Now, are you ready for your lesson?'

Gloria tried not to sigh. There Forrest was, off on another lark again. Yes, he was charming, but Forrest couldn't seem to talk about anything serious for longer than a few seconds. Though, really, he'd told her where his money came from – he'd inherited it. Why did Hank think any different?

She didn't want to spoil Forrest's good mood by asking about his father. Best to play along and hope he let something else about his past slip. As long as things didn't progress beyond flirtation, Jerome would understand.

Or at least, she *hoped* he would understand.

Gloria pasted on a smile. 'Okay, what do I do?'

'Get in front of me, quick. We can't have an unmanned ship for even a moment. I don't think Glamour would forgive us if we swerved and made her trip over those mile-high heels of hers.'

Gloria chuckled and stepped in front of Forrest, awkwardly placing her hands on the steering wheel. The wood was smooth under her hands. She took a sharp breath when Forrest put his arms on either side of hers, latching his hands onto the wheel as well. The warmth of his breath on her neck mixed with the cool early-evening air, giving her chills.

'Now we just want to make a slight left here, nice and easy,' he said softly.

She tried to keep calm as Forrest continued to give her instructions and critique her steering. But it wasn't a real lesson – Forrest was clearly just inventing an excuse to be close to her. Gloria had no idea where his sudden amorousness had come from. Had he finally given up on Ruby as a lost cause? Even if he had, Forrest knew about Jerome. Did he think things were over between Jerome and Gloria, simply because she hadn't heard from him in a while?

And what about Jerome – what would he think if he could see her *now*?

Gloria looked down at the others on the foredeck. Glitz and Glamour lay on their stomachs in the bathing suits they'd worn beneath their dresses, attempting to further deepen their already perfect tans. Ruby was still reading and Marty was still asleep beside her. If any of Forrest's guests looked up, they'd be able to see Gloria and Forrest perfectly.

They would even be able to see how Forrest's arms were looped around Gloria's.

It was hardly fair: Forrest could touch Gloria in public and no one cared. But every time Gloria had been out with Jerome, they had to remember *not* to hold hands or even let their gazes linger on each other for a beat too long. Every second they spoke to each other in public was a second they had to censor themselves for fear of inviting unwanted attention – simply because of the colors of their skin.

Gloria sighed and leaned back a little against Forrest. He wasn't even pretending to teach her anything now – he was content to steer on his own with his arms around her. Was there any way it could ever be like this between her and Jerome? Free and easy, without dozens of angry, narrowed eyes glued to them wherever they went? Maybe if they lived somewhere in Europe. But how would they ever get there?

'I'm not going to learn much if you just steer the boat for

me.' Gloria needed to get out of the circle of Forrest's arms. She felt too guilty.

'Fair enough.' Forrest beckoned for Otto to return to his post. When he did, Gloria slipped away, and Forrest followed her. 'Good job,' he said as they climbed back down the stairs to the main deck. 'Now if you want to steal the yacht for a late-night ride on your own, you'll be prepared.'

Gloria led the way back to the foredeck. 'Steal your yacht? You really think I'm capable of that?'

Forrest grabbed Gloria's hand, pulling her to him. 'I think you, Gloria Carmody, are capable of anything.' He gave a quick glance behind Gloria toward the foredeck. Then he moved still closer to her and tilted his face toward hers.

Gloria stiffened. She hadn't meant to lead Forrest on, certainly not to the extent that he thought he could kiss her. She'd just been trying to get more information. How could she get away without insulting him? He finally seemed to trust her – Gloria didn't want to lose that.

How ironic. A year and a half ago, it would've been a dream come true to have a handsome man take her out on his yacht and lean in for that big Hollywood kiss. Forrest was the sort of man Gloria had always wished Bastian could be.

But now she had Jerome. And as kind, handsome, funny, and clever as Forrest was, he would never win Gloria's heart. It already belonged to Jerome. Now and forever.

Gloria took her hand back. Forrest could go ahead and be insulted. He could kick her out of his villa, even, and send her back to Hank with nothing. A lifetime in prison would be better than betraying Jerome like that. 'We should probably get back to the others.'

'Gloria . . . ,' Forrest said. 'Listen. I know what it's like.' His intense eyes were fixed on the blue sea that stretched out in front of them.

'What *what's* like?'

'To follow your heart and damn the consequences! We understand each other, you and I, far better than you know.'

'Forrest, I don't—'

'What are you two up to over there?' Glitz called out.

If Gloria spent another moment alone with Forrest, it wouldn't be long before Glitz and Glamour started flapping their gums about the two of them to all of Long Island.

Gloria quickly walked the last few steps to the foredeck, and Forrest followed. 'Forrest was teaching me how to steer the ship,' she said, and sank into a deck chair.

'And I had to get Gloria alone to talk about her career,' Forrest added. 'I still can't get over how much everyone adored her Saturday night.'

'I'm absolutely green with envy, Glo,' Glitz called. 'I wish I were that good at something.'

'Don't be silly, Glitz!' Glamour said. 'You and I are both terrifically good at doing nothing. I challenge anyone to do nothing as well as we do!'

'You were wonderful, Gloria,' Ruby said from the other side of the deck. Even though she was giving Gloria a compliment, there was something acidic in Ruby's tone. 'I guess it's a good thing I wasn't able to perform, wasn't it?'

Forrest stared at Ruby for a moment; the two seemed to have a silent conversation with their matching eyes. They did this a lot – it made Gloria wonder how long they'd known each other.

Then Forrest turned to Gloria. 'Yes, well, I plan to make Gloria an enormous star.' He winked. 'If she'll let me.'

'Are we really talking about *work*?' Glamour turned over on her chair. She pulled off her black swimming cap and ran her hand through her short gold curls. 'Glitz and I are bored.'

Forrest sat on the empty chair beside her. 'Well, we can't have that. What would you ladies rather be doing?'

'I want to drink!' Glitz said. 'And dance. Possibly at the same time.'

'Hear, hear!' Glamour said. She winked at Gloria. 'Enough of you lovebirds puttering around the bay.'

Damn, Gloria thought. That wink meant that gossip about Gloria and Forrest was sure to be churning through the high-society rumor mill by morning.

Forrest looked out at the sun, which was beginning to dip in the pale blue sky. 'I guess it is getting a little late. I'll go tell Otto to bring us in.' He stopped by Gloria's chair and pointed at her. 'You better save me a dance, doll.'

Gloria reddened and looked across the foredeck to where Ruby was sitting with her husband. Marty was still asleep; his graying hair flopped over his lobster-red forehead and his white suit was rumpled.

Ruby was his polar opposite in a black halter dress and a

wide-brimmed white hat with a black scarf tied around it. The starlet was watching Forrest. Once he was out of sight, she shifted her gaze to Gloria. Her eyes were narrowed and she was frowning.

Gloria rose from her chair and walked over to Ruby's. 'So, how's it been going down here?'

Ruby shrugged. 'Just work, work, and more work.' She smiled, but again, something that was supposed to be friendly came off as bitter instead. 'I certainly haven't been having as much fun as you and Forrest.' Ruby's gaze turned wistful and Gloria followed it up to the foredeck, where Forrest was talking to Otto. From her vantage point, Ruby could see the steering wheel perfectly. And she'd probably had a better view of Gloria and Forrest at the railing than any of the others.

Now it was clear: Forrest hadn't developed sudden, inexplicable feelings for her. He'd simply been trying to make Ruby jealous! Gloria felt a rush of relief at this realization – and just tried to ignore the tiny pang of disappointment that accompanied it.

Gloria didn't love being used, but at the same time she understood. Ruby obviously had feelings for Forrest. But that didn't mean she was going to just up and leave her husband without a fuss. So by making her jealous, Forrest was really just trying to get Ruby to own up to her feelings and take the next step.

Still, after tonight, Forrest would have to find some other pawn to use in his games with Ruby. Gloria knew where his money came from now, and there was nothing shady about it. After they got home, Gloria would search the villa properly at last. She knew 'inheritance' wouldn't be enough to satisfy the bureau – but Forrest had to have some kind of documentation of his fortune, didn't he? Maybe a copy of his father's will or some bank statements?

She would call Hank in the morning. Tell him he'd been wrong about Forrest. Hank had told her to get information, and Gloria had gotten it.

She just had to hope it was enough for him.

It was nearly two in the morning by the time Gloria arrived at her bedroom. Her feet hurt from hours of dancing at a nearby beachfront club. She wanted nothing more than to sink into her cloud-soft bed. But Gloria knew that everyone else in the house was just as exhausted as she was. And that made it the perfect time to do some snooping.

Gloria hung up her dress and took out her pearl earrings. As she pulled a lacy white nightgown over her head, she heard a knock at the door. She groaned. Didn't Glitz and Glamour *ever* get tired?

She grabbed a silky blue robe and flung it over her shoulders, then yanked open the door, ready to dismiss those silly girls. She gasped at who was on the other side.

Not Glitz or Glamour.

It was Jerome.

'Oh my God!' she said, nearly fainting at the sight of him. He was wearing the white shirt, black tie, and white jacket all the servants wore. He had a bruise on one cheek and another near his jaw. And he looked so thin.

But he was *here*. Even handsomer than she remembered, which Gloria hadn't thought was possible. His brown eyes were nearly copper with the way they lit up at the sight of her. His full lips peeled back into a smile that warmed Gloria all over.

'Oh, Gloria,' he said, his voice breaking.

'Jerome! How did you get in here? What happened to you?'

Gloria couldn't look at him for a moment longer – she was too busy wrapping her arms around him and pressing her face into his shoulder. His strong arms rose to hug her tightly in return, and his hand combed through her hair over and over.

'God, I missed you,' Jerome murmured into her ear, dotting kisses along her earlobe and down her neck.

Gloria pulled back to give him a fierce, hungry kiss before she burrowed back into his arms. The two of them fit as perfectly together as they always had, as if no time had passed. His heart pounded against her ear, and she wanted to get even closer.

She walked backward toward the bed without moving out of his arms, and began to unbutton his shirt. She didn't know where Jerome had been, or what he'd been doing.

But Gloria knew this: She wasn't letting him go. Not ever again.

PART TWO

Nothing to Lose

'By the time a person has achieved years adequate for choosing a direction, the die is cast and the moment has long since passed which determined the future.'

— Alabama Beggs, in Zelda Fitzgerald's
Saw Me the Waltz

Chapter 12

CLARA

Clara wished she could've spent her Monday the exact same way she'd spent the past seven Mondays – sleeping off her hangover from the night before.

But thanks to Lorraine Dyer and her talent for ruining *everything,* Clara was sitting in a private investigator's office, not hungover in the least, digging around in her briefcase for her rapidly expanding file on Anastasia Rijn. She found it and withdrew the engagement photograph clipped to the first page of her notes.

Clara reached across Solomon's desk to hand him the photo. The desk was covered with teetering stacks of folders, old newspapers, and several open notebooks.

Solomon was as sloppy as his dim, cramped office. He was balding, and his black eyebrows were bushy enough to barely qualify as two separate entities. His checkered bow tie was coming loose, and mustard spots covered his collar and tweed jacket. If her colleagues at the *Manhattanite* hadn't spent the morning telling her so, Clara never would've believed this pudgy mess of a man was the best in the business.

Solomon stared at the photo for only a few seconds before tapping his finger over Anastasia's pretty face. 'She's cleaned up well,' he remarked. 'What name is she going under these days?'

'Anastasia Rijn,' Clara said.

'How'd you find her?'

'She's engaged to someone I know. A student who goes to school with Anastasia told me she thought there was something fishy about her. So I showed her picture to a few reporters at work, just to see if anyone had any dirt on her.'

'Makes sense,' Solomon replied. 'Salacious scandals are the *Manhattanite*'s bread and butter.'

'My thinking exactly. Our features editor didn't recognize her, but he gave me the number of his contact in the Barnard admissions office. I found out that Anastasia Rijn is a foreign transfer student at Barnard, speaks with a foreign accent. But she's only taking a *single* class, and I wasn't able to find anyone who knew about her background. She's telling people she's from France, and that she arrived in New York in the spring or early summer, but no one at Ellis Island was able to locate a record of her passage.'

Much as Clara hated to admit it, it seemed Lorraine had been right. There was definitely more to this girl than met the eye.

'You did all that today?' Solomon asked. Clara nodded. 'That's some fine detective work – better than what a lot of real cops were able to turn up on this particular dame.'

'Thank you. So you do recognize her?' She tugged nervously at the sailor collar of her blue-and-white plaid day dress.

Now that it appeared her sleuthing was going to dig up real answers, Clara almost didn't want to hear them. As soon as she knew for sure that Anastasia was up to no good, she would have to *do* something about it. It was one thing to long for Marcus from afar – it would be quite another to actually see him face to face.

'Sure I recognize her.' Solomon lit his cigarette and took a drag, filling the tiny room with smoke. 'She popped up in a couple of my cases, back when I was still working with the NYPD. This girl's been into a little of everything – robbing banks, tax fraud, even assault and battery.'

Clara had trouble keeping her breathing even. She hadn't thought the woman was a bona fide *criminal*.

'But she was never arrested?'

Solomon shook his head. 'She's a slippery one. She went under a different name every time. Deirdre Fitzsimons, Deirdre Dunwoody, Deirdre Jennings . . . Last time we were chasing her, we pinned down her real name as Deirdre Van Doren. But then she disappeared on us, like she always does. Looks like she wised up this time and used a totally fake name.'

'You're sure that's her?'

He gave the picture another glance. 'I wouldn't bet my life on it. But I'd bet . . . your life.'

Clara was taken aback. Then Solomon laughed. 'That was a joke, sweetheart.'

'Oh, um . . . okay. Well, ha ha!'

Solomon took a sip of what appeared to be a cup of cold coffee. 'This one started early. She's about twenty-one, I'd say. She's got a guy who does fake birth certificates and the whole shebang each time she decides to fleece somebody. Could I see that file of yours?' Clara wordlessly handed it over, and he shuffled through the pages. 'Sheesh, I would've thought a writer would have better handwriting.'

Clara shrugged. 'I failed my class in cursive, what can I say?'

Solomon snorted. 'You're feisty. I like that.' He stopped on one of the open pages. 'So she's in college. Must've thought she needed to step up her game to get herself hitched to someone who's really loaded.' He put the file down on his desk. 'It's a little hard not to admire a dame like that, I've gotta say. Who's the fool marrying her?'

'My old b— just, a, um . . . just a friend.'

Solomon frowned. 'Well, if you want to be a real friend to him, you better tell him to run as fast as he can.'

Clara swallowed hard. Solomon was right. The problem was, while Marcus would call Clara a lot of things, a friend definitely wasn't one of them.

Clara stormed into Hartley Hall looking purposeful.

A few boys in V-neck sweaters and breeches or checkered blazers and trousers sat in cushy chairs in the common area and played poker. Others gathered around a fellow telling an animated story at the bottom of the stairs.

Clara was going to have to send some kind of gift basket to Ricky in Features over at the *Manhattanite*. His Barnard admissions contact had put her in touch with a guy who worked in housing at Columbia. As soon as Clara had gotten hold of Marcus's dorm and room number, she'd taken the train straight up to Morningside Heights. She needed to warn Marcus about Anastasia right away. Before he made a terrible mistake.

A thick-looking boy at the poker table gave Clara a quick glance before returning his eyes to the cards. 'No girls in the dorm.'

One of the boys by the stairs – a particularly handsome

fellow with brown hair and light gray eyes – approached Clara. 'Don't be such a flat tire, Aaron.' He gave Clara a dazzling smile. 'I'm Thomas. Nice to meet you.'

'Clara.' She let her hand linger in his when he shook it.

'I'm afraid old Aaron's right, though. You'll get in huge trouble if someone catches you.'

'Oh no!' Clara said, raising her voice higher than usual and giving Thomas her best doe eyes. 'I'm sorry – I go to school across the street, and I was so curious to see what a *real* Columbia dorm looked like.' Clara stepped closer to Thomas and touched his arm lightly. 'Now I'll have to leave without even getting to see a dorm room.'

Thomas's eyes widened. He took her arm and led her a little away from the others. 'Go around back to the second door on the left. From there you can take the back staircase and no one will see you.'

'But won't the door be locked?'

'Naw, the lock on that door got busted a while ago. None of the RAs have reported it – they sneak girls in as often as we do.' He gave her a smug smile. 'My room's two twenty-five. I'll see you there in about five minutes?'

Sometimes boys made things so easy. 'I'll see you there.'

Clara walked around the deep-red brick, ivory-trimmed dormitory and found the door. She grinned when the doorknob gave right under her hand. She walked into a deserted, concrete-walled stairwell. She took a deep breath, gripped the iron railing, and began to climb. Once she reached the second floor, she pushed the heavy stair door open and walked into the hall.

It was like stepping out of a dingy cornfield into *The Secret Garden*. Clara marveled that this was merely a college dormitory. The walls were wood-paneled and masculine. Her heels sank into the plush rug and sconces hung between each of the doors. There were even elegant wooden benches against the walls, in case Columbia's men decided they couldn't make it the last five steps to their rooms before they needed to sit down. She knocked hard on 237 when she reached it.

And there he was.

For a split second, Marcus looked the way Clara always remembered him. He wore the half smirk of a man who knew that no matter what he said, it would always be charming and clever. He was dressed casually in a blue silk button-down with rolled-up sleeves and tan trousers. His blond hair was still a little damp from the shower, and Clara could smell his spicy aftershave. His blue eyes were bright and engaging, his lips were full and kissable, and he had those long black lashes any girl would kill for.

Marcus was the kind of handsome that always took Clara's breath away – not a handy thing when her nervousness was making it hard enough to breathe as it was.

But when Marcus recognized that it was *Clara* standing outside his room, his eyes hardened. Clara noticed his hands shaking a little, and he reddened when he noticed her noticing. He shoved his hands in his pockets and his lip curled. 'You're not allowed to be here.'

His words cut her like ice. He clearly did not want to see her.

And yet she pushed her way inside.

134

'Hey! What are you doing!' Marcus followed, rushing ahead and then turning on his heels to stop her – but they were already in the middle of the room.

It was huge, which made sense, considering Marcus's parents had built nearly half the school. The far wall had two expansive windows with checkered curtains. The room was surprisingly bare of personal touches, though there was a framed photo of 'Anastasia' on Marcus's desk.

Clara's breath caught in her throat when she saw the movie poster hanging on Marcus's wall. Buster Keaton stood in a straw boater and a long coat, his wide-eyed face as stoic and deadpan as ever. It was a poster for *Our Hospitality*: the movie he'd taken Clara to see on their first date in Chicago. Marcus was a Buster Keaton fan, sure, but why did he choose a poster for *that* particular film?

Marcus took a few deep breaths, attempting to cool down. 'You have to leave, Clara. I'm not kidding. Girls aren't allowed in the dorms, particularly not drunk ones.'

'I'm not drunk!'

He glanced at the gold watch on his wrist. 'No? Well, it's almost six o'clock. You'd better get a move on if you want to be half as zozzled as the other flappers at whatever speakeasy or party you're going to later.'

'Look, I know I'm the last person you want to see right now. And I'll go. But first there's something I need to tell you.' Clara crossed to Marcus's desk and picked up the picture of his fiancée. 'Marcus, this woman is not who she says she is.'

Marcus laughed incredulously. 'That's it? *That's* what you're here to say? No "Hi, Marcus, I haven't seen you in a month and a half. How's life been treating you?" No "You've started college since the last time I saw you. What's that like?" You skip right over all that and start taking shots at my fiancée?'

His hands started shaking again. 'Back in Chicago I liked you because you were different. You were smart, and funny, and you never felt the need to stoop to the level of the Lorraine Dyers of the world. But now you seem just like her.'

Clara focused all her energy on not allowing tears to spring to her eyes. 'No, Marcus, if you'd just listen—'

'Is this what you've stooped to now?' Marcus grabbed the photo from Clara and returned it to his desk. 'It wasn't enough for you to lie to me and break my heart, but you're now going to try and ruin the rest of my life?'

Clara could hear the anger giving way to hurt in his voice. She wanted nothing more than to admit how wrong she'd been to lie to him, to let him go so easily. She wanted to close the gap between them and feel his arms around her again.

Clara took a few steps forward. In response, Marcus's sky-blue eyes widened – was it from fear of her getting too close, or maybe in anticipation? Clara blinked. It was definitely fear. Her being here was making Marcus incredibly upset.

She stopped walking when she was close enough to brush Marcus's hair out of his eyes. His hair always dried messy and unruly before he had the chance to tame it with pomade – another thing Clara had always loved about him.

'Marcus, I—' Clara began, ready to confess how much she miss-ed him and how she'd do anything to have him back in her life.

She'd never given Marcus enough credit when it came to understanding all she'd been through in her old New York life, how hard it had been for her to pretend that the glitter and revelry of the flapper world didn't still call to her. Instead, she told lie after lie, then got angry at *Marcus* for being less than understanding about her new career as a journalist.

Marcus hadn't even told her to stop writing – he'd just encouraged her to go to school and take her writing more seriously. But Clara had decided that Marcus didn't support her career. If she tried to focus on Marcus's shortcomings, she could ignore how selfish she'd truly been at the end of their relationship.

But he'd been right. Parker and the *Manhattanite* team didn't take her seriously. Maybe if she apologized, *really* apologized . . .

The words were right there on the tip of Clara's tongue. But if she said any of them, how would he ever believe her about this Deirdre woman? He'd think she was only spinning lies in order to win him back. Marcus would probably go running back to his Anastasia as fast as his legs could carry him.

And protecting him from making the mistake of a lifetime was more important than confessing her feelings.

So Clara moved away from him, sank into the wooden chair in front of his desk, and avoided his gaze. 'Marcus, I'm not trying to ruin your life – this has nothing to do with you and me. I mean, there isn't even a "you and me" anymore. That's over and we're both over it, right? I'm here out of friendship. I just don't like to see a friend get fleeced.'

It pained her to say the words, because they weren't true. She wasn't over it. But if this was the only way to protect Marcus, then she'd have to bite the bullet.

Marcus was silent. He stood still, one hand resting on the black telephone on his night table. Had he called someone while her back was turned? Clara hadn't heard him say anything. His eyes narrowed, and Clara could tell right away that she'd said precisely the wrong thing.

'Friendship?' He scoffed. 'You and I were never *friends*, Clara, and we sure as hell aren't now. I loved you,' he said in a quieter voice. 'I wanted to be with you, and all you wanted to do was party and lie to me.'

Clara swallowed hard. 'I didn't *want* to, it was for a job.'

'A job you never told me about! For no good reason! Unless you didn't want me to know about the job because you didn't want me to know about your *editor*.'

'Nothing was going on between me and Parker then, and nothing is going on now.' At least she could say that honestly. Semihonestly, anyway.

'I don't believe anything you say anymore. You lied to me at first, back in Chicago, but I understood that. You were ashamed of your past. When we got here, though, I realized that wasn't it – it was just *you*. You got so caught up in manipulation and double talk as a flapper that now you don't know how to be honest with anyone.'

It was what Clara had always feared most. She'd watched enough girls lie their way into speakeasies, into relationships, into money, until they lied even when they didn't need to. And now here was Marcus, the boy who'd convinced her she was different from all those girls, telling her she was just like them.

'How was I supposed to keep loving you if I couldn't believe a word out of your mouth? Only a complete idiot would,' he said grimly. 'Do you really not understand what you did wrong?'

Don't cry, don't cry, don't cry, Clara said to herself over and over. It had kind of become a personal mantra these past few weeks.

Marcus held her eyes for a few moments, waiting for the apology Clara couldn't give him. If she told him how sorry she was, it would tumble into a confession of love that she wouldn't be able to take back.

Eventually Marcus exhaled heavily and looked away. 'You know what, it doesn't matter. I've found someone who wants to be with me, and I'm not going to let you screw it up. Do yourself a favor and leave. Now.'

'But I—' Clara began, when a sharp knock on the door interrupted her.

'Oh, too late,' Marcus said. He flung open the door to reveal two men in black uniforms with silver badges pinned to their chests.

Clara turned to glare at Marcus. He'd called security on her? Really?

'This drunk woman burst into my room. I've never seen her before in my life.' He looked at Clara with a hint of a smile. It was both sad and cruel at the same time. 'Please take her away.'

Chapter 13

LORRAINE

And Becky had said Lorraine's opera glasses would never come in handy.

It was early evening and the streetlamps that dotted Columbia's campus had just flickered on. The campus was fairly deserted this time of day – just a few students strolled down the cobbled path to the domed library on Lorraine's left. Wind brushed through the trees and made Lorraine wish she'd brought a sweater or jacket. Why couldn't summer do everyone a favor and last all year long?

From her bench on the lawn, Lorraine could nearly see through Marcus's window into his dorm room. She couldn't make out who Marcus was talking to, only that it was a girl who was *not* his fiancée. Lorraine pressed the glasses closer to her face and leaned forward. 'What *are* you up to, Marcus?' she whispered.

Lorraine had been following Marcus since she'd returned from Long Island two days earlier. Before, she'd only hung around outside Marcus's classes when she had a spare moment – but now tailing him had become her full-time job.

She'd been studying how much time Marcus spent with Anastasia/Deirdre, and what times of day she'd be most likely to catch the lying harlot alone. Soon Lorraine would tell Anastasia that she knew about her dirty past and that she'd

better come clean to Marcus. Or else Lorraine would . . .
do something. She hadn't really worked that part out yet.

Melvin had pointed out that Lorraine's 'research' was
remarkably similar to what she had been doing before she'd
even known Marcus was engaged. But while that might have
seemed to be the case to an oil can like Melvin, her motivations
had changed. Lorraine wasn't just a girl with a crush now: She
was a woman on a rescue mission.

She shivered and set her glasses on the bench so she could
rub her hands over her goose-pimpled arms. A sleeveless dress,
while fashionable, was not the best attire for spying. Lorraine
raised the opera glasses back up to her eyes and saw two security guards in black uniforms in Marcus's doorway. Where had
they come from?

The guards left nearly as soon as they'd arrived, the woman
Marcus had been talking to with them. Seriously, what was
going on up there? Lorraine slipped her opera glasses into her
purse, rose from the bench, and took a few hesitant steps across
the lawn toward Hartley Hall.

As her heels crunched over the fallen leaves, Lorraine specu-
lated as to who the woman might be. Was Marcus having some
kind of affair with a lady criminal?

When Lorraine was halfway across the lawn, the security
guards emerged from the dorm with the woman between
them. Lorraine stepped closer, squinted, and gasped.

Clara Knowles? What had *she* been doing in Marcus's room?

Back at Forrest Hamilton's party, Clara hadn't wanted
anything to do with Marcus. But clearly something had changed.

And now Clara was in trouble.

The security guards began to lead her across the South Lawn, and without another thought, Lorraine raced toward them. Ugh, her brocade T-strap heels were gorgeous, but they were horrid for running. She felt tempted to chuck them off – this damp grass had probably already ruined them anyway.

She nearly ran into a fellow lugging a huge stack of textbooks when she stopped short near Clara and the security guards. 'W-watch where you're going, y-y-you lousy dewdropper!' Lorraine yelled at the boy, out of breath. She needed to stop skipping her physical education class so often, even if it *was* at eight in the morning.

The boy caught his teetering books before any fell, scowled at her, and stalked off. How rude!

'Not another one,' the overweight, middle-aged security guard complained. 'What are *you* doing wandering around the campus after dark?' He, the other guard, and Clara all stared at her.

Lorraine froze. 'I . . . Opera!' She fumbled around in her purse and withdrew her glasses. They'd been so useful this evening! 'I'm coming from the opera, see?'

The guard frowned at Lorraine. 'Fine. Now, girlie, get back to your own campus and out of our way.'

'Do you want me to walk her back?' the other guard asked with a hopeful glint in his muddy-brown eyes. He had floppy brown hair and was barely older than Lorraine and Clara.

'No, let's just keep moving,' the first one replied.

The two men started to walk around Lorraine, but she caught

the younger one's shoulder. 'No, wait, she's my friend!' She rushed forward so she was standing in front of Clara and smiled wide at her. 'Where did you get off to, Clarabelle?' She flung her arms around Clara without waiting for an answer. It was a pretty awkward embrace since the guards were still holding both of Clara's arms. Not that Clara would've hugged her back anyway. 'I was so worried!'

'What do you think you're doing?' Clara asked through gritted teeth.

'Rescuing you,' Lorraine whispered back. 'Just shut your trap!'

'Step aside, ma'am,' the older security guard ordered, and continued walking.

Lorraine fell into step beside the younger guard, which caused the older one to harrumph and go faster. Lorraine practically ran to keep up with them, and the younger guard smiled at her.

'What's your problem with Clara? We're dear friends. I can vouch for her completely. I go to school at Barnard, that college just across the street—'

'We're well acquainted with Barnard, thanks,' the young guy said. His name tag said *Robert* while the middle-aged guy's said *Walter*. 'But one of our students said this girl was making a scene in his dormitory. He also seemed to think she'd been drinking. Now, if you'll excuse us.'

They pushed past Lorraine. 'Wait!' she said, urging her legs to keep moving. She approached them on the other side this time and tried to grab Walter's arm.

'Hands off, girlie!' He shook her off as they stepped from the lawn to a paved walkway, and Lorraine almost fell. The two men and Clara walked quickly to a redbrick building and climbed the stairs to its entrance.

'But you don't understand!' Lorraine said, stumbling up the stairs behind them. 'My Clara? Drinking? I've never heard of something so ridiculous. Why, I've never seen Clara drink *anything,* ever. Not even a glass of water—'

'Lorraine, you're not helping,' Clara said.

Robert and Walter led Clara into the building, which, judging by the men lounging in the common area and wall of mailboxes in the lobby, was also a dormitory. A few handsome boys in blazers rose from their armchairs to stare at Clara and Lorraine.

Lorraine followed the guards and Clara through a door to the left of the entrance and down the stairs to the basement. Walter scowled at Lorraine over his shoulder on the stairs. 'You're still here? Turn around, and don't stop until you're back on your own campus!'

Lorraine ignored him, and he couldn't do much about it, since that would've meant letting go of Clara. The security guards led them into a cramped, messy room. A few security guards as young as Robert were sitting at mismatched desks, reading textbooks and sipping steaming mugs of coffee. A half-full box of doughnuts and a stack of plates sat on an empty table with wooden chairs around it. Another positively ancient guard dozed on a couch against the wall.

'What is this place?' Lorraine asked Robert.

'Security headquarters,' he explained. 'And we've got

a holding cell in the back for the real troublemakers. That's where your friend is going.'

'You're putting me *where*?' Clara exclaimed.

'All right, I've got to take over the shift at Hamilton,' Walter said, ignoring Clara and checking his watch. He gave Lorraine one last glare before turning to Robert. 'You think you can handle this, Bobby?'

The younger man nodded, his shaggy hair flying as if he were a wet dog shaking himself dry. Bobby reminded Lorraine a lot of a Labrador, actually, with his big, eager-to-please brown eyes. Thank God he was the one sticking around. Lorraine would have Clara out of here in no time.

'Keeping booze and girls out of our dormitories is something we take *very* seriously here at Columbia,' Walter said to Clara. 'If you're going to get drunk, do it at your own school and let them deal with it.'

'For the last time, I'm not drunk! And I don't even go to Barnard!' Clara called, clenching her fists in frustration. But Walter was already steering his chubby form back up the stairs.

'Just come with me,' Bobby said.

He walked down a narrow hallway that branched off the office area, then took out a key ring to unlock the last door on the right. When he did, Lorraine could see over his shoulder that it was a supply closet of sorts. Cups of pencils and pens sat next to stacks of notebooks and folders on wide metal shelves. A few wooden chairs sat in the center of the tiny room and there was a coffeepot and mugs on a small table by the door.

Bobby ushered Clara inside. 'So like I said before, I'm going to have to ask you to cool your heels in our little holding cell here – just until you're sober enough to head home. There's coffee in there – that'll probably help.'

'I've said about twelve times that I'm not drunk,' Clara complained. 'Do you want me to walk in a straight line? Recite the Pledge of Allegiance?'

Bobby loosened the collar of his uniform. 'Sorry, but orders are orders. It's not like I even think drinking is such a big deal. Just last week my buddies and I went to this place called the Big Top—'

'Oh, fine!' Clara said. 'It's like talking to a damn wall.' She looked at Lorraine. 'Good job rescuing me.' Then she slammed the door to the supply closet shut behind her.

Bobby looked at Lorraine. 'You really need to leave now,' he said. 'Walter could get you in real trouble if you're still here when he gets back. I'll walk you out.'

Lorraine let out a heavy sigh and walked with Bobby back down the hallway. She needed to come up with a plan to free Clara, and fast. She'd prove that she *could* do something nice for someone else – whether that someone wanted her to or not.

Lorraine stopped at the end of the hallway.

'Why did you stop?' Bobby asked, halting as well. 'Is something wrong?'

Lorraine sidled up close to him, nearly pinning him against the yellow wall. She put her gloved hand on his arm and gave Bobby her best sexy sheba stare. 'I'm just dying to see the inside of a real jail cell, Officer!'

The security guard's face flushed and he blinked his big eyes a few times. 'I just do this to help pay my tuition. And it's not a real jail cell. We're in the basement of a dormitory.'

'I don't believe you!' she exclaimed. 'Of course it's a cell. You just said so yourself!'

'We call it that. It's really just a door that locks. You shouldn't worry about your friend – she'll be fine.'

'Doors don't lock! Not where I grew up!' Lorraine blurted out desperately. She looked between him and the door to the supply closet in mock wonder.

'Really? Where did you grow up?'

Lorraine thought for a moment. 'Amish country!' She could hear what sounded suspiciously like muffled laughter coming through the door.

Bobby eyed Lorraine's pleated navy-blue wool crepe Patou day dress. It barely reached her knees. 'Dressed like that?'

Lorraine had really picked the wrong outfit today, hadn't she? He would never believe her now. Unless . . . 'I'm trying to blend in. I'm on my rumspringa!' Lorraine looked down in concern. 'Isn't this what sinners in New York wear?'

Bobby laughed. 'You might've gone too far in the sinner direction.'

Lorraine gave him a coy smile and ran her fingertip down his skinny chest. 'Well, that does seem to be how, um, *non-Amish* girls get the attention of handsome boys like yourself. Now show me this 'locking door' of which you speak.'

Bobby, still blushing and a little dazed, walked back to Clara's 'cell.' He unlocked the door and opened it. 'See?'

'So,' Lorraine said, 'if I go in here and you close the door, I'm locked in?' He nodded. She walked through the doorway. Clara rose from her wooden chair with a hiked eyebrow. Lorraine ignored her and looked back at Bobby. 'Show me.'

Bobby closed the door on them and Lorraine tried to turn the doorknob a few times. Then she walked over to Clara's chair with a smug grin. 'You can thank me later,' she whispered.

Clara stared at her. 'Lorraine, what exactly are you—'

'The mouse is going to be your cue to run,' Lorraine whispered.

'What?' Clara asked.

'Try opening the door again,' Bobby called from outside.

Lorraine jiggled the knob and the door opened. She stood in the doorway with her hands on her hips. 'How do I know you weren't just holding the knob, using your muscles so that it won't turn?'

'Because it's a lock,' Bobby replied, somewhere between amusement and exasperation.

She crossed her arms. 'Back on the farm in Amish country, people used to tell tales about things like locks all the time. Like how buildings here in the city have these floating boxes that people ride in instead of climbing stairs! Can you imagine?'

'I should probably get back to work—'

'See, I knew you were lying! Locking doors, what a silly idea.'

Bobby sighed and walked past her into the supply closet. 'Okay, this time I'll let you close the door on me.' He took his key ring out of his pocket and handed a large silver key to Lorraine. 'But then you go home, all right? And maybe, well – my shift ends at nine . . . if you wanted to—'

Lorraine took the keys from him, then pointed at the corner in mock horror. 'A mouse!' she exclaimed. Before Bobby had a chance to look, Lorraine grabbed Clara's wrist and pulled her through the doorway.

She shut the door, locked it, and pocketed the key.

'Hey, you weren't supposed to bring your friend out with you!' Bobby called through the door. 'And I don't see any mouse!'

The girls ran into the hallway. 'Oh my God, I can't believe you did that!' Clara's voice was high with fear, anger, or admiration. Admiration, Lorraine decided.

'I know! What a rush!'

'What do we do now?' Clara whispered with wide blue eyes.

Ha! Clara Knowles was asking *her* what to do. Competency proven!

'Raine?'

'Run,' Lorraine said. 'There's a church nearby, Saint John the Divine. The guards would never chase us in there. It would be blasphemy or something.'

Clara looked doubtful but nodded.

'I don't see any mouse,' Bobby called out. 'And anyway, I was right about the lock. See? I can't get out.'

'Are you sure?' Lorraine asked.

The doorknob jiggled. 'Yeah, you've got the key, remember?'

'You're right, I do!' Lorraine called with a laugh. 'Bye!'

Lorraine gripped Clara's wrist and pulled her down the hall, away from Bobby and his poor, dumb Labrador eyes.

They ran past the security guards in the office, up the stairs, and straight out the door. They raced across campus, constantly looking behind them. A group of well-dressed Barnard girls and Columbia boys walked toward them – they were probably *actually* coming from the opera. The two girls veered out of the way onto the grass.

Finally they made it through Columbia's black gate and onto Amsterdam Avenue. They both laughed, relieved. 'We made it!' Clara said.

Lorraine looked back to the brick dorm they'd just left and saw two security guards running out the entrance. 'Not quite,' she said, pointing.

She grabbed Clara's hand and they ran straight down the sidewalk. A hulking Rolls-Royce honked loudly at them as they dashed across the street toward an enormous, beautiful Gothic stone church that looked like it had been yanked straight out of a piazza in Italy. The sight of its intricately carved archways, numerous columns, and rooftop spires against the night sky would've been gorgeous if Lorraine had had the time to appreciate it. The two girls rushed up the stone stairs and through the heavy bronze doors into the church.

Clara looked over her shoulder when the doors shut behind them. 'Do you think we lost them?'

'Definitely. They hadn't even left campus by the time we got here.'

Clara smoothed her hair under her headband as they walked down the center aisle. Lorraine found this surprisingly endearing. She'd never felt anything special when she walked into a church. To her, churches were just big, old buildings where people tended to get *very* angry when she pulled out a flask in a pew.

But the quiet wonder of this building did demand respect, no matter what religion a person subscribed to. They passed through the aisle under high, domed ceilings. Creamy white columns stood near the altar. The enormous stained-glass windows added splashes of warmth and vibrancy to the cathedral's otherwise somber atmosphere. An older woman dressed in black sat with a candle in her hands while a group of tourists marveled at the architecture in excited silence.

Clara and Lorraine slipped into one of the long wooden pews and sat down. 'It's not like an hour in the supply closet would've killed me.'

Lorraine shrugged. 'If I hadn't told you all that about Marcus, you never would've sneaked into his dorm.'

Clara met Lorraine's eyes. '*Amish,* Raine, really?'

'It worked, didn't it?'

'It did. Thanks, I guess.' Clara sank further into her seat. 'I'm sorry I didn't take you seriously when you tried to tell me about Marcus's fiancée. You were right. Her real name is Deirdre Van Doren and she's got some kind of record.'

'Like a criminal one? Then let's call the police, let them deal with her.'

'Shhh!' a frizzy-haired tourist hissed, glaring at them. Jeez,

Lorraine thought, just because she had horrible hair didn't mean she had to take it out on everyone else.

Clara leaned forward and whispered, 'No, I talked to an ex-cop who'd worked some of her cases in the past. He said he *thinks* Anastasia is Deirdre, but he can't provide anything that would hold up in court.' Clara fiddled with her aquamarine ring. 'So I'm going to have to make sure Marcus doesn't marry her myself. Even if he doesn't want to be with me, he deserves someone better than her.'

Lorraine studied formerly Country Clara and felt her stomach twist up. She'd known Clara wasn't really over Marcus – how could she be? It was *Marcus Eastman*. Marcus Eastman, the guy Lorraine had been in love with for the better part of her adolescence. As much as she wanted to save Marcus from ruin, part of her still wanted to be the girl he turned to once he was free of his duplicitous bride-to-be.

But the truth was like a fresh cup of coffee – it woke you up. Marcus would never want *her*. He was still in love with Clara. He never would've called security if he didn't harbor feelings for the girl. Being that angry took a lot of energy – energy Marcus wouldn't waste on someone who didn't matter a hell of a lot to him.

Lorraine stared at the high ceilings and felt a chill of piercing but revelatory silence. She could focus on the way Clara had put her down, how Marcus refused to notice her, how Gloria had abandoned her when she'd needed her most.

Or she could get over it and try to take the high road for once.

'I'll help you do the right thing, Clara. By doing the *wrong* thing. I'm an expert at that. We'll confront this quiff and chase her out of town!'

Clara nodded. 'And if she doesn't agree to leave, I'll publish an exposé on her. I managed to dig up a lot of dirt on her today. Maybe not enough to get her arrested, but it would definitely make Marcus's parents think twice about letting him go through with the wedding.' She paused. 'Provided Parker lets me do that. He might want me to focus on parties and gossip – it's what sells.'

'Whether Parker gives you permission or not, that shouldn't stop you from threatening Deirdre that you'll expose her.'

They both heard a man clear his throat and whipped around in their seats toward the aisle. A gray-haired man in a white priest's robe stood next to them with his arms crossed. 'I must ask you to keep your voices down. This is a place of worship.'

'Hey, it's not *your* church,' Lorraine snapped. Couldn't he see that they were in the middle of an important conversation?

Clara popped out of her seat and grabbed Lorraine's arm. 'We're very sorry. We'll finish our conversation somewhere else.' She paused. 'This church is really beautiful.'

The priest patted Clara's shoulder. 'You'll have to come back sometime, really take everything in. And be a bit quieter about it, if you don't mind.'

Lorraine stared at Clara's sheepish, genuine smile. She had thought that everything about Clara's country bumpkin act had been exactly that – an act. But she was beginning to see that at least some part of it had been the real girl peeking out.

Which made Lorraine appreciate Clara even more. She wasn't just the kind of girl who looked good in a designer gown. Clara could also appreciate the quiet brilliance of a nearly empty church on an early Monday evening.

'Yeah, I guess this place isn't so bad,' Lorraine commented as they left. 'Though I think they'd really benefit if they put in a bar in the back. Think how many seats they'd fill if you could get a martini with your prayer!'

Chapter 14

JEROME

Jerome didn't know a thing about croquet.

And yet he was pretty sure he could still play it better than Forrest and his guests.

The group was gathered on the wide lawn in front of Forrest's extravagant villa. Wickets were set up around the yard, and cushioned lawn chairs were laid out in a row. Forrest stood in front of the red ball with his mallet.

'Let's see if Forrest can aim for the right wicket this time,' a blonde sitting on one of the chairs called from under her large hat. Jerome was pretty sure her name was Glitter or Sparkle or some other such nonsense.

'I doubt it,' a darker blonde said from her seat next to the other one. 'His aim has never been very good. Have you seen how many times he's tried to hit Marty's balls out of the way? But you're here to stay, aren't you, Marty?'

Overweight, sunburned Marty was dressed for the game in white shorts and a white-and-red plaid sweater. He ignored the two girls completely and leaned on his mallet, the bulge of his stomach hanging out over his shorts. Marty's wife, Ruby Hayworth, wore a simple ivory day dress. The actress was a dead ringer for Clara Bow, only with dark brown hair rather than red.

Ruby rolled her eyes. 'Glitz, Glamour, lay off and let Forrest concentrate.'

She gave Forrest a warm smile and the playboy looked practically thunderstruck. She'd already bagged herself a rich husband – and now it looked like she had Forrest wrapped around her finger as well. Jerome wondered how Ruby managed to stay the center of attention with a firecracker like Gloria around. Sure, Ruby had charisma, but that was a given. You couldn't get far in show business without it.

Gloria had more charisma in her little toe than ten Ruby Hayworths. She was the last match in a matchbook – the one that managed to spark while the others lay dull and useless on the ground.

Gloria – his Gloria.

Today she was wearing a sleeveless lavender blouse and a pale gray skirt with a matching gray cloche. When Forrest managed to hit his ball through the correct wicket for the first time since they'd started playing, Gloria burst into delighted, musical laughter. 'I knew you had it in you,' she said to him.

'I'm actually a decent player on my good days,' Forrest replied. 'But how can I keep my mind on the game with so many lovely distractions so close by?' He winked at Gloria, and from fifteen feet away Jerome could see her blush. What was that – was Forrest flirting with Gloria?

Jerome brushed the idea out of his mind. Last night Gloria had told him how supportive Forrest was of their relationship – more than any white man she'd ever met. Forrest was a friend.

Well, sort of.

'Waiter?' Glitz called, and almost startled him into dropping the tray of gin and tonics in his hand. 'I think I could use another.'

'But your glass is still full!' Glamour remarked.

'Mmm, but my other hand is empty and not doing anything special. Why waste it when it could be doing something useful like holding my next drink?'

Waiter. The word pained him. Glitz took a drink from Jerome's tray without saying thank you or even acknowledging his existence. Jerome walked back to his post beside the row of lawn chairs. He stood with his tray held high and a towel over his arm: just another piece of furniture.

He used to be a musician. What had happened to him?

Jerome looked back to the croquet game. Apparently Forrest had convinced Gloria that he was a good enough player to teach her how to shoot. She bent over the ball with her mallet, laughing, while Forrest laid his hands on her arm and shoulder.

Too close for comfort.

Then Forrest called to Jerome over his shoulder. 'Waiter! I think this game is getting a little too sober for anyone's liking.'

Jerome took a deep breath and marched over to the two teams on the lawn. Forrest took drinks for himself and Gloria. He leaned in close and clinked his glass against Gloria's. 'To mopping the floor with these two,' he said, his lips close to Gloria's ear. Gloria's face was bright red now.

Jerome trusted Gloria, and Gloria had said that Forrest only saw her as a pal. So what the hell was Forrest playing at, pawing at Gloria like this? Jerome clenched his fists and told himself to calm down. Hank had worked hard to get him here – he couldn't risk blowing his cover. Thankfully, even if Forrest approved of him theoretically, the man had no idea what Jerome looked like – so Jerome was able to be at his estate without raising any suspicion.

Yet.

Before last night, Jerome hadn't spoken to Gloria in weeks – even though he'd been so worried about her. He'd seen in the papers that she'd been released from prison and hated that he couldn't go straight to her. But Hank had said he couldn't. So Jerome just had to wait and hope that Gloria was thinking of him even a fraction as much as he was thinking of and longing for her.

Then last night had been such a blur of pure joy and relief. The waves of her autumn-fire hair, those brilliant, pale eyes that held more intelligence and strength than Jerome had ever thought a silver-spoon dame like her could possess. God, he'd missed her.

The sun was already rising outside Gloria's window by the time they got to talking. Jerome lay on Gloria's enormous bed with her head on his chest, her soft, beautiful hair tickling his nose. He'd been ready to fall asleep in the heaven he'd found in Gloria's arms, but she'd pulled away and looked up at him with a mix of elation and concern on her face.

'I'm so happy to see you, Jerome. But what are you doing here?' she asked. 'I'm working to get us both out of trouble. Hank said—'

Jerome had put two of his fingers to her lips. 'Hank's the one who sent me here.'

He told Gloria how her father had left him in Middle of Nowhere, New Jersey. She gripped the silk comforter hard as Jerome told the story. At one point she interrupted him. 'Can you please stop calling that man my father?' A tear ran down her cheek, but her expression remained fierce. 'He lost his right to being called that a long time ago.'

Jerome looked at his fiancée for a moment, lost in sadness and admiration for her. Jerome's own father had never understood him, had done everything he could to tear Jerome away from music. He and Gloria had this in common. 'Well, anyway, I woke up on a tiny cot in a ramshackle house. A real sweet old couple, the Walkers, had found me lying on the side of the road not long after I passed out.'

'Thank God,' Gloria said.

'They insisted I stay with them for a few days to get my strength back up, then they directed me to the nearest pay phone in Hoboken. From there I called Hank, and he promised to help me out with Lowell if I helped you with Forrest.' Jerome looked away, unsure how Gloria would react to this next part. 'It took Hank a little bit of time, but soon he was able to get an investigation into your father's business dealings going. Now . . . well, Lowell doesn't have any time to worry about who you're planning to marry.'

Gloria smiled in relief. 'Good. One less problem for us.'

'So Hank set me up at a hotel in New York on the bureau's dime and worked to plant me here as a servant. Hank appreciates that it's probably been hard for you to get a chance to go through Forrest's things, being his guest – a servant would have a lot more access. He said I couldn't contact you. Otherwise, sweetheart, you know I would have.'

She nodded. 'I know. I'm just happy you're safe. And

Hank's right – I could use your help.' Gloria told him about Forrest's inheritance from his late father. 'So you see, he's not a criminal at all. Hank probably just got bored with gin busts and decided to target Forrest. But Hank will never believe me without proof. I've been waiting for the right moment to search Forrest's room so I can find his father's will and we can leave the past where it belongs: in the past. And move on with our lives.'

Jerome peered at Gloria, skeptical. 'What makes you think Forrest is telling the truth?'

'I know this mansion and the company he keeps might make you think differently, but Forrest really is a decent man,' Gloria said. 'You'll see.'

Jerome couldn't bring himself to dash the hope in Gloria's eyes. 'All right. The first chance I get, I'll search his room and find that will. Then we'll get out of here and it'll be just you and me.'

When Gloria fell asleep, he sneaked back to the servants' quarters happier than he'd been in weeks.

But now the joy drained from him as he watched Forrest manhandle Gloria. Forrest's hand had been on Gloria's waist for what felt like hours. It was too much for Jerome to take, no matter how *decent* Gloria insisted Forrest was.

Jerome abruptly twisted the hand holding the silver tray so that all five remaining gin and tonics splashed all over Forrest's navy-blue pin-striped jacket. Gloria squealed in surprise and Forrest jumped away from her.

'I'm so sorry, sir,' Jerome said half a second too late.

There was a tense, sickly pause in the air as Forrest pulled a white handkerchief out of his jacket pocket, wiping his hands with it. Then he did the impossible: He laughed.

'Ah, that was refreshing,' he remarked. 'I think a gin shower was exactly what I needed to up my game.' He glanced at Jerome without really looking at him. 'Thank you, good sir.' He took off his jacket, folded it over, and handed it to Jerome. 'I'm afraid I'll need a new one of these, though.'

Damn. Maybe Gloria was right after all. 'You're not angry?' Jerome asked.

Forrest waved him off. 'If even half the drinks that get poured around here survive, I count myself a lucky man. There's a similar jacket on the far right side of my closet.' He pulled a heavy silver key ring out of his pocket, pulled a brass key free from the rest, and handed the key to Jerome. 'I keep my bedroom locked, old boy.'

Jerome looked behind Forrest at Gloria, who eyed the keys in Jerome's hand and looked as though she was trying to suppress a delighted laugh. Gloria probably thought Jerome had orchestrated this whole thing so he'd be able to get into Forrest's room.

'Of course,' Jerome said to Forrest, 'I'll be right back with that for you, sir.'

Five minutes later, Jerome stood in the middle of what was easily the finest bedroom he'd ever seen.

The walls were paneled in soft mahogany, and a few tastefully abstract paintings hung in gilded frames. A four-poster bed sat in the middle of the room, and a few framed photos on the dresser and the desk by the window displayed Forrest next to gorgeous Follies dancers or famous actors.

Jerome crossed to the closet. It was full of fine silk shirts of every color and enough suits to clothe an army of gentlemen. Jerome removed the navy-blue coat Forrest had mentioned and hung it on the back of the desk chair. Then he moved to the desk and began shuffling through Forrest's mail. He didn't really know where Forrest would keep a copy of his father's will – he was a musician, not a detective. But he did have an advantage in this investigation that Gloria didn't: invisibility.

When Hank had first mentioned the possibility of Jerome's working as a servant in Forrest's home, Jerome had never thought it would work.

'We've paid off Forrest's head housekeeper. She hires all his help for him,' Hank had explained. 'You'll show up with a few other new servants, and it'll be your job to do your best to blend in. With any luck, Forrest won't even notice you're there.'

'But won't he recognize me? My face has been plastered in at least half as many magazines as Gloria's since everything that went down at the Opera House,' Jerome pointed out.

Hank had given him a pitying smile. 'Jerome, you're black. Put you in serving clothes and you'll be practically invisible to wealthy white folks like Forrest and his crowd. Forrest is the sort of man who, if he did read any of those *Manhattanite* articles, never would've looked past the pretty girl on your arm in the photos. A guy like you? You've only ever been an invisible man to him.'

Jerome had spent his whole life avoiding this kind of serving-the-white-man work. But Hank had made it clear that if Jerome wanted to escape Lowell and see his beloved fiancée anytime soon, he was going to have to get over his pride and do what needed to be done.

Unable to find anything out of the ordinary on the mahogany desk, Jerome began opening the drawers on each side. In the middle drawer on the left, he found a thick beige envelope. He withdrew two steamship tickets to Paris. The boat was leaving in a week. He also found a folded slip of notebook paper in the envelope. It was a sort of list written in impeccably neat handwriting:

Height: 5'2'
Weight: 105 lb.?
To Bring Along:
7 day dresses
7 evening dresses
4 skirts
4 blouses
Shoes? Ask Marlene at Bloomingdale's
Dial Madame Barbas/House of Patou as soon
    as we arrive

The handwriting looked masculine, but what was all this about skirts and blouses . . . unless . . . Forrest was planning to whisk a girl away to Paris!

Jerome felt his throat close up. From the way Forrest had

been acting outside, it wasn't too hard to guess who that girl might be.

Gloria had said she'd talked to Forrest about Jerome – it wasn't like this man had no idea Gloria was no longer available. What, did Forrest think that because Gloria was engaged to a black man, it didn't count as a real engagement? How dare Forrest try to steal his girl! It would serve the man right if Jerome ripped up these tickets right now.

But that was a big, stupid risk that Jerome knew he couldn't take. Besides, he knew if Forrest offered Gloria a trip to Paris, she'd refuse him. He returned the tickets and list to the envelope and put them back where he'd found them.

Jerome moved to the dresser. He went through it drawer by drawer and found far less clothing in the last one than there should've been. He reached through the stacks of polo shirts to the bottom of the drawer and grinned when the wood lifted easily under his hands. He cleared out the drawer and lifted the false bottom.

His eyes were drawn first to a small black velvet box in the corner. Inside? A ring that made Gloria's look like a child's plaything. It had a white-gold band, and several tiny diamonds were grouped into the shape of a flower at the center. Maybe the ring was just a family heirloom – maybe it had nothing to do with Gloria – but the sight of it still made Jerome queasy.

Jerome glanced at the door and listened hard for footsteps or voices, but the coast was still clear. He turned his attention to a large leather-covered book that took up most of the space in the bottom of the drawer. Jerome flipped through the photo album and recognized a handsome young boy with dark, glinting eyes as a younger version of Forrest. In one picture, the boy looked about five or six. He stood at the edge of a pond, fishing rod in hand. A mustached man in a casual checkered shirt and trousers stood behind Forrest with a hand on his shoulder. Forrest was laughing, but the man's expression was grave.

Jerome had to look at the picture for a few moments before he realized why the man seemed familiar. He hadn't been bald back then – he'd had dark, silky hair just like Forrest's, and it swept over his forehead in the exact same way. Though the man's pale eyes were more sinister, they had the same appealing glimmer as Forrest's – and like Forrest, the man was remarkably handsome.

This was before the man had gotten the scar that stretched across his face.

Without the scar, the resemblance between Forrest's man Pembroke and Forrest was unmistakable. The clefts in their chins, their long, straight noses, their lips that would've looked too thin on anyone else.

Pembroke wasn't Forrest's manservant, or bodyguard, or goon. Pembroke was Forrest's *father*.

But Gloria had told Jerome that Forrest said his father was dead. Why had he lied? And why was his father pretending to be a butler?

Jerome heard the grandfather clock in the foyer begin to chime. He'd been up here for half an hour already! Far too long to merely fetch a jacket. He reassembled the drawer as fast as he could and replaced the clothes.

He turned, ready to bolt out the door. And he met a pair of pale, bloodshot eyes. The same ones in the photograph.

Jerome gulped and dropped the jacket in his hands on the floor. He stumbled backward, bumping up against the cold metal handles of the dresser drawers. A framed photo of Forrest and some dancer fell on the floor, the glass shattering. Jerome looked quickly out the window, searching for some other escape. Then he stared into those eyes and they chilled him to the bone. What could he do now?

Pembroke stood in the doorway and chuckled, low and deep, at Jerome's distress.

His arms were crossed, but the doorframe still seemed too small to contain his bulk. Pembroke's lips curved into a garish, crooked smile beneath his bushy gray mustache. Like his son, he was dressed in a blue pin-striped suit. But his pale blue eyes held none of Forrest's good humor. They were flat and soulless – a killer's eyes.

Pembroke clucked his tongue disapprovingly. 'A floozy singer and a colored boy. They must not think much of my son over at the bureau if this is the cavalry they send after him.'

Pembroke continued to grin, making his jagged scar even more unsettling. He moved a few steps closer and Jerome backed away from the dresser and farther into the room, until he was against the wood-paneled wall. Then Pembroke pulled a hefty black pistol from his side holster. Jerome didn't know much about guns, but he knew a gun that size at this range would take his head clean off.

Pembroke pointed the gun at Jerome's temple. 'So. Did you find what you were looking for, Detective?'

Chapter 15

GLORIA

Gloria was beginning to understand why none of Forrest's shows had done well.

'Hey, Gretchen!' Earl slurred, slumped on his piano bench. 'You ready to run through "A Penny for Your Thoughts"?'

'It's Gloria,' she replied, 'and I'm not sure that's—'

'Come on, Glo!' Glitz called from her cushioned golden chair at the other end of the salon. She and the others sat by the floor-to-ceiling arched windows in the informal audience area. 'Keep going! It's all been jake so far. Ain't that right, Glam?'

Beside Glitz, Glamour clapped. 'Encore, encore! These songs are just the rage, Forrest. Much better than the ones in your other shows.'

What are the songs from his other *shows like?* Gloria wondered. *Maybe the actors just scratch their fingernails across a blackboard for ninety minutes.*

Gloria stood next to a grand piano in a salon on the first floor of Forrest's villa, looking over the pianist's shoulder at sheet music from *Moonshine Melody*. The pianist was a middle-aged man named Earl with messy dark hair and a thin mustache, still dressed in the tuxedo he'd worn to Forrest's party the evening before. He was more than a little tipsy, his fingers drunkenly caressing the black-and-white keys.

After the bright, sugar-sweet intro, she began to sing:

Oh, how I wish you would hold me tight
And tell me all that keeps you up at night,
All your greatest dreams and fears
Words that would bring you to tears.
Only then will I truly know your love
And believe you were sent from above
To give me strength and happy thoughts
So here's a penny, a penny for your thoughts.

There were so, so many things wrong with the song – even discounting obvious mistakes like rhyming *thoughts* with *thoughts*. The timing was off and the song was filled with sappy clichés. Who on earth was the lyricist Forrest had hired?

It wasn't like Forrest was paying attention anyway. When he had proposed that Earl run through a few songs from Forrest's new show with Gloria, she'd been so excited. Forrest was really considering her for a lead role – a role he'd previously wanted a star like Ruby Hayworth to fill!

But instead of watching Gloria perform, Forrest spent the whole time staring at Ruby. Finally the glamorous actress met his eyes and smiled at him. Then she turned to her husband. 'Marty, could you get me another rum and soda?'

'Tell the waiter,' Marty replied tersely.

'Oh, but no one can make rum and sodas the way you do.'

Marty harrumphed and left with both their glasses. As soon as he was gone, Ruby scooted as close to Forrest as her seat would allow and whispered something in his ear. They both laughed softly and didn't break eye contact for a second.

'This salon is gorgeous,' Ruby said to him, touching his wrist lightly and looking around at the gold sconces on the wall and crystal chandeliers hanging overhead.

Forrest covered her hand with his. 'Is it? I hadn't noticed.'

'You really are doing well for yourself these days. It's nice of you to let us enjoy your success with you – thank you for that.'

'No, *thank you*. I didn't enjoy it at all – not until you showed up.' Ruby positively glowed at this.

The two whispered through Gloria's song, touching each other with a casual ease that astounded Gloria. You'd think they'd been a couple for years.

Ruby and Forrest backed off when Marty returned, but they still caught each other's eyes every chance they got. Meanwhile, Marty just gripped the arms of his chair hard and drank down shots of Scotch faster than the waiter could bring them.

Gloria looked away from them and tried to focus on her performance. But she just couldn't get into it – the song was terrible.

Jerome had once given Gloria a talk about committing to the material no matter what it was. 'Chances are, you're not gonna love everything they hand you to sing. But if it's what they want to hear, you've just gotta deal with it and thank God, your manager, and Fate itself for giving you the chance to do what you love for a living.'

But Jerome wasn't here to give her a pep talk. He hadn't shown up at her room after the party last night, and Gloria had thought maybe he was just being careful after what had happened during the croquet game yesterday afternoon. But when she hadn't seen him this morning, she'd questioned Forrest about it. He'd said that after the bit with the jacket, his man Pembroke had found Jerome going through Forrest's things in his bedroom. So Pembroke had fired him on the spot. 'You just can't find good help nowadays,' Forrest had said with a shrug and a smile.

Gloria planned to call Hank as soon as she got a moment alone. She hoped that somehow Jerome had hooked back up with the FBI and they were looking out for him. Maybe Jerome had even found the will before Pembroke had caught him. Gloria prayed that he had. She'd had enough of this place. She wanted to go back to the city, back to Jerome. This gilded mansion was starting to feel as imprisoning as actual prison had.

Gloria finished singing, and after a moment, Ruby and Forrest remembered to tear their eyes away from each other and clap with the others.

Forrest stood from his chair and patted Gloria's shoulder. Now that he had Ruby's undivided attention, Gloria was his buddy once again. 'Fantastic work, my friend! And now you've put me in the mood for a musical. What do you say we head into the city and see my show *The Cat's Meow*?'

Glitz pursed her lips. 'No offense, Hammy, but I don't think you could pay me to see that show again. I should get a medal for sitting through it on opening night.'

'Mmm,' Glamour agreed. '*The Cat's Screech* would've been a better title.'

'What if I paid you in food and booze?' Forrest asked. 'We'll stop by Twenty-One beforehand. Drink enough of their martinis and it'll be the greatest show you ever saw, I guarantee it.'

'Now you're talkin'!' Glitz said, fanning herself.

'How about you, Glo?' Forrest asked as the others rose from their chairs. 'I'm afraid the show's as awful as they say. The playwright used to be brilliant, and when we met in a gin joint, I thought it was fate. Too late I realized that these days, that man is *always* in some gin joint or other. He's been hitting the bottle too hard for years, and so the script is basically nonsense. But I'll make sure we get a chance to go backstage after the show. You can get more of a sense of the Broadway world, what it's like behind the scenes. Maybe it'll help you decide if it's the kind of place you might want to work.'

'I'd have a lot to learn before I could ever really think about a Broadway career,' Gloria said. But even so, her mind swam with images of packed theaters, beautiful love stories made even lovelier by song, and a dozen red roses waiting in her dressing room by a mirror ringed in lights.

'You've got talent and more charisma than any leading lady I've seen on Broadway,' Forrest said. He looked at Ruby, who stood gossiping with Glitz and Glamour while Marty moved toward the door. 'Don't you think, Ruby?'

Instantly Ruby was at Forrest's side. 'Absolutely,' she said. But she was looking at Forrest, not Gloria.

'Ruby, are you coming?' Marty called from the doorway impatiently.

'You go ahead, Marty,' Ruby replied dismissively without

171

even looking at him. Before, Ruby had at least pretended to care about her husband, but now she only had eyes for Forrest. Was she really getting up the courage to leave Marty?

Forrest smiled dreamily at Ruby for what felt like a full minute before he looked back at Gloria. 'Sorry, what were we talking about?'

'You were saying how Gloria could be on Broadway, and I was agreeing,' Ruby answered, her eyes glittering with delight.

'Right, right. Anyway, the other stuff can be learned easily enough,' Forrest said to Gloria. 'You'll have plenty of opportunities in your life to sing your heart out on the Great White Way – there's no doubt in my mind.'

Gloria paused to think. This adventure into the city would mean she wouldn't get a chance until tomorrow to call Hank. But she couldn't hide her excitement. Jerome would *want* her to seize this opportunity, wouldn't he? She could meet producers and other people in the industry. That way, once she was free of the charges against her for good, she'd have a way to support them both.

Gloria had been eager to see a show since she'd arrived in New York. She couldn't think of a better introduction to the wonders of Broadway than doing so as the producer's personal guest.

'Thank you, Forrest, I'd love to!' she replied.

'Fantastic!' Forrest said. 'Then put on your glad rags, girls, and do it fast! I expect to see you outside in half an hour.'

'Half an hour!' Glamour exclaimed. 'That's barely enough time to get my eyelashes on!'

At five-thirty, the group gathered around Forrest's black Lincoln and Marty's surprisingly rusty old red Model T.

Gloria had never seen a smart set dressed more smartly than Forrest and his friends. He and Marty both wore gray suits, but the similar outfits only exaggerated the differences between them. Marty looked short and pudgy in his ill-fitting suit and bright red shirt – what had Ruby ever seen in him? Forrest's suit was like an expensive second skin that accentuated his trim, muscled build. He wore a pale yellow shirt with a white collar that looked delicious against his tanned skin and made his dark eyes even more arresting. His hair looked carelessly tousled; the effect was sexy enough to make Gloria wonder why so many boys bothered with slicking their hair back.

Glamour was a ray of sunlight in a gown of gold brocade. Glitz's outfit coordinated well with her friend's – she wore an ivory dress with a gold lamé hip band.

Ruby looked possibly the most beautiful Gloria had ever seen her. She wore a full-length burnt-orange dress with Grecian-style beading on the shoulders, and diamond earrings dangled from her ears. Her dark, wavy hair was parted far on the side so that a wave fell over one sparkling dark brown eye. Her dress was easily the longest of the four girls'. But Ruby was a girl who didn't need to dress sexy to be sexy – her sheer essence gave her all the sex appeal she would ever need.

Gloria knew she didn't look too bad herself. She'd chosen a Jeanne Paquin dress made almost entirely of sea-green lace, with two satin panels on the sides. The dress brought out her eyes, especially with her matching jade earrings.

'So I guess we should figure out who's driving who?' Ruby asked. There was something a little strained and nervous about her typically musical voice.

'What?' Forrest asked. He'd been staring at her in stupefied silence since she'd walked out the front door.

Ruby smiled. 'I was just about to say that Gloria could come with me in Marty's jalopy and you all can have Pembroke drive you. You don't mind, do you, Marty? Gloria wanted me to give her some advice on auditioning and I just don't want to bore you.'

Gloria hadn't even noticed Forrest's manservant near the marble steps to Forrest's front door. Wearing a black suit, he stood with his hands clasped behind his back like a silent but horrifying ghost. Just *looking* at the older man gave her the shivers. She'd be grateful not to be stuck in a car with him.

Ten minutes later, Pembroke didn't seem so bad. Ruby was a gorgeous girl of many talents – but driving was certainly not one of them.

'Um, how long has Marty had this car?' Gloria asked lightly. She wasn't sure if talking would help Ruby's swerving or make things worse.

'About a hundred years,' Ruby replied. 'He's rich as they come, but he won't replace this car until it stops dead in the street. If I knew more about cars I'd probably try to speed up that process somehow.'

Gloria laughed. 'So, have you seen *The Cat's Meow*?'

Ruby took her eyes off the road for a horrifying moment. 'Let's cut to the chase, shall we?'

'About auditioning, you mean?'

Ruby snorted. 'I know you've been snooping around here.'

Gloria felt the blood drain from her face. She stared out the windows as rain began to fall. 'I don't know what you're—'

'Save it, honey.' Ruby honked the horn and hollered, 'Get outta my way, nutty!' then dashed into another lane.

This is it, Gloria thought. *I'm going to die.*

'Forrest is as good a man as God has ever created,' Ruby went on. 'If there's anything dirty in that house, it's not him.'

'Are you implying that somebody *else's* dirty laundry might be hanging somewhere in Forrest's house?' Gloria asked. Had the inheritance story been a lie after all? But why would Forrest lie if he really had done nothing wrong?

'It's complicated,' Ruby said after a few moments. 'But how about we make a deal: It'll take me a few days, but I'll get you the information you need. *And* I'll make sure you snag the lead role in *Moonshine Melody.* In return, you're going to make sure no coppers come after us when Forrest and I disappear on Saturday night.'

'I'm listening,' Gloria said in a measured voice. It sounded too good to be true. Freedom for her and Jerome, and the lead in a Broadway show? Sure, the show clearly wasn't great, but it was still a *Broadway* show. Thousands of girls would kill for that kind of shot, and those were girls with tons of experience.

But if Gloria had learned anything in the past year, it was

175

this: If something seemed too good to be true, it probably was.

'Forrest and I were in love a few years ago,' Ruby explained. 'I was in the choir at my church back then, and Forrest always used to walk me home. He was so handsome, and smart, and . . . well, he was just the same as he is now. Only he was poor, and my father was set on my marrying Marty. Forrest and I talked about eloping, but in the end I was too afraid.'

Interesting. That made sense – their chemistry was too deep to have only developed over just these past few weeks. No wonder Forrest had been so fixated on Ruby! She was the one who got away. Now he finally had the money to get the girl, but it was too late. Or was it?

'Why are you telling me this?' Gloria asked.

'Because I know your story,' Ruby replied. 'I've read all about you. You could've married that Sebastian Grey, had a horrible life – like mine. But you followed your heart. And now it's time I did the same thing. Only I'm gonna need your help.'

Gloria watched the road blur by through the window, the trees combining in a mass of deep green through the rain. She'd wondered before what might've happened if she had stayed in Chicago and gone through with her marriage to Bastian. Living with Jerome in their closet of an apartment in Harlem, she'd even wondered if she'd made the wrong choice by running away from her easy, hassle-free life.

But looking at Ruby, Gloria could see that the hassles were what made life worth living – so long as love was waiting on the other side. Ruby was married to a wealthy man, had a dream of a career, was young and beautiful. All she could see, though, was the absence of the one man who had ever made her truly happy.

This was something Gloria understood herself. It was the same way she would have felt if she hadn't picked Jerome. She *had* to help Ruby.

And also . . . the prospect of taking over Ruby's part didn't hurt.

'All right, Ruby, I'd say we've got a deal. You get me proof of where Forrest's money comes from – something tangible I can show to the FBI – and I'll help you get away.'

Gloria gasped when Ruby swerved out of their lane, nearly crashing into a honking blue Cadillac. She parked on the shoulder of the road, twenty feet away from the tollbooths into New York City.

Ruby turned and gave Gloria an exhilarated smile. She extended her hand. 'A deal isn't a deal without a proper handshake.'

Gloria shook her hand. 'I really hope you're right about Forrest and that things work out for you two.'

'Thank you. I hope the best for you and Jerome, too.'

Jerome. Gloria's stomach swirled at the sound of his name. Now that she had a clear path to some professional success, she had to turn her focus to reuniting with the love of her life – before anything else terrible happened to him.

Chapter 16

CLARA

It was Clara's first visit to a bridal salon and she was here with Lorraine Dyer. *By choice.* Life certainly was full of strange surprises.

Lorraine nudged her side as they passed by the first rack by the door. 'You see the third one from the left? With the halter top and the lace?'

Priscilla's Bridal Salon had looked elegant enough through its expansive front windows, but it was positutely gorgeous inside. Embossed lavender wallpaper covered the walls, and glass tables topped with fresh flowers were sprinkled throughout the shop. Several floor-to-ceiling windows let in tons of natural light and illuminated the racks of dazzling white dresses.

'Umm . . . I think so.' Clara looked around and saw dresses in every shade of white, from the blinding snow to nearly pale yellow. The tastefully placed silver racks were a riot of stunning lace detailing and luxurious silk. Clara recognized the Coco Chanel gowns by their short hemlines and long tulle trains.

'You think my dad would get angry if I bought it now?' Lorraine bit one of her fingernails. 'I mean, of course I'm going to get married *eventually,* right?'

Clara couldn't help but share a little of Lorraine's enthusiasm. She pointed to a dress on her right with beautiful little cap sleeves and some of the most intricate beadwork she'd ever seen. 'That one's my favorite.'

Only a few months earlier, she'd fantasized about wearing a dress just like that opposite Marcus. She'd never imagined a big, swanky event – certainly not the Plaza. It had always just been the idea of looking deeply into Marcus's too-blue eyes throughout the ceremony and knowing she'd get to keep doing it for the rest of her life.

But now his gaze belonged to someone else – the very someone Lorraine and Clara had been following from Barnard's campus since she'd gotten out of her one and only class. (Which was *French,* by the way. What kind of French girl needed to take French?)

'Where is she?' Lorraine asked, craning her neck.

'I don't know,' Clara said. 'Maybe you shouldn't have tried on so many shoes across the street.'

'You said we had to bide our time! I was simply biding my time trying on shoes!'

Clara rolled her eyes. '*Twenty* pairs?'

A woman in a tailored gray suit appeared next to them, startling them both. Her gray hair was pulled into a severe knot at the nape of her neck, and her drawn-on eyebrows were downright terrifying. She stood with crossed arms and scowled at Lorraine and Clara. 'Can I *help* you?'

Clara smiled at Lorraine and looked back at the woman: *Marguerite,* her name tag said. 'My best friend, Julia, here is about to get married!' Clara exclaimed. 'It's so exciting.'

'And Becky here is going to be my maid of honor, *of course,*'

Lorraine said, looping her arm through Clara's. 'We'd love to try on a few dresses.'

Marguerite's expression didn't change. 'You don't have an appointment.'

'I know,' Lorraine said. 'But I saw these beautiful dresses through the window and I just couldn't resist! My fiancé, Renaldo, would just die if he saw me in one of these lovely creations. I mean, of course, he wouldn't really die – he's got to stick around for the honeymoon! We're going to Paris, you know, and—'

Marguerite stared at Lorraine's hand. 'Where's your engagement ring?'

Lorraine raised her eyebrows and seemed lost for words, but only for about half a second. 'Where's *yours,* you old maid!' She began to pace in front of the desk. 'Do you have any idea who my father is? Clar – uh, I mean, Becky, can you believe the way she's treating us? Why, if my father knew you were being so rude, he'd buy this place right out from under you and you'd never work in this town again! He'd turn this shop into storage for his golf clubs, he'd—'

Clara left Lorraine to her tirade and wandered farther into the store, past more racks of dresses, and peered through a doorway into a circular room with multiple full-length mirrors. Sweet little lavender couches to match the walls were gathered around a platform where Anastasia now stood.

Marcus's fiancée was even more beautiful in person than in her engagement photo. Her auburn bob had finger waves and framed her delicate cheekbones beautifully. Her eyes were a warm chestnut brown, the sort that inspired trust – a very handy trait for a con woman.

She was wearing a blindingly white monster of a dress. Ugh, was Marcus really going to let his bride wear something so unfashionable? Clara was pretty sure there was even a hoop-skirt hiding under all that taffeta. Two women in suits cut like Marguerite's, though theirs were respectively burgundy and dark brown, knelt on either side of Anastasia with pincushions in hand.

'Irene, could you raise the hem about half an inch on your side?' the woman in brown asked the other.

'Could I trouble one of you for a glass of water?' Anastasia asked in a French accent as light and feathery as the rest of her.

The woman in the brown suit rose and walked through the doorway past Clara. Clara glanced at her name tag as she walked by: *Jacqueline*. Lorraine showed up beside Clara a few moments after Jacqueline left, and peered through the doorway. 'Now we've got her right where we want her. How do we get her alone, though?'

'Let me worry about that,' Clara replied. 'How'd it go with the dragon lady?'

'She's picking out dresses for me. By the way, if anyone asks, my last name is Rockefeller.'

Clara rolled her eyes – of course that was the name Lorraine had used. 'You ready?' she asked.

Lorraine nodded. 'Let's get this lousy quiff.'

Clara and Lorraine walked through the doorway. 'Excuse

me, Irene?' Clara said. 'A lady named Jacqueline said she needed you for something.'

Irene blinked a few times. 'I'll be right back, dear,' she said to Anastasia.

As soon as they were alone, Lorraine and Clara approached Anastasia. The platform made the girl even taller than Lorraine. Not ideal for intimidation purposes, but what could they do? They had to rile Anastasia up before either of the bridal shop employees came back, which could happen at any moment.

So Clara cut right to the chase. 'We know who you are.'

'Yeah, cut the accent, Deirdre!' Lorraine chimed in.

In the split second before Marcus's fiancée remembered she was supposed to be an innocent ingenue, her eyes hardened and her mouth leveled into a thin line. Anastasia might have looked like a porcelain doll, but there was clearly a layer of steel underneath the delicate surface. Then, like magic, the anger was gone. Anastasia looked from Lorraine to Clara in wide-eyed confusion without batting an eyelash. 'I zink you must 'ave me meestaken for someone else. And you are not supposed to be 'ere.' She squinted at them as if she had forgotten her glasses and was trying to make out their facial features.

'*You're* not supposed to be here!' Lorraine poked a sharp finger into Anastasia's chest. 'If he knew the truth about you, Marcus would never look twice at you, much less marry you!'

Anastasia stepped off the platform to get away from Lorraine. She clasped the material of her long veil in her hands as if it would somehow defend her. 'I don't know 'oo you are,

184

but if you do not get out of 'ere I will call ze police! Irene, Jacqueline!'

Clara swallowed hard. 'Maybe we should all just—'

But then Lorraine lunged at Anastasia and pried the long veil from her hands, yanking it straight off her head. Several bobby pins clattered to the floor. 'Not so cocky without your veil, are you, tramp?' Lorraine spat. 'Clara, catch!'

Lorraine threw the veil at her. Clara caught it, bewildered. 'Lorraine, what are you—'

'You geeve zat back right now!' Anastasia growled, and ran straight at Clara.

Clara took off, running around the room with Anastasia chasing her. She threw the veil back to Lorraine, laughing. This was definitely one way to intimidate a girl.

They tossed the veil back and forth a few more times, taunting Anastasia. The girl was enraged as she ran back and forth between them like an angry little poodle desperately seeking a favorite chew toy.

After a few minutes, Lorraine ran with the veil toward a door marked ONLY USE IN CASE OF EMERGENCY, and Anastasia followed. 'Here you go,' Lorraine said, handing the veil back to Anastasia. As soon as she started to pin it back on, Lorraine caught the train of her wedding dress and pulled the enormous skirt straight up over her head.

And, yes, there *was* a hoopskirt underneath.

'*Que faites-vous!*' Anastasia screamed, her shrill voice muffled by the taffeta skirt now covering her face. '*Lâchez-moi! Lâchez-moi maintenant!*'

Lorraine bunched the hem of the skirt in a wad over Anastasia's head, reaching on her tiptoes to make sure Anastasia couldn't punch it open with her fists. 'Open the fire door!' Lorraine called to Clara.

'What!' Clara exclaimed. 'Are you insane? We're supposed to get her to admit the truth – not kidnap her!'

'I'm not going to kidnap her. We'll probably never get another chance to talk to her,' Lorraine replied as she fought a squirming Anastasia, who was kicking and screaming, trying to tear away at the dress. 'Now *open the fire door*!'

Of course she was going about it all wrong – it *was* Lorraine, what else could Clara expect – but she also had a point. Clara wrenched the door open and the room filled with the urgent, ringing sound of an alarm. Lorraine pushed Anastasia into a deserted alley behind the salon, letting the door close behind them.

They stepped out onto dirty gray bricks; the back of a beige stone building faced them. Anastasia's screams were even more grating now that Lorraine had let go of her skirt. Half of it fell down, back to her ankles, while the other half hung stubbornly over her face. *'Chiennes! Dingues! Salopes!'*

Clara didn't know French, but it was clear Anastasia was calling Clara and Lorraine every nasty insult she could come up with.

'You make sure she stays put!' Lorraine said, and left Clara the lovely deed of holding Anastasia by her arms. Clara could only pray the skirt didn't slip all the way back down. Anastasia was definitely the sort who would resort to biting if necessary.

Lorraine walked back to the door and pulled off one of her green pumps. She jammed it through the door handle and big hasp. The shoe would keep the shop ladies out of the alley for now, but it probably wouldn't hold for long.

Lorraine hobbled back, trying to keep her shoeless foot off the grimy brick street. She didn't care about practically kidnapping a woman or setting off a fire alarm, but heaven forbid her stockings get dirty. 'All right, we need to make this girl talk,' she said, 'and this is the way it's done in the movies!' She pulled the skirt completely away from Anastasia's face.

The con woman narrowed her brown eyes and looked back and forth across the alley, searching for help.

'No one's coming for you, so you might as well listen to what we have to say,' Lorraine said. Anastasia scowled. 'Now, you're going to call off your wedding to Marcus.'

'And why would I do zat?'

The woman *did* do a fantastic French accent. Clara felt a tickle of doubt in her stomach. What if Solomon had been wrong? But she pushed it away. Solomon was the best PI in New York – he wouldn't have gotten where he was without some sharp eyes.

'Because if you don't, we'll expose you,' Clara said.

'Zere is nuzzing to expose!' Anastasia yelled. 'You are both just *ravisseurs diaboliques*!'

'How *dare* you!' Lorraine raged. 'I don't even know what that means, but I am *highly* offended.'

Just then, Clara heard banging on the fire door and looked at Anastasia. They didn't have much time. 'We know what you're doing,' she said quickly. 'You're only marrying Marcus for his money. Just admit it!'

'But I love Marcus,' Anastasia whimpered.

'The only thing you love is lying, you filthy ... liar!' Lorraine said, shaking her fist.

'Stop trying to play us like you do everyone else,' Clara said. 'I know all about you, *Deirdre Van Doren*.' Anastasia's brown eyes widened just a fraction and gave Clara the courage to keep going. 'About your record – the burglaries, the assault charges, how you've tried to swindle about a dozen other beaus before Marcus came along. If you confess now and break your engagement to Marcus, we'll let you leave gracefully. You don't want to get arrested *again,* do you?'

'Yeah!' Lorraine said. 'Throw yourself upon the mercy of the court!'

But the woman wouldn't budge. 'I 'ave no idea what you are talkeeng about. Now un'and me!'

More banging on the fire door. 'Listen, Deirdre, I write for a little magazine called the *Manhattanite,* maybe you've heard of it? If you don't call off that wedding, I'm going to write an exposé, and everyone in New York, including Marcus, will read it. And I've got plenty to expose – believe me.'

Anastasia stared at her in silence for a moment. Was she going to come clean, admit the truth? But then she made a move to run away and Clara and Lorraine caught her by her arms. 'You are assaulting me!' Anastasia said. 'I will call ze police!'

'Go ahead and call them!' Lorraine said, digging her sharp nails into Anastasia's bare arms.

If the police came and saw this scene, who would they believe? The dignified young woman in the wedding dress, or the two girls who'd dragged her from her fitting and held her hostage? It had been foolish to come here like this.

They'd tried intimidating Anastasia, they'd tried reasoning with her . . . what else could they do?

Then Clara had an idea.

'Lorraine, let her go,' Clara said, taking a step away. She looked at Lorraine over Anastasia's shoulder and mouthed, *Trust me.* Lorraine hesitantly stepped back as well.

'We must be mistaken,' Clara said, her voice eerily calm. Lorraine opened her mouth to object, then closed it before speaking. Clara continued: 'You look like someone else. We're really sorry. We're just going to run away now.'

Clara opened her handbag and withdrew her silver cigarette case. 'Before we go, though, could I offer you a Gauloise? It's the least I can do to make up for this whole mix-up.'

Anastasia stared at her for a moment, squinting, then relaxed. 'I could use a cigarette after all ze stress.'

Clara lit the cigarette for her and watched as Anastasia inhaled. 'Good smoke?'

'Mmm, *oui*,' Anastasia replied, and took another puff.

'Aha!' Clara said, clapping her hands. 'That's a Lucky Strike! A real Frenchwoman would know immediately that that isn't a Gauloise! Those French cigarettes taste like tar buckets!'

'Gotcha!' Lorraine called triumphantly, as though she'd

had any idea of what Clara had been doing. 'Who's the *raveesur diaboleek* now, eh?'

As though someone had flipped a switch, the girlish distress slipped right off Anastasia's face. She didn't look scared, happy, angry, or anything else – the woman was utterly blank. A fanciful, girly name like Anastasia no longer fit her. They were looking at Deirdre now.

The con woman stood up straighter and crossed her arms. She shrugged and gave a menacing little laugh. 'Oh, fine, it doesn't matter,' she said in an unaccented voice that was about an octave lower than it had been before. 'No one will believe you two idiots, anyway.'

Suddenly the fire door banged open against Lorraine's shoe, which fell to the ground. While Lorraine ran for her shoe, Deirdre pointed at her and Clara. 'Zey are robbing me!' she cried in her thick fake accent.

'Stop, thieves!' Marguerite called out. She, Irene, and Jacqueline stepped out into the alley. Even little old biddies like them would catch Clara and Lorraine if they didn't get out of here now. 'The police are on their way!'

Police? Clara turned to Lorraine, who was still stumbling into her high heel.

'Run!' Clara shouted.

Chapter 17

LORRAINE

'Well, that didn't work out as planned,' Clara said with a nervous glance out the window.

Lorraine peeked out from underneath her oversized black felt hat. 'Sing it, sister.'

They'd probably be sitting in the big house right about now if Clara hadn't thought to run straight from the bridal salon to a street vendor. They'd hastily bought disguises – the hats, for one, as well as feathery white shawls – and worn them into the diner across the street from the shop.

Now they could sit by the window and keep an eye on the police cruiser parked outside Priscilla's without worrying about the fuzz spotting them. The diner was a greasy sort of joint with stuffing bleeding out of half the red booths, and smudged windows.

Deirdre stood in front of the shop, talking to two police officers. Marcus's fiancée twisted her veil nervously in her hands, leaning on Marguerite for support. The old hag of a shop manager patted Deirdre's shoulder and pulled a handkerchief from her suit pocket. Lorraine guessed bitches like them had to stick together.

'Thank God that woman doesn't know who we are!' Clara said. 'Otherwise she'd be giving our names away to the cops!'

Lorraine gave a little laugh. 'Um, yeah! *By the way*' –

she paused and put on a smile – 'you didn't happen to grab my purse, did you? Because I might have forgotten it. In the bridal shop. With all of my identification inside of it.'

Clara's gray-blue eyes widened. 'Raine, how could you do something so—'

'Don't worry, Clara, I know *just* the guy to go back there and get it for us. A total, um . . . sheik. Well, maybe a sheik-in-training.' Lorraine stood and headed toward the pay phone in the corner of the diner. She spoke to Clara over her shoulder. 'He'd do anything for me!'

Melvin already looked silly in his lumpy gray sweater vest, wrinkled red button-down, and checkered bow tie. But carrying Lorraine's alligator clutch as he walked into the diner took him to a whole new level of ridiculousness.

Lorraine waved him over. 'Poor thing,' she whispered to Clara. 'He's desperately in love with me. Says if I don't kiss him, he'll die! Can you believe it?'

Clara rolled her eyes. 'Hardly.'

'Hmmph.' Lorraine watched as Melvin approached them. So maybe he'd never said those words *exactly* to her . . . but no reason for Clara to know that.

Melvin held the clutch low against his thigh, trying to hide it. But he was so awkward about it that he made the purse even more obvious. A little girl eating an ice cream sundae pointed as he passed. 'Look at the man with the purse, Mommy!'

A woman in a frumpy day dress didn't look up from her issue of the *Queen*. 'That's nice, honey.'

'I never should've believed this was just about a purse,' Melvin said, and slouched in the booth beside Lorraine. 'There are cops in that dress shop! Things are never simple with you, Raine.'

Lorraine frowned. 'Simple? Who likes simple!'

Clara extended her hand across the table. 'We can't thank you enough. I don't think we've been properly introduced – I'm Clara Knowles.'

'Right, from Forrest Hamilton's party. Melvin Delacorte.'

'I really can't tell you how much we appreciate this. I hope we didn't pull you away from anything important.'

'Oh no, I was just working on my art history paper on Millais.'

Clara clasped her hands to her chest. 'I love his *Ophelia* painting!'

'I do, too!' Lorraine had never noticed what a sweet smile Melvin had. Or maybe he just didn't smile that way around her. 'His depiction of the flora around the river is just amazing.'

'I always thought Ophelia was the best part of *Hamlet* – much better than Hamlet and all his I-have-to-do-something-but-I'm-too-depressed-to-do-something hooey,' Clara said. 'Make up your mind!'

'Ah, I always like Rosencrantz and Guildenstern best. Every good story needs its double-crossing spies,' Melvin replied.

Lorraine looked at them. Clara wasn't trying to seduce Melvin, was she? He wasn't her type, but still – the girl did have a habit of stealing men right from under Lorraine. Not that Lorraine wanted Melvin, of course. She just didn't want Clara to want him.

Besides, it wasn't like Lorraine didn't know that painting, too. It was of a dead girl floating in a river. What was so *amazing* about that?

Clara nodded at the purse. 'I hope it wasn't too much trouble?'

'No, it was actually really easy,' Melvin explained. 'I just told them that my cousin, recently released from a sanatorium after having been jilted at the altar, has a penchant for attacking brides.'

Clara burst into laughter at this. Lorraine cracked a smile, too, though she doubted anyone had really believed the story. 'Erm . . . good one, Melvin.' She looked down at her light green floral-print day dress with its ruffled skirt and her perfectly matching heels. Could a crazy girl put such a fantastic outfit together? She thought not. 'Whatever gets the job done.'

'I had to pay some damages,' Melvin went on, 'and they put your name on a watch list, but they're not going to press charges.'

Lorraine raised her eyebrows. How much had he paid for her bad-cop routine gone wrong? Melvin was at Columbia almost entirely on scholarship – he didn't have much money to throw around. Lorraine threw her arms around his neck in a sideways hug and kissed his cheek. 'Aw, Melvin, thank you so much! I'll pay you back.'

Melvin's face turned bright red and he scooted away from her. 'I can't believe this is why you called me – to involve me in your petty crimes. I thought something serious had happened, and when I got there, well . . .' He shook his head, at a loss for words. 'I helped you out this time, but don't call me for any more of these shenanigans.'

'Shenanigans? I can't get in trouble with the cops again!' Lorraine exclaimed. 'You know that, Melvin! You, Mr. Squeaky Clean, could probably steal a car right in front of the owner's eyes and he'd still never suspect you.'

Melvin wiped his brow with one of the napkins from the table. 'Raine, you're not asking me to—'

'No, no! Believe me, my career in crime is over.' Lorraine took off her hat and plopped it right onto Melvin's head. 'Though I'm not sure you should end yours. You'd look pretty spiffy in a fedora.'

Melvin chuckled and scooted back into the booth. He slid Lorraine's chocolate milk shake away from her and sipped it. It was the rudest thing Lorraine had ever seen him do, and also the most attractive. Was Melvin finally growing some backbone?

'All right, so tell me what this is all about,' he said with the hat still on. The way it flopped over his forehead, Lorraine couldn't see his face – it was a good look for him.

'Well,' Lorraine said, 'we're trying to stop Marcus from marrying that gold digger. Clara here – she's a reporter for the *Manhattanite* – found out all sorts of dirt about her. The woman's changed her name about a thousand times, and she's wanted for robbery and assault. And those are just the things the cops know about! Once Clara digs a little deeper—'

'I'm not going to pursue this any further,' Clara cut in.

She was looking wistfully out the window. The coppers were finally leaving, and Deirdre was back in her normal clothes: a peach crocheted day dress with little black bows down the front where buttons would usually be. It was still hard to believe such a delicate flower of a woman had committed all those crimes.

Which was probably exactly how she'd gotten away with them.

'What?' Lorraine exclaimed. 'Why? Now we *know* it's her – she confessed!'

'If Marcus wants to marry that Deirdre woman, it's his business.' Clara reached over to take a French fry from the basket they'd been sharing ('These are more French than that lying harlot,' Lorraine had commented when the waiter brought them) and nibbled it. Lorraine noticed sadness in Clara's eyes. 'I need to stop pretending it's mine.'

'Applesauce, it's not,' Lorraine said. The cheerful bell over the door jingled as an elderly couple left. 'Don't be an idiot like me! Haven't you learned anything from my example?' She looked at Melvin. 'Marcus is only with this Deirdre girl because he misses Clara, who lied to him and broke his heart.'

'Thanks for that,' Clara said.

'But I thought *you* liked Marcus,' Melvin said.

'Oh, that was *so* three weeks ago,' Lorraine replied, waving him off. 'Nope, Clara's the only girl for Marcus – anyone but the two of them could see that in a second.'

It was only when Lorraine said it that she truly believed it. Clara and Marcus really did belong together. With their runway-ready looks, neither of them had any business being as smart and sensitive as they were. They needed to get back together, get married, and have beautiful blond children. Who would probably also be charming and clever enough to take over the world.

Clara raised her eyebrows at Lorraine and opened her mouth, surely to object, but Lorraine wouldn't let her.

She met Clara's eyes. 'The only reason that girl's spell works on him is because he can't see straight. He got hit so hard by you. Like he was hit by a brick. Yep, that's it exactly – he was smashed in the head by a brick full of love.' Lorraine let out a tiny cough. 'For you. Not me at all. Definitely for you, Clara.'

For a second, Clara looked as though she might start crying. Lorraine dug into her purse, readying a tissue, but then Clara blinked, took a deep breath, and composed herself.

'Do you really think so, Raine – that he, you know . . . the love brick? For me? He was so cold when I went to see him . . . not that I didn't deserve it.'

Clara was asking Lorraine's opinion as if it actually mattered to her. The way Gloria used to, back before everything had gone so wrong between them.

It felt really nice.

'Probably because you told him you were only there as a friend,' Lorraine said. 'He wanted you to tell him that you're lost without him, that you want a happily-ever-after with him, so that he could sweep you into his arms, and—'

'It's true,' Melvin chimed in. He took off the hat now, and swept his hair back with his hands. Actually, it was a good head of hair, Lorraine thought. 'Men don't really want to be friends with women.'

Lorraine elbowed him in the ribs. 'What's that supposed to mean? You're friends with me, right?'

Melvin glanced away sheepishly. 'Yeah, but—'

'No buts about it!' Lorraine said. 'Clara, you need to snap out of it. We have to stop this devil woman *together*.'

What she didn't say out loud was that not only did she want to help Marcus, but she wanted to help Clara, too. After all, they were starting to become ... *friends*. Weren't they? Stranger things had happened. Lorraine had been manager of a speakeasy before she'd turned eighteen, after all.

'Spare me the theatrics, Raine,' Clara said. She straightened her hat and grabbed her briefcase. 'I'm gonna get out of here.'

'Where are you going?' Lorraine asked lightly.

Clara sighed. 'The *Manhattanite* offices. I've got to talk to Parker, see if he'll actually let me write something about this Deirdre.'

Lorraine's lips spread into a big smile. They *were* friends. It was such a relief to finally have a real girlfriend in the city. She had Becky, she supposed. But she and Becky really didn't have much in common. Lorraine had started to wonder whether Becky was joking about that matronly stuff at all. She'd made shortbread the other day, and it had been *delicious*.

'Melvin, you mind letting me out?' Lorraine asked.

'Of course not.' He drank down the last of her milk shake and stood.

Lorraine sprang from the booth and gave Clara a hug.

'Sorry for fouling everything up earlier. I'll try to keep my flair for the dramatic in check from now on. Though you do have to admit . . . Deirdre looked much better with the dress over her head, don't you think?'

Clara swatted her back. 'You're so bad, Raine.' She giggled. 'But seriously – if all this works out, and if Marcus ever speaks to me again, I'll be sure to tell him everything you've done. I think he'd be impressed by how far you've gone to help him.'

While Clara made her way to Midtown, Lorraine and Melvin began the long walk to the Columbus Circle subway station. Lorraine had already blown enough money on the cab she and Clara had convinced to follow Deirdre's town car to the dress shop.

They moved past Bloomingdale's on Fifty-Ninth Street and Lorraine felt a pang at the sight of the enormous store and its windows full of mannequins modeling Patou and Chanel. But she could shop another day. Right now it was time to just be happy she wasn't in jail.

In the distance she could see Pulitzer Fountain burbling in front of the Plaza Hotel, and the trees of Central Park beside it. She glanced at Melvin. It was kind of nice to spend time with him off campus. He seemed like less of an insufferable brain without that constant tower of books in his arms.

'Hey,' Melvin said as they walked. 'That was nice what you said to Clara back there. About Marcus and everything. You used to like him a lot, didn't you?'

'Yep, I wrote bad poetry and everything.' Lorraine's cheeks

pinked at the fool she'd made of herself over Marcus Eastman in prep school. 'I was so far gone over him – I used to crash his base-ball games and ask for his help on math homework I'd already finished just so I'd have an excuse to stare at him.'

She'd wanted so badly for Marcus to feel the same way about her. Lorraine's face still flushed every time she thought of the one and only time they'd ever kissed. They'd been at the Green Mill with Gloria and Clara, and Marcus was already so clearly beginning to fall for Clara. She'd leaned in to kiss him and he'd pulled away, horrified. She'd had to cover, say that she was drunk and being silly – but really, she'd been as sober as a judge.

The worst part of that memory was how long Lorraine had persisted in the senseless crush *after* it had happened.

And then in New York there'd been Hank. Their whole relationship had been a big fat lie, but Lorraine had walked away from it having learned a big fat truth: It was really, really nice when the boy you liked actually liked you back.

Now she could hardly believe how long she'd chased after Marcus, thinking she could convince him to have feelings for her. Why go to all that trouble when there were boys out there who would like her all on their own? Surely there had to be a few lining the streets of New York. She just had to find them.

She shrugged at Melvin. 'But Marcus never liked me that way. I should've realized that a long time ago.' How lovely it was to finally admit that, without it feeling like her whole world would come crashing down. 'How about you, Melvin, have you ever been in love?'

His cheeks got a little rosy and he gave her a quick glance. 'Well, there is this one girl I sort of like . . . but I don't think she likes me the same way.'

'Well, then she's crazy. You're a real catch, Melvin.' Just like when she'd said Marcus and Clara belonged together, Lorraine had to say the words to realize that she believed them. Melvin really was a great guy.

'You think so?'

'I do.'

They walked in silence for a few minutes, with the park on their right and the hulking skyscrapers of the city on their left. Lorraine watched a few picnickers pack up their blankets as the sun began to set.

'So why do you want to help Marcus?' Melvin asked. 'If you're not trying to get him to like you?'

'It'd just be nice to have him back as a friend. Maybe then some of the Barnard girls would give me the time of day.'

'Ah, so you *do* have an ulterior motive. I should've known.'

She glanced over at him, ready to be insulted. But his smile made it clear he was kidding. He really did have such a nice smile – how had she never noticed? 'Of course. I'll leave true selflessness to you – you're much better at it than I ever could be.' She paused. 'Like what you did today. I don't know how I can ever thank you.'

Lorraine looked at him then – *really* looked at him – walking with his hands plunged into his pockets. He didn't walk with his chest puffed out like Marcus or Hank, men who knew how charming and attractive they were. But Lorraine was beginning to find that she *liked* that about Melvin. He didn't think about how he appeared to anyone else – when he walked he thought about deeper things, like books and art. And Lorraine, maybe. People he cared about.

Melvin was funny, and not in the biting way Marcus had always been. And he was the sort of boy who got better looking the more you got to know him, though it wasn't as if he were handsome. Still, as long as he kept his glasses on, Melvin's strong chin, sculpted cheekbones, and full lips were practically swoony. He didn't have to spend all his time at Lorraine's beck and call. There were plenty of brainy girls at Barnard who would be happy to give Melvin the attention he deserved.

She stopped in the middle of the sidewalk and turned to him. 'You do everything for me, and you never complain, and I never do anything for you. Why?'

He glanced down at her with his head cocked to the side. 'Why do you think?'

Could it be . . . did Melvin do all this because he *liked* her? Could Lorraine be the girl he'd been talking about before? But no . . . he'd just said Lorraine did everything with an ulterior motive. He'd been joking, but would he really joke that way with the girl he carried a torch for?

'I'm your friend,' Melvin explained.

Ah, right. Friends. Of course.

'Now come on,' he said, 'you're gonna help me study for U.S. *and* European History. You owe me.'

Lorraine linked her arm through Melvin's. 'Oh, all right. Can we skip over Queen Victoria, though? She's such a bore.'

'You'd be surprised. She and Albert actually had a pretty saucy marriage.'

'*Really?*' She paused. 'Well, I guess that's not actually so surprising.'

'Why not?'

'Well, in my experience, the people who seem dull at first can turn out to be some of the best people you'll ever meet.' She peered at his brownish eyes behind his glasses and tightened her arm around his. 'Once you get to know them.'

The two of them walked past the last bit of Central Park and a cool wind blew Lorraine's hair back from her face. She smiled at the leaves of the trees beside them. They were just beginning to change color – a little flash of yellow on one tree, a bit of orange on another. The shift was only just starting, but soon it would be as though the trees had completely new leaves.

And now it looked like Lorraine, too, had new leaves after all.

Chapter 18

GLORIA

Gloria was tired.

She'd been ready to fall into bed when the group had gotten back from a drunken scavenger hunt in Great Neck Plaza the night before. But Forrest had decided that it was the perfect time to set up the tightrope he'd just bought in the backyard. Gloria wasn't sure how no one had broken any bones – though the mattresses the servants dragged outside had helped.

Gloria still hadn't been able to dig up anything else on Forrest. And to make matters worse, Hank didn't know where Jerome was. Thank God Ruby had agreed to help them, or Hank probably would've sent Gloria back to prison by now. Ruby would bring the information the feds needed to Marcus's wedding tomorrow. Then, with Hank's blessing, Ruby and Forrest would run off to Paris. And Gloria would be free to focus her attention on finding her fiancé.

But for now, she was still stuck here. After three weeks at Forrest's villa, she'd almost started to think three a.m. beach bonfires and sled rides down the grand staircase were normal. Talking to an old friend helped her remember how absurd Forrest Hamilton's lifestyle really was.

'What are Forrest and his pack of vamps getting up to now?' Marcus asked over the telephone. 'Sparking some fireworks in the living room? Parachuting off the rooftop?'

'I'm not sure even Glitz or Glamour would be dim enough to try to set off fireworks indoors,' Gloria replied. 'I should mention the parachute idea to Forrest, though – sounds right up his alley. But no, they're all playing chess.'

'I don't believe it. Sounds far too civilized for his crowd.'

'Well, it *is* human-sized chess. Forrest had the tiles out on the terrace painted to look like a chessboard.'

'Ah, there we go. Has anyone chucked a pawn off the terrace yet?'

She sat up from the sofa, looking out at the broad terrace through the wood-paneled den's ornate French doors. The chessboard took up almost the entirety of the terrace. Larger pieces like the king and queen were more than half as tall as Forrest and his houseguests. Forrest and Glitz controlled the aquamarine pieces, while Marty, Ruby, and Glamour pushed the ivory ones.

Marty was the only one who seemed to be paying the least bit of attention to the game. Glitz and Glamour were using their respective bishops to have a sword fight of sorts. Ruby twirled her skirt this way and that and sang while a besotted Forrest applauded. Ruby had been singing soft, sweet songs in French all morning.

'No, but it's only a matter of time,' Gloria replied with a laugh. 'I'm sure you're no stranger to this sort of thing now that you're an experienced college man.'

'You forget I was nearly engaged by the time school started. I've been behaving myself these days, unlike you.'

'Well, I hope you haven't *completely* reformed. The scoundrel Marcus Eastman is the one who's been my best friend all these years.'

'I'm still me, don't worry. I've just got my head on a little straighter. And you're one to talk – I hope I'll even recognize you at my wedding. You've turned into this singing jailbird who cavorts with shady billionaires. Doesn't sound like the Gloria Carmody *I* used to know.'

Marcus was joking, but Gloria recognized the truth in his words. Would the girl Gloria had been in Chicago, president of the Honor Society and example to all the other debs in town, even recognize the woman Gloria had become?

Gloria didn't think so. And she was so glad.

When Marcus spoke again, his tone was more serious. 'Really, Glo, what are you doing out there? You're way too good to spend your days as one of Forrest Hamilton's girl toys. And now he's coming with you to my wedding?'

'Just as friends,' Gloria corrected quickly. That way Forrest and Ruby would be able to flee the wedding directly and catch their ship to Paris. 'You don't want to know what I'm doing here, believe me.' Gloria peered outside again. She couldn't see Forrest anymore – he'd probably returned to his own side of the chessboard, which Gloria couldn't quite see from her vantage point. 'It's complicated,' she told Marcus in a whisper. 'I'm working for the FBI, but I can't really talk about it. Forrest thinks I'm here as a guest, more or less – he doesn't know that I'm trying to bring him down.' Gloria thought of Ruby. 'And I'm very close to getting what I need to satisfy the FBI and have him locked away.'

'I figured it might be something like that, considering you went straight from prison to that fellow's house.' Marcus's voice was tinged with worry. 'But your detective work better not keep you from your role in my wedding. I can't get married without my best friend there by my side.'

Gloria felt a rush of affection for her old friend. Maybe she didn't agree with his getting married so fast, but she did have to admit this was the happiest she'd heard him in a while.

'Don't worry,' she replied. 'They'd have to lock me up again to keep me away.'

They said their goodbyes and Gloria returned the telephone to the mahogany end table. She let her hand rest on the receiver for a moment. In Chicago, Marcus had been such an integral part of her world. Here in New York, he was nothing more than a ghost. And now that he was getting married . . . would he disappear forever? Would their only communication be via Christmas cards and family photos?

Then it hit her: Would she and Jerome even send Christmas cards? What would be the point – who would they send them to? Vera and Evan, maybe, but that was it. She sighed and fingered the chain around her neck – she hadn't taken it off since Forrest's party, Hank and his rules be damned. Jerome kept disappearing on her. Wearing the ring around her neck, close to her heart, was the only way Gloria could ease the pain of his absence. Now she would just work on getting him back. It was only September, after all. They could worry about Christmas cards later.

Gloria stood and made for the den's door.

And she found that she wasn't alone.

Forrest sat at the other end of the peach velvet sofa, perched on its arm. He must have left the terrace while she'd been on the phone, and entered through the other set of French doors that led to the room beside this one. He held an empty martini glass in each hand and raised one to her in a mock toast.

'One of these was for you,' he said. 'But I was so engrossed by your conversation that I drank both without realizing it. Silly me!'

He placed both the glasses on an end table and moved toward her. His dark eyes had none of their usual sparkle – they were nearly black. Gloria had never seen him without a touch of mirth on his face, some joke on the tip of his tongue. But now Forrest's expression was utterly grim and his face was pallid.

'Tsk, tsk, tsk.' He clicked his tongue against the roof of his mouth, making Gloria feel uncomfortable. Nervous. 'So you really *are* on the bureau's side. I thought I'd won you over, but you're still intent on uncovering some dirt about me, aren't you?' His voice was harder than Gloria had ever heard it.

She had to think of a lie, and quickly. 'No – at least, not anymore,' Gloria said. 'Not after what Ruby told me last night.' The moment she mentioned Ruby, Forrest's face softened. 'She told me everything, Forrest, about how you two are going to run away together to Paris. And I'm so happy for you. I know you two have real love. I just said that stuff to Marcus so he wouldn't be suspicious.'

Forrest blinked a few times, then sank onto the couch.

After a moment he looked up at her with hope in his eyes. 'She really said that?' He smiled a little. 'I've been begging her for weeks to agree . . . I've been so scared she would change her mind.'

All the canoodling, the secret conversations Gloria thought she'd been witnessing – they really had been going on. She wasn't crazy. Ruby was going to leave her husband for Forrest.

'I'm sorry I wasn't honest with you, but it's not like you haven't been using *me,*' Gloria said.

Forrest looked at her, confused.

'Oh, come on. The flirting, the compliments – you were just trying to make Ruby jealous.'

Forrest glanced away, his cheeks turning red. 'Fair enough,' he said.

Gloria held out her hand. 'So we're even?'

Forrest studied it for a second, then extended his own. 'Even.'

'Besides' – Gloria sat down beside him – 'Ruby also said she loves you more than life itself. She said she doesn't care about money or fame just so long as she can be with you.'

He turned to give her a wide smile. He wasn't a self-assured playboy billionaire or a possibly shady businessman now; he was just a boy in love. 'I'm so excited, Glo,' he admitted. 'Tomorrow Ruby and I are going to sail off into a new life together, just her and me. It's what I've always wanted. No one will know who we are: no more questions about my fortune, no more insufferable Marty. We'll be free to do whatever we want, and we'll never come back.'

Then he saw something behind Gloria that wiped the joyful expression right off his face.

'Oh, so is that the plan?' a gruff voice said.

Pembroke.

Standing in the doorframe.

His presence sucked the happy energy out of the room like a vacuum, and suddenly the den was dark and desolate. Pembroke's gaze had the same effect on Gloria as an ice cube sliding down her spine. She was surprised the older man's burly shoulders were even able to fit through the doorway. But though Pembroke was a big man, he moved gracefully, crossing the Persian rug like a lion stalking its prey. His bushy gray brows lowered over his eyes, and cold fury radiated off him in waves. Back in Chicago, Carlito Macharelli's rages had been like wildfire – burning, passionate, and unpredictable. But there was something so much more frightening about the combination of Pembroke's intimidating size with his cool, unruffled manner. It was as if he could snap Gloria and Forrest in half without a blink of his pale, eerie eyes.

Now those terrifying eyes fixed on Forrest. 'And you didn't even think to include me? I suppose I shouldn't be surprised. You always were a selfish boy.'

Pembroke pulled a wooden chair away from the desk in the corner. He turned it away from Gloria and Forrest and sat to face them, straddling it and resting his muscled arms on the back. He chuckled, and the smile twisted the lower end of his scar into a disturbing J. 'I should have known better than to let you squander my money on Broadway shows. A stupid kid like you always gets romantic notions.'

Gloria looked between Pembroke and Forrest. What made Forrest's servant think he had the right to call Forrest selfish or stupid? 'Excuse me, but what business is it of yours?'

Pembroke threw his head back and laughed. 'It's all my business, sweetheart. Forrest doesn't have two wooden nickels to rub together.' He turned back to Gloria. 'All he's got is the money I let him launder while I set up a new life for myself in Europe. And yet he seems to think he could make it without me.'

'No, Dad, Gloria's got it all wrong,' Forrest said, his voice high and nervous. 'I'm . . . not running away with Ruby. Honestly.'

Gloria's head whipped between the two men again. *Dad?*

'Damn right, you're not!' Pembroke yelled, causing Ruby and the others to look at them through the French doors questioningly. Forrest summoned a shadow of his usual charming smile and waved off their concern.

Once the others were back to their drunken shenanigans, Pembroke stood up and pointed at Gloria. 'And you aren't going to say a word to anyone about anything.' He paced and stroked his mustache pensively for a moment. 'I still haven't decided what to do with your colored boyfriend.' He held his hands out, weighing them back and forth. 'Kill him? Leave him locked up till he starves to death? Let him go?'

Without thinking, Gloria leaped up from the couch and seized Pembroke by his shoulders. 'Where is he? Let him go!'

Pembroke looked down at her and laughed. Then he effortlessly shoved her away from him, hard enough that she fell to the ground.

'You weren't kidding, Forrest, this girl's a real bearcat,' Pembroke observed. 'Moxie's something I respect in a woman, and I plan to treat you and your boy real nice if you promise to treat me the same. I'll let you know where he is after you do what I want. But if you don't play by my rules . . . well, there won't be much left of him to find.'

Gloria swallowed hard and sat back down next to Forrest. She looked into Pembroke's eerie eyes and nodded.

Pembroke sat down as well. 'Forrest. When did you say your tickets were for?'

Forrest gulped, wiping sweat from his forehead. 'Tomorrow night. After the Eastman wedding.'

Pembroke nodded, then pointed at Gloria. 'So here's how things are gonna work: Forrest and I are going to be on that boat.' Forrest sucked in a sharp breath and Pembroke laughed again. 'That's right, Son, you're taking *me* with you – not your old flame. Ruby's got a sweet deal, being a *real* producer's wife. I'm sure she'll thank me someday for keeping her from ruining her career for a punk like you.'

Pembroke leaned forward to pat Forrest's knee. 'That's something you still need to learn from me – how to know when something's over. You and Ruby were finished a long time ago, and now I'm finished with this country. Things have gotten too hot here, and too many people know that I'm still alive. It's time to get out, and I'm taking you – and my money – with me.'

Gloria stared at Forrest, sure he was going to scream, or storm out, or do *something*. She knew how much he loved Ruby. Was he really going to let his father steal his and Ruby's one chance to be happy together?

But Forrest just stared at the floor and gave a small nod. 'Yes, sir.'

Gloria could feel the chill of Pembroke's gaze on her. 'You, Gloria,' he said, 'are going to be at that wedding. My contacts tell me your G-man expects you there. And we'll be there with you, because I don't trust you and we're not letting you out of our sight. So long as you don't misbehave, afterward you can spring your boyfriend. By then we'll be long gone.'

Gloria peered quickly at Forrest, who still seemed to be trying to read some kind of hidden wisdom in the carpet.

'All right,' Gloria said. What choice did she have? 'But if you hurt Jerome, you'd better believe you'll be climbing onto that boat with a bullet in your back.'

Pembroke laughed again and slapped his thigh. 'You really took that thing I said about moxie to heart, didn't you? That's what makes you a good performer, kid – you know your audience.' He stood and put the chair back by the desk. He turned back to Gloria and Forrest and clapped his hands. 'Great, so we all know the roles we're playing here.' He glanced at the others outside, then at Forrest. 'I believe you have a chess game to finish.'

Pembroke moved in front of her when she tried to follow Forrest through the French doors. 'Meanwhile, Miss Carmody, your telephone privileges are cut off.' He leaned closer so that he was speaking directly into her ear. 'And believe me, I'll know if you try to place a call here or anywhere else. I've got eyes and ears everywhere.'

Then Pembroke approached the end table where the telephone Gloria had used earlier was sitting. In one swift move, he yanked the telephone straight out of the wall. It fell to the floor with a jangle.

He cracked his knuckles and glanced at Gloria. She tried not to let him see her hands trembling.

'Now,' Pembroke said, his voice an older version of Forrest's when he was at the height of his charm. 'Why don't you go out and enjoy the day with my boy and his friends? After all, it is a *lovely* time of year.'

Chapter 19
CLARA

Clara sifted through the contents of her file on Deirdre Van Doren. 'I don't see why *I* have to go to the wedding.'

She and Parker sat around the expansive oak table in one of the *Manhattanite* conference rooms with Solomon, the private dick who had proven invaluable to Clara's research on Deirdre Van Doren. The rumpled PI was actually a real swell once you got past that top layer of snark.

They'd been working for hours – it had been early morning when they'd started and now Clara could hear reporters chattering outside about which restaurant to order lunch from. Clara had forgotten all about food. She'd been subsisting purely on cup after cup of strong coffee.

'I know you're not too keen on watching Lover Boy marry someone else tomorrow afternoon,' Parker said with a cruel grin. He wore a deep-burgundy suit today with a skinny blue silk tie. 'But you're just going to have to suck it up. Real journalists learn to put their feelings aside.'

Clara picked up a photo of Deirdre that Solomon had taken. 'Not having them in the first place must make the job real easy for you, then.'

Solomon scratched his neck. Clara could tell he was getting annoyed – sitting here while she and Parker fought like children. Solomon had been tailing Deirdre for the past week on the *Manhattanite*'s dime, and doing a much better job of it than Clara and Lorraine.

Clara raised the picture, held it underneath the shoddy light from one of the lamps. Deirdre wasn't doing anything incriminating in the photo, but the way she happened to be looking over her shoulder as she walked across the Barnard campus had a distinctly smarmy feel to it. It would be great for the cover of next month's *Manhattanite*.

Provided Clara got enough evidence to write the exposé at all.

'Stare at that long enough and you'll give yourself a headache,' Parker said, taking a swig from the coffee cup in his hand.

Clara ignored him and walked to the corkboard on the wall, which was quickly filling with everything from copies of old police records to notes Clara had taken on a napkin from that greasy diner across from Priscilla's. She tacked the picture right next to her invitation to Marcus's wedding.

Then she turned to Solomon. 'Can't we just tell Marcus what we know and stop the wedding?'

'I'm afraid not, doll.' Solomon put out his fifth cigarette of the morning in the ashtray and went straight for another.

He offered her a Lucky Strike straight from the carton – she doubted he knew what a cigarette case was, much less ever carried one. She gladly accepted. She was pleased when he failed to offer a gasper to Parker. She was pretty sure Sol liked him about as much as she did – which, at this point, was very little.

'We don't have any real evidence that this Anastasia Rijn girl is Deirdre Van Doren,' Solomon said. 'Nothing but your testimony and that of your friend Lorraine, who sounds a hell of a lot less credible than you.'

Clara wasn't going to argue with that. Once upon a time she would've argued hard against the 'friend' part . . . but now she felt okay about letting it stand.

'You've already told Marcus once and he didn't listen to you,' Solomon went on, puffing out a cloud of smoke. Clara looked away – she'd neglected to mention to Solomon and Parker that Marcus had turned her over to campus security. It was far too embarrassing. 'What makes you think he's going to listen to you at his wedding? We need proof. We need it in a way that can't be denied.'

'And that's where *you* come in,' Parker said.

Parker withdrew a booking photograph of a skinny fellow with a dark, thin mustache from a manila folder. The man in the photo looked about twenty-five. 'We found one of Deirdre's old beaus, Benji Stafford, who did time for a con job she put on him. Benji has quite the grudge against Miss Van Doren, and he's willing to testify to her identity in court. Sure, he's an ex-con, so his testimony isn't as credible as we'd like. But it's all we've got – and it's better than nothing.'

'That's great. But what does it have to do with me?' Clara asked.

'We need you to smuggle Benji into the wedding as your date,' Solomon explained. 'Benji's the only one who can give us a positive, indisputable ID on Deirdre, and we need that to be able to arrest her without a confession. So we're going to confront Deirdre before the ceremony.'

215

'First we'll give her a chance to come clean,' Parker chimed in. 'Our exposé will be that much better with a confession of guilt from the woman herself. And having Benji there should put the fear of God in her. We're hoping that the sight of a familiar mug like his will put Deirdre in the mood to be as cooperative with the fuzz as possible.'

'Even if she doesn't say a word,' Solomon said, 'once Benji gives us our confirmation, my buddy on the NYPD will be able to arrest her before the wedding gets under way.'

Clara studied the picture of Benji and frowned. Even if Benji was innocent of that particular crime, his dark, flat eyes made her sure he was guilty of *something*. 'And when do I get to meet this dream date of mine?'

'He doesn't get into town until tomorrow morning,' Solomon said. 'It's the fastest he could come. We'll have to pick him up at Grand Central and bring him straight to the ceremony. I'd much rather confront Deirdre quietly at her apartment today than arrest the girl in front of hundreds of wedding guests. But we don't have much of a choice.' He reached his pudgy hand over to pat Clara's. 'It's the best we can do, hon. Parker here will get his juicy story, and Marcus – well, he'll be spared an ugly marriage.'

Clara crossed her arms. 'Great. My date to the wedding of the man I love is going to be an ex-con named Benji.'

'Could be worse,' Solomon replied. 'I once booked a con named Knifey McGee. His real name – I had the boys dig up his birth certificate to be sure.'

Clara picked up a copy of last month's *Manhattanite* and

pretended to flip through it for a moment, then met Parker's pale green eyes across the table.

'Tell you what – get enough dirt on this woman tomorrow and you can consider the 'Glittering Fools' column officially folded.' Parker paused, letting the words sink in. 'You're too good a writer to spend all your time out gallivanting with those spoiled little rich kids anyway. You can write the exposé you've always dreamed of. Be a real journalist.'

Clara felt her heart flutter. She had more or less forgotten about her own career – she just wanted to help Marcus. Only . . . what would Marcus think if she exploited his personal life for a story? He'd always wanted her to write about something serious, but she doubted he meant himself and his personal life. He'd be hurt enough once he knew the truth about Deirdre. What would an exposé like this do to him – to them?

Clara winced. There wasn't a *them* anymore.

And yet she still felt she owed him something. 'Parker, I don't think I can do this to Marcus. I'm already going to ruin his wedding day. Do I really need to make things worse by showing up with an ex-con?'

'What makes you so sure he'll even care?' Parker asked with a sneer. 'I think he'll be focused on the girl he's marrying – not an old flame who always seems to want what she can't have. When you were with him it was me, and when you were with me it was him. If I didn't think this exposé would sell a heap of magazines, I'd tell Marcus he was better off with the lady criminal.'

Clara's face flamed red. She glanced at Solomon, but

his expression remained utterly blank as he lit yet another cigarette.

She pointed a finger at Parker. 'A real man wouldn't ask a woman he cares about to pretend to be an ex-con's date at her ex-boyfriend's wedding.'

Parker leaned back in his chair and gave her his best film-star smile. 'That, my dear, is why I'm asking you. I'm over' – he looked Clara up and down – '"us." Do you know how many women I turned down in the hope that you might come around? Real women, too, not immature girls still hung up on boys stupid and gullible enough to get themselves engaged to con artists.'

Clara stood in silent shock for a moment. How dare he! But then her lips twisted into a smile. 'Well, I'm *so sorry* to have deprived the women of New York of a prize like you for so long. I hope none of them mind that you take longer primping in front of the mirror than they do.'

She turned to Solomon. 'I'm sorry you had to witness this. I'm usually quite the professional.'

Then she flung the copy of the *Manhattanite* she'd been holding straight at Parker's head.

One thing Clara loved about New York: It had endless sidewalks for a girl with too much on her mind to wander.

After she'd left the *Manhattanite* offices hours before, Clara had thought about going home to Brooklyn. But the lonely anonymity of the crowded city streets suited her frame of mind far better than an empty apartment. Here, among the thousands of people who walked the streets, Clara felt invisible. Hidden. The wind bit at her cheeks, and the fall leaves were scattered across the pavement in beautiful shades of reds and oranges and yellows. In a way, the colors reminded her of home – before New York, before Chicago. Home with her parents, when her concerns were so few and her life was simple.

Clara pulled her coat tighter around her waist, passing by shop windows full of furniture and clothing, and a bakery with the scent of freshly baked bread wafting through the door as customers entered and left.

Then and there, on the street, she made a vow. Marcus had been set on Clara's going to college before she pursued her writing career. At the time it had made Clara feel like he wasn't confident in her abilities. But now she knew that even the best writers in the business admitted that there was always more to learn.

She left the crowds crammed outside the string of theaters on Broadway, moved a few avenues east, and turned onto Park Avenue. She passed upscale shops and stopped walking when she found herself outside Sherry's Restaurant. Bushes flanked the restaurant's entrance, softening the skyscraper's appearance. She knew that inside there was a huge ballroom with crystal chandeliers and enough linen-covered tables to seat hundreds.

A lifetime ago, she'd attended a charity gala there with Marcus. He'd only just found out that Clara had been keeping her job at the *Manhattanite* a secret from him. Marcus had still wanted to make things work with her.

She stood across the street from the entrance, letting the memories of being in love with Marcus fill her body and soul, warming her on this cold fall day.

And then, out of nowhere –

One of the large double doors opened, and Marcus and Deirdre walked out and stood under the entrance's red awning.

At first, Clara was light-headed at the coincidence. Then she remembered: Not only was Sherry's the site of the beginning of the end of Clara's relationship with Marcus, it was also where Marcus and Deirdre's rehearsal dinner was taking place.

Clara crouched behind a bush and peeked around the side. Marcus was devastatingly handsome in a traditional tuxedo. His hair was Brilliantined, and a handkerchief that matched his eyes peeked out of his pocket. Clara could remember the way the Brilliantine mingled with his spicy cologne, how she would practically taste it on her tongue when she kissed his neck.

Deirdre's coppery hair was expertly curled and pinned away from her face with diamond barrettes. She wore a sleeve-less deep-green velvet gown. The top was sheer, but it became opaque at just the right point on Deirdre's chest to remain respectable enough for the tables of old society biddies inside. The girl was positively glowing. And why wouldn't she be? Half the Eastman fortune was about to be hers.

Marcus lit a cigarette and held it to Deirdre's to light it. His hand lingered on her tiny waist as he did so. 'I hope tonight hasn't been too painful for you,' Clara could dimly hear Marcus say.

'Painful?' Deirdre gave a charming little laugh. 'I adore your entire family. Your fazzer ees so kind and welcoming, and your muzzer ees beautiful! Zough zat ees not so surprising, you being as wonderful as you are.'

He tucked a stray curl behind her ear. 'I'm glad you like them. They'll be your family too soon enough.'

Clara looked away as the two leaned in for a big Hollywood kiss. Even though she'd heard the truth from Deirdre's own lips, it was hard to believe someone so seemingly lovely was a con artist. And Marcus looked so happy.

She was beginning to understand what Marcus saw in his fiancée. Through all her lies and sneaking around, when was the last time Clara had remembered to tell Marcus something as simple as how wonderful he was?

As soon as she heard the door creak closed, she stalked away from the restaurant. It wasn't fair – *she* should be the one standing across from Marcus on Saturday, telling him how much she loved him and how happy she would be to spend the rest of her life with him.

Instead, she'd show up to the wedding with a former criminal as her date, and would work her hardest to ensure that Marcus's bride-to-be would be walking out in handcuffs rather than walking down the aisle.

Clara loved Marcus so much. And yet she was about to do something that would make him never want to speak to her again.

Chapter 20

LORRAINE

Lorraine was sure the Eastman-Rijn wedding was the reason words like *swanky* and *elegant* existed.

Tramp though Deirdre was, it was kind of a shame such a gorgeous event was destined to go down in flames before it even began. It would be like that time Lorraine had dropped the latest issue of *Vogue* in the bathtub while she was still flipping through the ads in the front.

Melvin whistled. 'What do you figure they spent on candles alone?'

Lorraine shook her head. 'I don't even want to think about it. I'm all for extravagance, don't get me wrong. But spending a fortune on sticks that are just going to melt? That's just applesauce.'

Though as Lorraine looked around the ballroom, she couldn't deny the romantic, almost ethereal effect the dim lighting and hundreds of candles had. The candlelight bounced off the coffered ceilings and onto the enormous arched mirrors that lined the walls. The white linen canopy set up on the sleek wooden platform at the end of the aisle and draped with wisteria glowed with some sort of inner light.

Lorraine grabbed Melvin's hand and pulled him deeper into the crowd. There must have been at least a hundred and fifty people milling around the rows of cushioned gold chairs, and probably twice that were still munching on hors d'oeuvres in the lobby downstairs. Lorraine had spied her own parents talking to Mr. and Mrs. Eastman in the lobby when she and Melvin had arrived – exactly why she'd hightailed it upstairs. She'd have to suffer through dinner with her mother and father later – she didn't want to give them more opportunities to bore her than necessary.

Lorraine smiled with approval at the sight of her pink lips and rouged cheeks in one of the mirrors. The low lighting made her look positively angelic. She looked around for Gloria. She hadn't spied her old friend yet, and she wasn't sure what she'd do when she did. Hide? Say hello? Apologize for everything, and ask if there was any way they could possibly start over?

She recognized more than one gorgeous heiress from the pages of society magazines, or from passing by them on campus at Barnard. Sure, they never actually stopped to speak to her, but . . . who cared about a silly little detail like that.

'Sabrina! Hello!' Lorraine waved to a girl she recognized from her European History class, who was sipping from a champagne flute. Her father was some oil magnate. Or was it steel? The details were always so confusing.

'Do you know her?' Melvin asked.

'Of course,' Lorraine replied, waving even harder. 'She's one of my dearest friends.'

Melvin coughed. 'But she's ignoring you . . . and now she's walking away.'

Lorraine's shoulders slumped as Sabrina shot her a confused look, then continued across the room. 'Oh, that's just a game

225

we play. She pretends to ignore me, I pretend to ignore her . . . hysterical, don't you think? That Sabrina is such a hoot.'

Just then, another girl passed them by – Lorraine had to stop Melvin from stepping on the velvet train of the blonde beauty's dress. The bodice was completely covered with intricate gold embroidery, and Lorraine was instantly envious.

The girl was hanging on the arm of a handsome fellow in his mid-forties. He wore a midnight-blue double-breasted suit. He laughed uproariously and squeezed the blonde closer to him.

'You see the man in blue?' Lorraine whispered. 'That's Senator Jimmy Walker – people are saying he's going to be our next mayor. He's also sugar daddy to just about every chorus girl in town.' She pulled Melvin away from that couple before he could react. 'Oh, and there's Gloria Morgan Vanderbilt! Doesn't she look beautiful? Gloria, hello!'

Old Reginald Vanderbilt, heir to the family's railroad fortune, stood beside his new bride and smoked his pipe. His raven-haired wife wore a royal-blue satin gown that dipped scandalously low in the front *and* back. A pin inset with diamonds was fixed to the front of the dress and Gloria Morgan wore a necklace and earrings to match.

'I think *you* look beautiful,' Melvin said, surveying Lorraine's pale green silk charmeuse gown.

Lorraine smiled. It was the most formal dress she'd ever worn, and it had the longest hemline she'd worn since puberty. It was sleeveless and was embroidered with gold thread. There were deep aqua panels on each side, and a seashell-shaped gold pin gathered the fabric before it draped into a train in the back. Lorraine hadn't expected to love the long Callot Soeurs number as much as she did when she'd tried it on in the store, but it made her feel like some kind of mermaid princess.

Even Stella Marks, one of the Laurelton girls who'd tortured Lorraine after she'd made a drunken scene at Gloria and Bastian's engagement party, had gushed about how much she loved the dress when Lorraine and Melvin had arrived in the ballroom. 'I wish I had one just like it,' Stella had said.

Lorraine had given Stella her brightest grin. 'For your sake, Stella, I wish you did, too. Then you wouldn't be wearing that puke-colored monstrosity.'

'Thank you,' Lorraine said to Melvin now. 'You don't look too shabby yourself.'

To think Melvin had said no when she'd first asked him to come today! 'I told you I don't want to get caught up in any more of your wild shenanigans, Raine,' he'd said.

'This isn't anything like that!' she'd replied. 'I just . . . I'd like you to come. With me. I'll have to deal with all these Chicago bluenoses, and it'll be nice to have a friendly face around. Plus I bet you'll look absolutely dapper all dressed up.'

She'd been right. Melvin's traditional tuxedo with its too-wide lapels wasn't going to start any fashion trends, but at least it fit. He was even wearing some classy silver cuff links that his grandfather had given him when he graduated from high school. Lorraine had been surprised – Melvin was from Wisconsin; she hadn't thought anything classy existed there.

225

'Raine—' Melvin began, the candlelight doing his cheek-bones and strong chin all kinds of favors.

But Lorraine saw two more familiar faces over Melvin's shoulder, and she knew them from more than just the society pages. She pointed toward the entrance to the ballroom. 'What do you know? Clara and her editor are here to put their plan into motion.'

There was an unspoken rule that women needed to look their very best when there was a danger of running into an old flame. And boy, was Clara abiding by that rule. She wore a sleeveless floral-print silk voile dress. Beads and sequins dotted the print and caught the light beautifully. A beaded belt sat low on Clara's hips, and she wore a long pink beaded necklace. Gold heels peeked out from under the dress's long, artfully uneven hem.

Parker wore a gray pin-striped suit with a matching waist-coat. In his pocket was a delicately folded green handkerchief, which matched the color of his tie. A gray bowler hat covered his dark, wavy hair.

The two of them stood with two middle-aged men, neither of whom was dressed formally enough for a wedding. One was overweight and dressed in a tweed suit. Half his shirt was untucked under his jacket. The other was a nondescript fellow with wrinkled worry lines crawling across his forehead, wearing an equally nondescript brown suit.

Despite the fact that Clara and Parker were possibly one of the best-dressed couples at the wedding, neither looked happy. They seemed to be in the middle of an argument.

'C'mon,' Lorraine said. 'I smell trouble.'

Melvin allowed her to pull him toward Clara and Parker. 'That could just be the potpourri. There's one crystal bowl too many of that stuff here, if you ask me.'

'What's the rumpus?' Lorraine asked once she reached Clara and Parker.

But they were still in heated conversation. 'It's all up to you,' Parker said to Clara. 'There's no one else. You have to stand up when they ask and accuse her.'

'I can't do that!' Clara exclaimed. She was getting into a lather. 'I can't cause a scandal and ruin Marcus's big moment!'

Lorraine cleared her throat loudly – Clara and Parker finally looked at her. 'Cause a scandal? That sounds like my cue.'

'You must be Lorraine,' the overweight man standing with them said. 'I'm private detective Leonard Solomon' – he gestured toward the man beside him in the brown suit – 'and this is Lieutenant Robby Skinner.'

'Well, my, my.' Lorraine reached out to shake their hands, incredibly flattered that they knew who she was. Clara probably bragged about having a friend as intriguing as Lorraine all the time. 'Nice to meet you, gentlemen. So what are you two talking about?' Lorraine looked back and forth between Clara and Parker. 'And where's that hard-boiled character you were supposed to sneak in here?'

Clara let out a heavy sigh, looking close to tears.

'Benji missed his train,' Parker explained. 'And now Clara's going to have to accuse Deirdre during the ceremony.'

'Except I *can't*.'

'Except you *have to*,' Parker fired back. He smoothed his dark hair and turned back to Lorraine. 'Without Benji, we've got no one to identify her. The police won't arrest her without a positive ID.'

'So what will you do?' Melvin asked.

Parker shrugged. 'Hope that Deirdre will slip up when Clara confronts her in front of all these people.'

'She's a hardened criminal, Parker,' Clara said. 'I don't think a roomful of senators and socialites is going to scare her.'

Lorraine nodded. 'She is a pretty tough cookie.' She glanced at Clara. 'You said he was a tall, skinny guy, right?'

Clara nodded.

'Have you got a picture of him on you?'

'I do,' Detective Solomon said. He opened his black leather briefcase, pulled out a thick manila folder, and withdrew a booking photograph. 'Here's Benji.'

Lorraine studied the photo: The skinny man had beady brown eyes and dark hair, a dusting of freckles across the bridge of his long nose. She turned back to Melvin. 'Take off your glasses!'

His face scrunched up. 'But you're always telling me not to!'

'Just this once,' Lorraine replied. Melvin reluctantly took his glasses off and put them in the pocket of his jacket, and Lorraine tried not to cringe. Melvin's poor eyesight really was a blessing – for his face.

She looked at the photo again: In it, Benji was wearing a newsboy cap. Lorraine plucked Parker's bowler hat off his head, eliciting an angry 'Hey!' from him. She ignored it and started banging the hat hard against her knee.

An older woman in a lavender suit walked in on the arm of her son and stared at Lorraine questioningly.

'Love your suit!' Lorraine called, still thwacking the hat against her leg. 'What is that, Chanel?'

The woman shook her head and hurried away.

Once the hat was shapeless, she plopped it on Melvin's head. It mostly hid his flaming-red hair. 'Perfect,' she said.

Clara looked at the photo as well, with a small, wondering smile on her face. 'He has a mustache and a mole, though,' she said, referring to the picture.

Lorraine fished around in her gold, shell-shaped purse. 'I can fix that!' She withdrew her black eyebrow pencil.

Melvin stepped backward when she aimed the pencil at his face. 'You're not even going to ask my permission first?'

Lorraine threw her hands up. 'This is a life-or-death situation, Melvin!'

'No, it's not!' Melvin replied. 'Why would you even say that?'

She paused. 'Okay, but a friend of ours, the man Clara *loves,* is about to ruin his life. Are you really going to let him do it, knowing you could've done something to help?'

Melvin stared at her with his tiny brown eyes for a few seconds, then sighed. 'Oh, fine.' He held still so Lorraine could draw a thin mustache above his lips and a mole on his left cheek. It didn't look too bad, if Lorraine said so herself.

It was clear from Parker's face that he didn't agree. 'That'll never fool anyone.'

'Not unless she's blind,' Solomon agreed.

'But that's just it,' Lorraine replied. 'She basically is! Clara and I saw this girl up close. She squints; she's nearsighted.'

Clara nodded in confirmation. 'She's right. Vain girls never wear glasses.'

'If we keep Melvin here far enough away, she won't be able to be sure he's not this Benji jamoke,' Lorraine said. She looked at the others, ready to receive her praise for coming up with such a brilliant solution.

Solomon took the photo back and glared at Melvin. 'Even if she thinks it's him, the moment he opens his mouth, she'll know the truth. Benji has a serious Southern accent.'

Lorraine waved him off. 'The man's name is *Benji*. How serious could his accent be?'

'Serious enough,' Parker said. 'But Clara's going to do all the talking.'

'What?' Clara asked, incredulous.

They all looked up when they heard the sound of strings. The white-suited wedding band was seated next to the canopy and was starting to warm up. The guests took this as their cue to take their seats.

Lorraine walked toward the aisle with the others trailing behind her. Her plan was good, she knew it was – even if no one else thought so. Plus, it wasn't like they had time to come up with anything else.

It was now or never.

Chapter 21

GLORIA

Forrest mopped at his forehead with his handkerchief and used his other hand to offer Gloria his gold-plated flask.

'Here, kid. You look like you could use it.'

Gloria took in the stately wedding guests crowded around them in the Plaza's marble-floored lobby. The debutante on her left fingered the feathered skirt of her peach gown and confirmed to a reporter that, why, *yes,* they *were* real ostrich feathers. On her right was a crowd of Marcus's old prep school friends from Chicago, enthusiastically discussing Babe Ruth's latest home run. The stately room – with its high ceilings and countless tall windows bordered by gold curtains – was packed to the gills with a rainbow of wedding guests dressed in the finest clothing that money could buy.

When Marcus asked Gloria to be his 'best girl', Gloria had expected to wear the same flouncy dress as Anastasia's brides-maids. But instead, Marcus had commissioned a black silk halter dress with a white lace bodice. There was a black bow at the center of the bodice and a line of black buttons beneath it.

Gloria took a swig from the flask. She and Forrest could've filled a novel with all the tabloid pieces that had been written about them. But they were practically invisible in this sea of New York and Chicago royalty.

'You don't look so great yourself,' Gloria replied, handing

back the flask. Since she'd met him, Forrest had never looked anything but perfectly groomed. But now he was a sweaty mess. His nervous fidgeting had quickly loosened his pomade-tamed dark hair into unruly waves. Sweat dotted his brow, and he constantly tugged at his dark green silk tie.

Gloria tried to let the booze relax her, but it wasn't working. She could barely focus on the snooty guests crowded around them or the crystal chandeliers hanging above. When a waiter offered her a finger sandwich, she thought she might be sick.

When she recognized a gaggle of Laurelton Prep graduates, she tilted her head downward and hoped they wouldn't see her. They didn't, but she did hear her name:

'I wonder where Gloria Carmody is,' Anna Thomas said, twisting her unfashionably long brown hair between her fingers. 'Do you think she got a job in another gin joint?'

'I doubt it,' Helen Darling said, and slurped at her lemonade.

'She's probably off getting arrested again with her colored boyfriend,' Amelia Stone said. 'Remember the way we used to look up to her? It's positively *embarrassing* to think of it now.'

On another day Gloria might've been offended by their barbed words. But now all Gloria could think of was Jerome, and how Forrest's sadistic father had him locked up God knew where. Pembroke had refused to say anything about what he'd done with Jerome – only that he was alive. *Alive* was not necessarily synonymous with *safe* or *unharmed*. She couldn't stop imagining Jerome's soft brown eyes widened in terror, or his normally deep voice pitched in a cry for help that no one would hear.

'Where is Pembroke now?' Gloria asked Forrest.

'In the far right corner, by the vase of lilies,' Forrest replied immediately. His eyes hadn't strayed from his father for a moment since they'd arrived at the Plaza.

Gloria peeked over the many wide-brimmed hats and delicate headdresses. Pembroke stood as he always did, silent and imposing with his hands folded behind his back.

He wasn't playing the servant today – his black tuxedo was of finer quality than half the guests here. His black bowler hat pitched low over his eyes and made his garish scar less obvious, but Gloria could still feel his stare. When Pembroke made eye contact with Gloria, his lips peeled back to reveal a smile that was more of a sneer.

Gloria tugged on Forrest's sleeve. 'Come on, I've got to join the wedding party.'

They made their way through the crowd and under the domed ceiling of the Plaza's Palm Court. Large tables were already set up with place cards and more silverware than one person could ever need for the reception that would follow the ceremony. Gloria and Forrest walked between the columns and began to climb the steps.

'You don't have to go with your father,' Gloria pled with Forrest under her breath. 'You're a better man than he is.'

Forrest refused to look at her. 'I have to help him. He's my dad.'

'Yeah, well, your *dad* is holding my fiancé hostage. And I doubt he got that scar rescuing small children.'

'He's not a good man, I know,' Forrest admitted. 'But

without him, I'm just another poor boy – no mansion, no musicals, no shot to win the heart of Ruby Hayworth.'

'But you *were* planning to leave him,' Gloria said when they reached the second floor of the hotel. They walked quickly past the entrance to the ballroom, where several men and women mingled and smoked cigarettes. 'You wanted to run away to Paris with Ruby,' she whispered. 'What happened?'

He gave her a bleak smile. '*You* happened, Gloria. How am I supposed to leave now, knowing you'll probably turn my father over to the feds before my boat's even left the harbor? I owe everything I have, everything I am, to my father.'

They reached a long hallway. Gorgeous landscapes and portraits of women in elegant gowns hung between the doors. Gloria stopped walking and leaned against the wall. Her bare arm brushed up against the rough texture of the painting behind her. From here she could see the ballroom entrance to their right and the stairs beyond it. Pembroke was nowhere in sight. 'What happened between you and Ruby? She said you two were planning to elope when you were younger.'

Forrest stopped as well and leaned on the wall beside her, a gold candelabra sconce right above his head. 'We were seventeen,' Forrest said in a dreamy voice. 'Even before she was onstage, a spotlight seemed to follow Ruby Fredericks everywhere she went. I could hardly believe my luck, that a girl like that would even notice me, much less love me back.'

'Why, though?' Gloria asked. 'You're a charmer, Forrest, and you're not too horrible to look at, either.'

Forrest frowned as the memory slipped away. 'I was poor. And to people in Ruby's world, that was all that mattered.'

Gloria could understand that. Even if Jerome had been white, her family never would've accepted her love for a penniless piano player.

'She said the money didn't matter to her,' Forrest said. 'But it did, in the end. Money kept her from running away with me, and sent her straight into the arms of that block of wood, Marty. I was so angry with her at first. But then I realized I couldn't blame her. I had expected her to walk away from everything she'd ever known. All the little comforts she'd grown so used to would be gone.'

Gloria flinched at the heavy sadness in Forrest's voice. Ruby wasn't as blameless as he claimed, Gloria didn't think. Giving up a life of comfort – that was exactly what Gloria had done to be with Jerome.

'I didn't know my father back then – he left my mother when I was only seven. All I knew was that he was a shady businessman, that my mother expected better of me. But Ruby left me, and my mom died not too long after. I didn't have any brothers and sisters – my whole life it had just been my mom and me. I'd never been so alone.'

His voice broke on the word *alone*. Gloria's heart twisted.

'I had no choice but to track Dad down. I found a few of his letters that Mom had never given me, and went to the return address. He took me in, brought me into his insurance business.

'I didn't have much of a head for the work – numbers and

I don't get along so well. Which is why I didn't realize until it was too late that my father was engaged in ripping off thousands of people.'

So Forrest *was* innocent. And he'd only sought out his father because he'd been backed into a corner. Gloria knew from experience that desperation had a way of glossing over red flags where money was involved.

Gloria looked over at the ballroom entrance and saw that everyone milling around it had gone inside. 'We'd better get going.' She walked fast down the hallway, her heels sinking into the fluffy peach carpet. 'Is Pembroke even your father's real name?'

'It isn't, but I'm not planning on telling you what it really is.'

'Is Forrest Hamilton *your* real name?'

'Yes. Hamilton was my mother's maiden name.'

For some reason it made Gloria feel better that she knew Forrest by his real name. 'So Pembroke got caught?'

'Only after he'd illegally made enough money to buy this hotel a dozen times over.' Forrest gestured at the chandeliers they passed under and the crystal doorknobs that probably cost more than some people's houses. 'When the cops came to arrest him, we fled across the country and made new identities for ourselves. I convinced my father that we could hide on Long Island. Ruby was in Manhattan with her new husband, and I wanted to be close by while I became the man she needed me to be.'

'She needed you to be a criminal?'

'She needed a man who could take care of her.' Forrest's

expression grew hard. 'The feds never came looking for me – they just wanted my dad. So I could pretend to be a high roller and disguise my father to keep him safe. I invested in shows, laundering his money, all the while hoping Ruby might recognize my picture in the newspapers. Eventually she did, and she showed up at one of my parties.'

The two of them stopped outside the last door on the left, room 219. Gloria knocked and looked back at Forrest while they waited.

A smile had appeared on his face when he mentioned Ruby, but it dissolved as quickly as it had come. 'I can't leave my father to the authorities, though, not now. If it's got to be one or the other, I've got to leave Ruby behind.' He let out another world-weary sigh. 'She probably would've changed her mind at the last second anyway. Dad's right. She'd regret ruining her career for a punk like me.'

'You're not a punk,' Ruby said, surprising him. 'Just an idiot.'

Ruby stood in the doorway of room 219, looking stunning in a deep-purple sleeveless gown. Flowers were embroidered in silver thread all over the dress's bodice. A rhinestone headband held Ruby's luxurious waves in place.

'Ruby, what are you doing here?' Forrest asked. He glanced anxiously down the hall in the direction he and Gloria had come.

'Don't worry, I think we lost him when we came upstairs,' Gloria said, following Forrest into the room and closing the door behind her.

They walked into the parlor of a luxurious suite, complete with a gold chandelier, floor-to-ceiling windows, and a grand piano in the corner. There was a brown velvet couch in the center of the room with two matching armchairs on either side. Marcus sat on the couch in his tuxedo. His golden hair was slicked away from his face and showed off his sculpted cheekbones.

Somewhere along the line, Gloria's best friend had shifted from a prep school rake to a devastatingly handsome man. His golden skin glowed with a fading summer tan, and long, sooty lashes framed his arresting blue eyes. But when he grinned and his dimples sank into his cheeks, Gloria was still able to see the boy who'd first taught her how to sneak out her bedroom window.

He rose from the couch and hugged her. 'You're finally here! Agent Phillips said he hadn't heard from you since yesterday, so I offered to let him and his men wait for you in here. And then another agent brought Mrs. Hayworth in just a second ago. I loved you in *The Girl from Yesterday,* by the way,' he said to Ruby. Then he leaned in close and said in Gloria's ear, 'Something go wrong with that bureau business of yours?'

'Maybe for a minute,' Gloria said. 'I think it's all on track now, though.' Marcus sat back down and she sat beside him.

Burly men in black suits stood by the windows. They had the bored, slightly angry expressions Gloria had come to associate with FBI agents.

'I'm glad you were finally able to pull this off,' Hank said. Special Agent Hank Phillips sat in one of the chairs. The handsome FBI agent sported his usual five o'clock shadow and skinny tie. He gave Gloria a half-smile. 'Took you long enough.'

Gloria looked back to Forrest, who clutched both of Ruby's hands in his own.

'What are you doing here? I didn't think I'd ever see you again.' Forrest tucked a dark curl behind Ruby's ear and she leaned into his hand. They fell into each other's arms and Forrest held her tightly, whispering, 'Ruby, oh, Ruby,' over and over.

Finally Ruby pulled away. 'You let *me* walk away once – I'll be damned if I let *you* do the same thing. I love you, Forrest. Let's forget the past and start fresh in Paris.'

'Only if you brought what was promised,' Hank cut in sternly.

Ruby stepped away from Forrest and picked up the fat leather binder of papers sitting on the coffee table. She handed it to Hank. 'It's all in there, Agent Phillips. It's not Forrest, it's his dad. He's alive – the two of them faked his death.'

Ruby looked back at Forrest and gestured toward the binder. 'I was scared when we were kids, but not of being poor. I mean, that *was* part of it. But mostly I was afraid to leave everything I knew – of losing my parents and friends from my life forever. But now all I'm afraid of is losing you again. I don't care about your money or anything else, Forrest, I care about *you*.'

Gloria leaned her head on Marcus's shoulder and tried not

to cry. She felt exactly the same way about Jerome, but wasn't sure she'd ever put it as clearly as Ruby just had.

But Forrest paled and his eyes narrowed at Ruby. 'I trusted you!'

Hank set the binder on an end table, rose from his chair, and approached Forrest. 'You were right to trust her. Special Agent Hank Phillips.' He extended his hand, but Forrest refused to shake it. 'Listen, if everything checks out according to what Mrs. Hayworth has told us and you agree to be a witness against your father, we can reach a deal whereby you serve no time.'

'I can't believe this!' Forrest exclaimed. He turned to Ruby; he didn't look angry so much as desperate. 'You ran out on me once, and now you're sending my father to jail? How could you betray me again?'

Ruby put a hand on either side of his face. 'No, this time I'm giving it all up for you,' she said calmly. 'I've already told Marty I'm leaving him.'

Forrest raised his hands to cover hers. 'What about your career, and the money?'

'I don't care about any of that! All I care about is *you*.'

Forrest stared into her eyes for a few long moments. He looked pained and elated all at once. 'But he's my *father*,' he said, his voice tight.

'He's a dangerous thug who doesn't care about anyone but himself. The only reason anyone could call you a criminal is because he forced you to become one. You don't belong with him. You belong with *me*.'

'My father's been there for me all these years, Ruby. Unlike you. Now you want me to repay him by selling him out to the feds? All so I can go to Paris with you? How do I even know you won't just run off on me again when we get there?'

'I won't, I promise I won't,' Ruby said fiercely. 'I'll be happy as long as we're together. Please, Forrest.'

Forrest was silent for several moments. Then his face crumpled. He jerked away from her. 'Maybe you'd be happy, but I wouldn't. Not knowing that my father is rotting in a cell and that the woman I love is the person who put him there.'

With that, Forrest stormed out of the room and slammed the door behind him. Ruby gasped and rushed out after him.

Gloria looked at Hank. 'Aren't you going to go after them?'

Hank flipped through the binder Ruby gave him. 'You heard Mrs. Hayworth – Forrest's father is the fish we really want.' He pointed to a page in the binder. 'I *knew* there was something shady about that butler of his. Callum Morrison pulled off the biggest insurance scam this decade – I didn't recognize him with the scar. And I didn't even know he had a son.'

Gloria put two and two together: Callum Morrison was Forrest's father's real name. Not Pembroke.

Hank pulled a silver pistol from the holster on his hip and checked the bullets in the cylinder. Then he nodded to the men standing by the windows. Immediately the other agents checked their guns as well. 'We're going after *him*.'

'What about Jerome?' Gloria asked, her voice breaking a little. 'Pembroke said he had Jerome somewhere. I got you your information. You owe it to me to find him!'

'As soon as we bag Callum, my boys and I will head over to Forrest's place. We'll search it from top to bottom,' Hank said. He patted Gloria's shoulder. 'You've done good work here, Gloria. We'll make sure Jerome makes it back to you safe and sound.'

Once Hank and the other agents were gone, Gloria slouched into the couch cushions beside Marcus.

Marcus let out a low whistle. 'You really do know how to liven up an event. If you're not getting ripped offstage by your fiancé, you're singing for gangsters in a basement club or running away from home and living like a ragamuffin on the streets of New York. All I need now is for Lorraine to barrel in drunk and spoil things.'

'Just like old times,' Gloria said. 'Though I hear she's staying sober these days.'

'Well, we both know the booze was only part of Raine's problem.' Marcus knocked his shoulder against Gloria's. 'Anyway, I'm glad we got all of this taken care of before the big event. I intend to have you by my side when I finally hang that golden noose around my neck – I mean, put a ring on my finger.' He squeezed her hand. 'You're my best friend. Always were, always will be.'

Gloria swallowed hard. She could hardly believe it – Marcus, getting married. 'You're my best friend, too. And it looks like my detective days are over, so now we might actually get to see each other.'

Marcus nodded. 'And you'll finally have a chance to get to know Ana. She wants to meet Jerome, too! She's French –

they're all much more relaxed about that sort of thing over there.'

Gloria tried to smile back at him, but she couldn't fake it. Marcus *was* her best friend. Which was exactly why she had to risk hurting his feelings. 'Marcus, what on earth do you think you're doing?'

He blinked. 'What do you mean?'

'Do you even really know this girl? You got engaged so fast after you and Clara split.'

Marcus scooted away from her. 'You could've picked a better time to voice your concern, Gloria.'

'I'm sorry!' Gloria placed her hands on his shoulders and stared directly into his eyes. 'I was afraid of hurting you, and our friendship, by saying something. But now I know I wouldn't be a real friend if I *didn't* tell you that you're making a huge mistake, and that you belong with Clara. So I'm asking: Do you still love her?'

Marcus shrugged her off and stood, walking halfway across the room. 'Why are you asking me about Clara? I'm getting married to someone else. Maybe you've mistaken the occasion here. Did you even read the invitation I sent you? Come to think of it, I don't recall getting your RSVP. If you were hoping to have the filet mignon for dinner, too bad – we're fresh out.'

'Come on,' Gloria said, 'don't make a joke of this, Marcus. I'm serious.' Forrest had managed to dodge enough of her questions with questions – Gloria wasn't going to let Marcus do the same. 'It's not too late to stop this. Not if you really love Clara.'

Marcus looked down at the floor for a long time, breathing hard. When his blue eyes rose to meet Gloria's, they weren't angry anymore. They were sad, hurt, and so confused. He looked just the way he had when he'd come to visit Gloria in prison, right after he and Clara had split. God, he hadn't gotten over their breakup at all, had he? He'd just hidden away in this new whirlwind romance so he wouldn't have to think about his feelings.

'I just don't know, Gloria,' Marcus said softly. 'I shouldn't. I know I shouldn't. But then she came to see me last week. I was so angry with her, at the lies she'd told me. She wouldn't even apologize! And still I had to call security to make sure she left before I took her in my arms and kissed her right then.'

'Wait, you called security on Clara?'

'Not my finest moment,' Marcus said, chuckling. He paused. 'I miss her so much, Glo. Nothing seems as fun, or interesting, or exciting without her. She just . . . makes life better, you know?'

Gloria did know. 'That's what the people you love tend to do.'

He let out a heavy sigh. 'Clara doesn't love me, though. She told me so.'

Gloria took her black beaded purse off her shoulder so she could smack Marcus with it. She didn't hit him hard – just hard enough to make her point. 'Don't be an idiot. Clara is so clearly in love with you – if she told you otherwise, it was for a reason, to protect you somehow. But that girl is sick with her love for you.'

There was a flickering of something in Marcus's eyes – hope? – but then it faded. 'It's too late now. We're at my wedding! People came all the way from Chicago for this. I can't disappoint everyone out there. Not to mention Anastasia. That poor girl . . . what would she do if I backed out now?'

Gloria thought back to when she'd run away with Jerome. There was hardly anyone in her life she *hadn't* disappointed by choosing her life with him. 'Marcus, sometimes disappointing people is just a part of life. Just because you're afraid of letting some people down, that's no reason to marry a girl you don't love! This is *your* life you're gambling with. You should do what will make you the happiest.'

'Do you really—'

The door's crystal knob turned and a man with dark golden hair peppered with gray stood in the doorway. Even pushing fifty, Mr. Eastman cut a very handsome figure in his tuxedo.

'Come on, Son, we're waiting on you to begin,' Mr. Eastman called. 'Oh, hello, Gloria!'

Marcus wiped the hopeful expression off his face and, without another word to Gloria, marched after his father down the hallway.

The first thing Gloria noticed as the bridesmaids went down the aisle to the band's wedding march?

They were all so *tall*.

They were also all willowy blondes Anastasia had probably met at Barnard. The girls walked down the aisle of the ballroom toward the linen canopy in their pink sleeveless dresses. Fabric roses dotted the dropped waistlines of the dresses, and rows of flounces formed the skirts.

Every few seconds, a flashbulb went off. Gloria couldn't imagine how many reporters were in attendance, though she could pick out at least a dozen photographers sitting in the rows of gold chairs. Some faces Gloria had only seen in magazines – senators, socialites, even literary bigwigs like playwright Marc Connelly and Ruth Hale, who had helped to get women the vote. Then there were Gloria's old sort-of-friends from Chicago – witless Ginnie Bitman (now witless Ginnie Worthington), for example, who sat in the front row with her new, bored-looking husband on her arm.

The bridesmaids held the same white lilies that were in pale blue vases all over the ballroom. The bouquets were all tied with blue ribbons that matched the vases. A long stretch of white linen paved the girls' way down the aisle, and Gloria couldn't help thinking it was a waste of such beautiful fabric if people were just going to walk on it.

A full, white-suited orchestra sat beside the platform and played a slow, jazzy version of the wedding march with ambling piano and silky horns. The candlelight bounced off the enormous mirrors on the walls and the crystal chandeliers above onto the guests, bathing them with a hushed glamour.

It wasn't exactly the sort of wedding Gloria would've wanted. Gloria didn't need crystal or designer dresses or enough candles to light every Christmas tree in the city come winter. But the feel of it – something quiet yet utterly sophisticated – appealed to her.

It reminded her of a gilded version of the underground speakeasy world where she and Jerome had first met.

As the last of Anastasia's bridesmaids neared the platform, Gloria stepped forward and whispered in Marcus's ear. It was speak now or forever hold her peace – and she wasn't too good at holding things in these days. 'You need to fight for love, Marcus. Nothing wonderful in life comes easily. That's why I'll suffer anything to be with Jerome. And I know you'd do the same for Clara.'

As the wedding march swelled in the background, Gloria's mind filled with memories of her own beloved fiancé: the first time she'd seen Jerome playing at the Green Mill, their first kiss, running away together to live in New York and almost losing him, that night at the Opera House when he'd proposed. What was it he had said to her the night they boarded the train and left Chicago behind them? Oh yes: *It won't be easy. Easy is over with.*

And it certainly hadn't been easy. Mobsters. FBI. Evil fathers back from the not-so-dead. But fighting for love with Jerome was worth it – it always had been and it always would be. After watching Forrest turn his back on Ruby and Marcus do the same to Clara, Gloria was even surer of her love for Jerome. Men like Forrest and Marcus seemed to have everything – money, charm, good looks. But what was any of it worth without true love? The other trials Gloria could take. But a life without Jerome? Never.

Gloria absently felt for her engagement ring around her neck and pulled the necklace out from under her dress.

She held her ring and prayed that Jerome wasn't in danger,
wherever he was.

She glanced back at Marcus. Her closest pal since she was
little. She had to stop him from making the hugest mistake of
his life.

Chapter 22

CLARA

Marcus was getting married – to somebody else.

Clara's only plan to stop him had more than a few flaws.

And she was sandwiched between 'Benji' and Parker.

Could this wedding possibly get any worse?

'Just look at that jailbird standing up there with good, decent society like Marcus,' a woman's voice whispered. 'I'm surprised she's not on the arm of that Negro boyfriend of hers.'

Yes. It could. The old women sitting behind her were gossiping.

'Let's hope she doesn't cause some kind of ruckus,' another lady scoffed. 'She's already tarnished the Carmody name enough. She doesn't need to bring the Eastmans down with her.'

Clara studied Gloria, who was standing next to Marcus and looking beautiful in a black-and-white number with buttons down the front. She was whispering something in his ear. What was she saying?

'We're lucky she didn't try to smuggle a gun in here! I heard she had a whole room of them in that Harlem hole she was living in.'

'I hear she *does* have a gun,' Lorraine whispered just loud enough for the row behind them to hear. 'And that gossipy old ladies will be the first to go.'

That shut them up in a hurry.

Lorraine caught Clara's eye, and Clara couldn't help but smile. Then her gaze drifted to Melvin and the smile faded into a frown. A *nervous* frown.

His eyes were squinted into slits – the boy was nearly blind without his glasses. He looked ridiculous with his obviously drawn-on black mustache and his clashing red hair peeking out from under a hat that looked like a car had run over it. Clara had to hope Deirdre was as vision-impaired as Melvin, or they would most certainly be in trouble.

Clara turned her attention back to the processional and ran through each unsavory fact she'd learned about Deirdre Van Doren in her mind. She could only hope it would all be enough to rip Marcus away from the quiff for good.

The old biddies in the row behind them started up again. 'Marcus looks so dapper – though not as happy as a groom should, eh?'

'Young men always get cold feet. And this was a short engagement. I hear Bea Carmody and her bridge ladies didn't even have enough time to change the dates of their annual retreat so they could attend. Thank goodness – avoiding that ruined woman at parties has become such a *chore*. Marcus got engaged right after he broke things off with . . . oh, what was her name? The Carmodys' cousin who had that affair with Harris Brown and abandoned her baby?'

'Clara Knowles. Or was it Cara? Don't recall. Anyway, she *lost* the baby. The scandals in that family . . . Marcus dodged a bullet, getting away from that one.'

250

The ladies' voices drifted away as Clara focused on Marcus. He stood in the center of the platform beneath the canopy with Gloria and his groomsmen gathered behind him. His crystal-blue eyes were narrowed, and a bead of sweat rolled down the side of his sculpted face. He smoothed a hand over his already perfectly slicked golden hair and tugged a little at his white bow tie. Marcus's dimples were nowhere to be seen – he didn't look happy, he looked scared.

Suddenly Marcus's eyes fixed on hers. It was hard to be sure at this distance – she was seated in the middle of a crowd of hundreds – but Clara swore she could feel the warmth of Marcus's gaze on her. Why had she told him she didn't love him anymore? Raine had been right. That night, in his dorm room, she should have told him the truth: that she was still head-over-heels, madly, truly, deeply in love with him.

Friends? No thanks. She wanted to be his girlfriend.

But now some other woman was going to be his wife.

Marcus continued to look in her direction. Was he just surprised to see her? His eyes held a lot more than surprise, though – Clara could see hurt, confusion . . . and yet his mouth turned up the slightest bit at the corners. His eyes were bright in a way Clara hadn't seen since he had come to pick her up at Grand Central at the beginning of the summer. When the first words out of his mouth had been 'I love you.'

Could he still love her?

She tore her eyes from Marcus's and glanced back at Lorraine and Melvin. Melvin whispered something in Lorraine's ear and she laughed. The old Lorraine wouldn't have looked twice at a boy like Melvin, especially when he was wearing that silly disguise. Seemed like Clara wasn't the only one who'd learned a thing or two about love since she'd arrived in New York.

Beyond them sat Solomon and Lieutenant Skinner, both looking bored by the festivities. Sol was heinously under-dressed in his tweed suit, but it was probably the finest outfit he owned. Clara just hoped he would be able to make it through the ceremony without sneaking out for a smoke.

On Clara's left, Parker sat beside the *Manhattanite*'s top photographer, his pencil poised over the notepad in his lap. Some people could be happy being married to their careers.

Clara just wasn't one of them.

The crowd turned as one to watch Deirdre, or *Anastasia*, walk down the aisle. She wasn't wearing the same dress she'd worn that day at the bridal shop – Lorraine might have ruined that one beyond repair. But really she'd done the con woman a favor.

This dress was a sleeveless ivory satin gown with a cluster of handmade cloth flowers at one hip. It had a V-neck, and the skirt was made of tiers of elegant lace. Deirdre's light gray feathered headdress covered most of her bob. A veil lined with even more lace flowed from the headdress and draped onto the floor. She walked on the arm of Marcus's father – she'd probably fed Marcus some sob story to account for her absent parents. Ugh, that girl made Clara sick.

The crowd filled with appreciative whispers as Deirdre walked down the aisle, everyone remarking how gorgeous the bride looked. Deirdre smiled widely at Marcus when she reached the platform. *Come on, Marcus; just back out on your own so I don't have to do this to you . . .*

'Dearly beloved,' the minister said in a deep, booming voice, 'we are gathered here today to join Marcus Edward Eastman and Anastasia Juliet Rjin in holy matrimony, which is commended to be honorable among all people, and therefore, is not to be entered into lightly, but solemnly and only after serious thought.'

'Amen,' Lorraine murmured.

'Into this holy partnership these two now come to be joined,' the minister continued. 'If any person objects to this union, let them speak now or forever hold their peace.'

Clara fiddled with her wedding program, twisting it until it tore. She took a few deep breaths but couldn't help grimacing at what she was about to do. She just had to hope that Marcus would understand. She waited, her heart rattling in her chest, for Melvin to make his move.

After a moment of silence, Clara nudged Melvin hard in the side.

'Oof!' Melvin sprang out of his chair, pointed at Deirdre, and bellowed, 'Tarnation!' in the most absurd Southern accent Clara had ever heard.

Guests all around them looked at Melvin in surprise and began whispering to each other, filling the room with noise. 'How'd he get in here?' a mustached man whispered to his date.

'He looks like he escaped from the carnival,' the brunette replied.

Melvin looked at Clara with desperation in his eyes. This was as far as his part was supposed to go.

Clara stood beside Melvin and cleared her throat. 'Excuse me, I have something to say.' She patted Melvin's arm. 'Hold your horses for a moment.'

The whispers around them doubled in volume. At least half the people here knew who she was. Getting tangled up in scandals in New York and Chicago didn't exactly make for anonymity.

But the only person whose reaction Clara cared about was Marcus. His blue eyes were enormous; his mouth gaped open.

The boy was dumbfounded.

'I object,' Clara said, causing more than one wedding guest to gasp. A woman whipped out a feathered fan and began flapping it in front of her face as though she might faint. 'Marcus, I don't believe you can love that woman – Anastasia or Deirdre or whatever her name is.'

Clara nudged through the row so she could stand in the aisle. She'd been sitting in the eighth row of guests. Not a bad seat if all you wanted to do was watch a wedding – but Clara couldn't have this kind of conversation with Marcus from a distance.

She rushed closer to the platform, careful not to trip over her dress. She couldn't get the courage to climb up onto the platform. Plus she was a little scared of what Marcus's fiancée might try to do to her if she did. So she stopped just in front of the platform. Clara ignored the stunned gazes of the wedding party, Deirdre's affronted scowl, Gloria mouthing *What are you doing?*, and the weight of the hundreds of eyes on her back. Clara couldn't look at or think of anyone but Marcus, not if she was really going to go through with this.

'If I let you marry that viper beside you,' Clara said to him, 'not only will you be making the biggest mistake of your life, but so will I.'

'Why, you—' Deirdre began, her dainty hands clenching into fists.

Marcus held up a finger to shush Deirdre. 'The minister said it himself: This is the part where people are allowed to speak. So what exactly *are* you saying, Clara?' he asked. Marcus's eyes were bright again, and he looked like he was fighting a smile.

That gave Clara the courage to keep going. 'I have made some big mistakes in my life. But my biggest mistake was letting you go. But it stops here: Marcus, I love you. I want to spend the rest of my life with you, if you'll have me.'

''Ow dare you!' Deirdre screeched at Clara. She turned back to Marcus and grasped his wrists with her tiny hands. The minister took a step or two away from them and stroked his gray beard nervously. 'You should 'ave zat woman arrested. She's ze one 'oo attacked me at ze bridal shop!'

'Oh, shut your trap, sister!' Lorraine yelled before Marcus could react. She barreled through the row, stepping on feet left and right. 'You get your hands off me – I'm not sitting in your lap on purpose!' she yelled at a leering, bearded man sitting by the aisle after she tripped and nearly fell.

Lorraine pulled up her dress enough to expose part of her

lacy white slip and ran down the aisle. She stopped beside Clara and heaved a few deep breaths.

'Lor*raine*?' Gloria asked, holding her hand to her chest. Gloria looked between her old friend, Marcus, and Clara. 'Will someone please tell me what's going on?'

'All in good time! Love your dress, by the way. You're like some kind of classy penguin,' Lorraine said.

'Thank you?' Gloria said, blinking.

Lorraine pointed at Deirdre. 'And *you,* drop the fake French accent. The closest *you've* ever been to Paris was when you looked at a map . . . of Paris!'

The crowd gasped, and now guests didn't even bother to whisper their suspicions.

'Could it be true?'

'But she's so beautiful!'

'They did get engaged quickly . . .'

'Never trust the French – that's what I always say.'

'Our buddy, Benji,' Lorraine went on, beckoning to Melvin, 'he knows what we're talking about. You two used to date, isn't that right?'

Clara could see a glimmer of fear in Deirdre's copper-flecked eyes. 'I do not know what you are talkeeng about.'

'Oh yes you do,' Clara said. 'Just like you know you're wanted in three states for armed robbery. You were nearly arrested outside a restaurant in New Orleans for destruction of property and, oh, right, attempting to stab the owner with a steak knife.'

'That was you?' a middle-aged woman with her black hair piled on top of her head asked from the second row. She rose from her chair. 'My sister lives in New Orleans – she told me all about it. The town was scared half to death when they couldn't catch that madwoman.'

The crowd gasped again, and the word *madwoman* echoed around the room. 'Yes, thank you, ma'am!' Clara called to the woman. She looked back at Deirdre with more confidence. 'Then you changed your game. You fell off the radar, went through about a dozen aliases, and focused on trying to get rich the old-fashioned way – by marrying the money rather than stealing it.'

Deirdre turned to Marcus. '*Sacre bleu!* She eez lying!'

'One of your schemes almost worked, Deirdre,' Clara said. 'Once you figured out that a boy fresh from a recent heartbreak would be less likely to question you. But the lies and deceit end now. So how about you drop the act and get away from the man I love, before Benji here starts telling some stories of his own.'

Marcus stared at Deirdre now, withdrawing his wrists from her grip. 'Is this true? Do you know that man with the strange mustache?'

'Of course not!' Deirdre exclaimed. 'Obviously your ex-girlfriend eez just jealous of me.' She pointed at Clara, scowling. 'And she has mistaken me for zis Deirdre person! She must be very good-lookeeng. But I never—'

A look of dawning realization spread across Marcus's face. He put up a hand to stop her. 'You know what? It doesn't matter.'

Deirdre stopped cold. 'What do you mean?'

'I don't care whether you're this Deirdre person or Anastasia or the Yellow Kid,' Marcus replied. He glanced at Clara and gave her a smile that made her heart lighter than it had been in months. 'What Clara's saying is true: I don't love you. I love her. And I've just been using you to get over my broken heart. For that I really am sorry.'

Clara had no time to relish the fact that Marcus still loved her: Deirdre let out a high-pitched shriek. She raised her skirt, jumped off the platform, and turned her fierce glare on Clara. 'You can't do this to me!' she exclaimed without a trace of a French accent. Her voice had also dropped about an octave. 'I – I'll sue!'

Lorraine burst into laughter. 'Oh, please. You've duped so many men, I'm sure one or the other of them will press charges once they learn where you've ended up. Clara's got more than a few names in that file of hers.'

Clara nodded. 'You're right, Raine, I do.'

Deirdre's eyes widened in white-hot fury and she lunged at Clara, who moved out of the way, knocking into an elderly man with a monocle seated on the edge of the aisle. A few women in the row raced from their chairs and left the room, not wanting to get caught up in the commotion. Meanwhile, two little boys a few rows behind rose up on their knees in their chairs and shook their fists, chanting, 'Fight, fight, fight!'

Gloria rushed from the platform to help Lorraine and Clara, while Marcus approached his parents in the front row. Mr. Eastman was standing in the front row with a sobbing Mrs. Eastman on his arm.

'Marcus, explain this!' Mr. Eastman yelled.

'Sorry, Dad, I really don't think I can . . . ,' Marcus replied.

The rest of the wedding party remained on the platform, rooted to their places with shock.

Gloria caught Lorraine's arm just as she was about to punch Deirdre in the face. Deirdre moved to attack Lorraine and Gloria yanked her out of the way. Deirdre dove straight onto the linen cloth that covered the aisle, while Parker's photographer called, 'Smile!'

Clara laughed as Deirdre pulled herself to her feet. 'Thanks for that, Deirdre,' Clara said. 'You can look for that photo in next week's issue of the *Manhattanite*.'

'I won't be in this country by next week,' Deirdre growled.

She chucked the bouquet of calla lilies she'd been holding right at Clara's head – Clara ducked, and Lorraine caught the bouquet easily. 'I've always wanted to do that!' she exclaimed, holding the bouquet in the air as a trophy and yelling out into the crowd. 'Guess all those years of softball at Laurelton Prep really paid off!'

Deirdre raised her skirt and went running straight down the aisle.

'Stop her!' Mr. Eastman yelled. 'Someone stop that woman!'

Mrs. Eastman had stopped crying, and now her arm was around Marcus. She wiped the last of the tears from under her eyes. Her expression was pure venom. 'No one hurts my Marcus and gets away with it!'

Clara reminded herself to step lightly around Marcus's mother in the future.

'Don't worry, ma'am, she won't!' Solomon's police companion called to the Eastmans. 'Not if I have anything to say about it!'

Lieutenant Skinner rose from his seat and took off after the con woman. Clara didn't doubt the copper would catch Deirdre and have her in cuffs before she reached the lobby.

The murmuring crowd had been shocked into complete silence. Clara breathed deeply in and out, her heart hammering. She jerked when she felt a hand on her arm. 'Clara, why didn't you tell me you were looking into Marcus's fiancée?' Gloria asked. She moved her hand back and forth – maybe she'd hurt her wrist in the fight. 'With . . . Lorraine?' Lorraine looked up hopefully at Gloria's mention of her.

'You and Marcus are so close – I was afraid you'd tell me to stop,' Clara said. 'Plus I know you've been busy.'

Her cousin pulled Clara into a hug. 'No, I'm so glad. You two belong together. And I have been busy.' When she pulled away her face was distracted. 'Actually, that reminds me, I need to go check on something.'

'Secret bureau stuff?' Clara asked.

'Exactly.'

Gloria turned and began to walk down the aisle to the exit.

'Gloria!' Lorraine called, and Gloria turned. 'Thanks for saving me from that roundheel!'

Gloria smiled brightly at Lorraine. 'Thanks for helping Clara save Marcus from *her*!'

Then she rushed away, leaving Lorraine glowing.

The members of the orchestra, as well as several guests, rose from their chairs and followed Gloria out. Clearly there wasn't going to be a wedding now.

The rest of the guests were still quiet after the others left, watching Clara and her friends with amused disdain. The only sound Clara could hear was slow clapping, and that came from Marcus. He still stood with his parents with a band of stupefied groomsmen on the platform behind them. His mother still had her arm around Marcus, to comfort him, but he just grinned at her.

He walked down the aisle toward Clara and Lorraine. When he reached them, his eyes flicked toward Lorraine while she sniffed at the bouquet in her hands.

'Oh, Raine,' he said, 'how I've missed you.'

Lorraine immediately got misty-eyed. 'Really? Because I—'

He patted her hand. 'I'll find you at the reception, okay? We'll catch up.'

Lorraine took the hint. She linked her arm with Melvin's and led him back to their seats.

Which left Marcus and Clara alone. Or at least, as alone as they could be in front of a crowd of people. Clara looked out at the women clutching at their pearls, the men leaning forward to get a better view. She should've felt utterly embarrassed to have caused such a scene. But looking into Marcus's beautiful blue eyes, she couldn't feel anything but pure elation.

'I think *you and I* have some catching up to do,' he whispered to her.

Without paying any attention to the hundreds of eyes fixed on them, Marcus wound his arms around Clara's waist and pulled her close. He leaned his forehead against hers. 'No more lies, okay? I think I've had enough of those for one lifetime.'

Clara nodded and tentatively placed one hand on the lapel of his tuxedo. 'Did you mean what you said to Deirdre? That you still . . . love me?'

Marcus gave her a sheepish grin. 'I've always loved you, Clara. And I always will. Now and forever.'

Clara felt everything inside go warm. She hadn't lost Marcus. Somehow, he'd come back to her – and she was very much aware that this was a second chance most people never got. She wasn't about to screw it up.

'Then kiss me, you fool,' she whispered.

Marcus didn't hesitate. He took her in his arms and pressed his lips to hers. Clara's entire body sighed: Kissing Marcus felt like coming home again. Yet Clara felt she was also traveling somewhere new and wondrous. She hadn't been sure Marcus would stay interested in her forever, once he got to know the real her. But now she realized he had always known the real Clara, far better than Clara herself did.

When Marcus pulled away, the crowd erupted into applause. Marcus's parents, much to Clara's relief, were clapping, too. Lorraine looked the most gleeful of all. Clara thought of the way Gloria had smiled at Lorraine before she left. Could there be hope for those two, after everything?

Marcus took Clara's hand, sending pleasant shocks up her arm. 'This will sound absurd,' he announced to everyone, 'but since we have already paid for a party, I'd like for us to have a party. There is food and dancing in the Palm Court, and an incredible band. So please stay and enjoy the near death of my bachelorhood.'

The crowd laughed and a few of Marcus's college pals stood, ready to kick off the party downstairs.

'It was a close call, friends. I almost married the wrong girl. But now I've got the right one back and I'm never letting go. And if that isn't a reason to celebrate' – Marcus met Clara's eyes and grinned – 'I don't know what is.'

Chapter 23

LORRAINE

Rescuing Marcus had been a lot more glamorous in Lorraine's imagination.

When she'd pictured saving him from Deirdre – and she *had* pictured it – she'd imagined hundreds of flashbulbs igniting in her direction, reporters asking, 'Lorraine, how can one woman be both so beautiful *and* intelligent?'

All the Barnard girls would cry how they'd been wrong, and wasn't Lorraine the zebra's spots, and she would instantly be invited to every collegiate party for the next four years, and she and all of her new best friends would sip gin fizzes and remark at how many boys there were for them to choose from, and Lorraine would say things like 'My oh my, I can't pick just one – that's why I'm dating five!' And all of her new friends would laugh and laugh and laugh, and she would graduate summa cum laude and marry someone tall, dark, and handsome and somehow, some way, befriend Gloria Carmody again and they'd dance together at Marcus and Clara's wedding.

But fantasy was much more engaging than reality.

And here she was, minus the flashing lights and newfound friends, alone with Melvin while everyone else raced to follow the Golden Couple to the reception – even though there wasn't a wedding, who'd turn down a free party?

All anyone could talk about was Deirdre, Marcus, and Clara.

No one even mentioned Lorraine.

'Oh, that was so romantic!' Ginnie Worthington exclaimed, clinging to her pudgy husband's arm. Her pale blue frock looked like it was wilting under the candlelight. 'Why don't you ever do anything romantic anymore, Wally?'

Wally raised his eyebrows. 'You want me to leave you for a con woman so I can come back? Let's just get some wedding cake so we can go home.'

Lorraine sighed – sure, she'd love a piece of cake. But it didn't exactly go with fitting into her dress. No, water would have to do. Well . . . and a teensy bit of vodka.

'You feeling peachy, Raine?'

She whipped her head at the sound of Melvin's familiar voice. He'd put his glasses back on – thank God – and was turning his white handkerchief gray trying to wipe the drawn-on mustache off his face. But without a mirror he was really just smearing dark smudges all over the lower half of his face.

Lorraine reached over and took the handkerchief. 'Let me do that. You look like some kind of deranged chimney sweep.'

Melvin smiled and let her scrub his face. 'But a chimney sweep who dresses *very* well for work.'

She laughed, continuing until his face was as clean as it was going to get without soap and water. She handed the cloth back to him, and there was a slight spark when they touched. Lorraine felt something rush through her – was it just static energy, or something else? 'Listen, Melvin . . . you did a good job earlier. Really great. You were a very believable Southerner. Nice improvisation with all the finger raising!'

'Think so?'

'I do.' She reached up to push his hat back on his head a little so that his flaming red hair waved over his forehead. He needed to wear newsboy caps more – the hat gave him a real scholarly-yet-dangerous look. 'And I love that hat on you!'

Melvin ducked his head and gave her a bashful smile. 'I know I told you not to get me wrapped up in any of your schemes after the incident at the bridal shop, but this one was pretty . . . copacetic. Definitely a change of pace from all that reading at Columbia.'

'And how!' Lorraine said. 'It's ducky to get up to some mischief on your own once in a while! The characters in books shouldn't have all the fun, right?'

'Right. And we were able to help Marcus avoid a terrible fate. Which means we both deserve some overpriced finger food and at least one dance, wouldn't you say?'

Lorraine took Melvin's arm and they moved through the nearly empty ballroom down the stairs to the Palm Court. Most of the crowd was already seated at tables beneath the domed glass ceiling; a group of black men dressed in white suits sat on a raised platform at the far end of the room, playing some springy jazz music. A few couples were dancing in the space between the stage and tables.

Clara and Marcus sat at one of the tables, guests on either side of them trying to get their attention. But they only had eyes for each other – and surprisingly, Lorraine wasn't jealous at all.

She leaned against one of the enormous marble pillars by the court's expansive archway. 'Those two look so happy.'

'Yeah,' Melvin replied. 'Isn't it nice knowing you helped that happen?'

Lorraine crossed her arms and pouted. 'But no one else knows! All anyone can talk about is Clara. It's like I wasn't even there.' The dreams of all the Barnard girls hearing about her amazing detective work and wanting to befriend her, or the Columbia boys wanting to date her, suddenly seemed so far out of reach.

'That's how it should be! Sometimes you do something because it's the right thing to do, not because you're going to get the glory.'

Lorraine let his words sink in. 'I guess you're right.' She glanced at Melvin out of the corner of her eye. He was a genuinely *nice* boy. So different from Marcus, who had never seen her as anything more than a floozy, or Hank, who had lied to her and used her for his own personal gain. Melvin was here because he wanted to be. It was a good thing, too. If she was going to keep working on this whole being-a-decent-person-without-an-ulterior-motive thing, she was going to need a teacher.

Melvin took a deep breath and moved to stand in front of her. 'Besides,' he went on, 'we got to know each other much better because of this. And I have to say, Raine, you're quite the kitten's pajamas.'

'Really?' Melvin *had* always been willing to do everything for her. But he'd said himself that he only did that because he was her friend. There had been that moment at Forrest's party when he'd held her . . . And then after the bridal shop debacle, he had said that he had a crush on someone. Someone he didn't think felt the same way about him. Had he been talking about . . .

She felt her mouth stretch into an enormous smile. 'You really think so?'

Melvin took a step closer to her, whipped off his glasses, and wrapped his arms around her. Lorraine barely had time to process what he was doing before he pulled her close and kissed her – hard.

There was passion, there was heat. Melvin kissed like Lorraine imagined men did in the movies – the kind of kiss that really *meant* something. She felt a thrilling tingle shoot from the tips of her toes to the top of her head. Her arms moved as if they had a mind of their own, winding around Melvin's neck, her fingers getting lost in his impossibly soft hair.

Who could've guessed that brainy Melvin was such a good kisser?

And Melvin was a boy who really, truly liked her. Despite her laundry list of flaws.

Maybe even *because* of them.

Lorraine pulled away and looked at Melvin – it was almost as if he were an entirely different person now. He wasn't the man she'd always imagined, but he was the man she needed. She gave him a wide smile, which he returned. Unfortunately the smile looked a little creepy with those tiny eyes twinkling down at her.

'Oh, Melvin. The smooching was great and all, but you really need to put your glasses back on.'

He chuckled and did as she'd said. And instantly he was handsome again – those frames were magic! Lorraine couldn't believe she'd never noticed how attractive he was before, like a sexy professor, or maybe a writer. Handsome in an under-stated, *intellectual* way.

'Better?'

Lorraine grabbed his lapels and pulled him closer. 'Much.'

But just as Melvin leaned in for another round of necking, there was the unmistakable crack of a gunshot.

Lorraine trembled, shocked. Who had a gun – and where was the shooter? Melvin instantly stood in front of Lorraine to protect her – he really *was* one of the good ones – and she peeked over his shoulder. A bald man in a tuxedo stood in the archway and held a stunning young brunette at gunpoint. Several guests were cowering under tables and looking around frantically for another exit. Lorraine didn't recognize the man with the gun. A jagged scar ran across his nose.

She gasped when she studied the brunette in the purple dress more closely. Was that Ruby Hayworth?

'I want all the cops to clear out. Then I'll let this lady go,' the thug bellowed.

Two men burst through the doorway behind the man, then approached him and Ruby slowly. Lorraine recognized one of them as Forrest Hamilton – rich, dark, and handsome. How was it that he wasn't married?

Lorraine's eyes widened at the other man. What was *Hank* doing here? Though she'd preferred the casual vests and trousers he'd worn as a bartender, his pressed black suit didn't look *too* bad. Men dressed just like Hank followed him.

Hank and Forrest both held up their hands. 'Violence won't get you out of this jam, Callum. How about you just let the girl go and save yourself the murder charge?'

But the hard-boiled character – Callum – turned to Forrest. 'You were going to hand me over to the bulls just so you could run away with this floozy!' He tightened his bulky arm around Ruby's neck, pressing the gun harder into her temple. 'That is not how a son honors his father.'

Ruby blinked, and mascara-blackened tears dribbled onto her cheeks.

Lorraine heard glasses and silverware clatter to the ground as guests stood from their tables or ducked for cover. Men and women both cried out for help, and many pressed up against the back wall of the court, as far from Callum and his gun as they could get. There was a jumble of people by the stairwell, which was clogged with people trying to get away. The room filled with tense whispers.

'First the bride's a con woman and now someone's holding a guest at gunpoint?' a woman in a red dress complained to her husband under a nearby table. 'I *told* you I didn't like your friends.'

The rest of the crowd stood and watched, as motionless

as Lorraine and Melvin. Lorraine could hardly believe this Callum was Forrest Hamilton's father. All the good genes must've come from his mother.

'You're right,' Forrest said. His voice was shaky and he seemed much more like a boy than a man. 'But don't blame her – blame me. Hold me hostage instead of her!'

'You're not worth anything,' Callum spat. 'They'll just shoot the both of us.'

Callum gestured to Hank with the gun for a split second – but that was all Forrest needed to attack.

Suddenly he was in the air, soaring into his father. Ruby cried out and ducked to the ground with her hands over her head, out of Callum's hold and out of Forrest's way.

Forrest pummeled into the older man's chest with such force that Callum toppled over, hitting the floor with a sickening smack.

The pistol fell to the floor.

Forrest reached for it, his limbs tangled with his father's. Ruby jumped up and tried to help Forrest, grabbing Callum's coat and attempting to yank him away.

But before Ruby could do any damage, Hank was by her side, pulling her to safety.

A few FBI agents attempted to separate Forrest and his father, but Callum was rushing after the pistol and then it was difficult to see what was going on – there were FBI men everywhere, screaming things, and guests hovering in fear underneath the tables, praying for help.

There was something silver sliding across the floor – the

pistol? A hand grabbed it, but in all the commotion, Lorraine couldn't see who the hand belonged to. She tried to lean forward, but Melvin stood firmly in front of her.

Lorraine heard someone – Ruby? – cry, 'Forrest!' and then there was another gunshot.

Melvin dove to the ground, pulling Lorraine along with him by her arm. She hit the floor on her elbows and flinched at the impact, the carpet scraping her skin as she slid forward. As soon as Lorraine was down, Melvin covered her body with his. She could feel him breathing hard and fast.

She and Melvin weren't the only ones with this idea – the sound of glass breaking and chairs falling filled the room as guests dove for cover. In mere seconds, everyone in the room was lying or kneeling on the plush burgundy carpet in fear.

Callum was the first to rise, making a quick run for the lobby. But Hank took him down in a flying tackle before he even reached the doorway.

'I did always love the way that man moved.' Lorraine glanced at Melvin over her shoulder. 'You should have seen him behind a bar.'

Melvin rose to his feet and offered her his hand. 'You don't think anyone got hit by that second shot, do you?'

A crowd was gathering around the front of the court, near the arched entrance, where the struggle had taken place. The room was noisy, but not as loud as it should've been. The guests could only speak in hushed, terrified whispers. People gasped, and Lorraine saw an older woman clutch what looked like a rosary with closed eyes.

Lorraine pulled Melvin through the crowd, trying to get a glimpse of Forrest, Ruby, Hank, and Callum.

Someone *had* gotten hurt, hadn't they?

A wail that sounded more like it came from an animal than a woman pierced the air.

Hank had Callum in handcuffs, but the older man wasn't fighting now. He stared, stricken, at the ground where Ruby knelt beside a motionless figure.

It was Forrest Hamilton.

His brown eyes were open and glassy, staring up at the domed ceiling without seeing it. Lorraine stared at his broad chest and willed it to rise and fall. But the young millionaire was utterly still. Blood trickled from his mouth, which was open in a surprised O.

Forrest's hand rested on his chest, over a deep red circle staining the center of his crisp white shirt. Blood sank into the burgundy carpet around him, turning it brown.

'No, no, no, no,' Ruby said over and over. She clung to Forrest and shook with sobs. 'You big idiot,' she cried. 'What'd you go and do that for?'

Behind her, Hank pushed the handcuffed Callum out into the lobby, followed by most of the other agents. Two of the suits stayed behind; one put his hand on Ruby's shoulder. She shook him off violently and remained beside Forrest, leaning over his body. Blood from his chest seeped into the bodice of her dress, making it look as if she were bleeding, too – but no one was moving to stop her or do anything except watch the horrifying scene playing out before their eyes.

Lorraine turned to Melvin and wordlessly put her arms around him. She made herself a silent promise: No matter how many ill-fitting suits Melvin wore or how many times he begged her to run through yet another set of annoyingly specific flash cards, she would never forget how thankful she was to have him.

It was better to risk loving *too* much before it was too late and all you were left with was regret.

Chapter 24

JEROME

Despite everything that had happened in the past twenty-four hours, being on the water made Jerome feel calm.

He and Gloria stood on the foredeck of the steamship, watching the island of Manhattan get smaller and smaller as they floated away. The night air was chilly, and Jerome could practically taste the salt coming off the harbor. Several of the boat's passengers were braving the cold with Gloria and Jerome so they could say their silent goodbyes to the lights of New York City.

Gloria hadn't taken her arm from Jerome's or looked at anyone but him since they'd boarded the ship to Paris. Jerome had noticed more than one passenger staring at them from their deck chairs. Some had even left in a huff, retreating to their cabins.

Well, let them stare. Let them leave. Nobody had any idea what they'd been through. What they'd survived in order to be here.

Jerome glanced down at his arm, where Gloria's engagement ring glinted on her finger. Seeing it on her made him feel whole again.

Gloria turned to him and tugged at the scuffed collar of his white shirt, then looked at her formal gown and laughed. 'I think our first stop once we get there will have to be to some kind of clothing shop. These aren't exactly traveling clothes. And you're still stuck in that servant's uniform!'

The gruesome wedding was barely two hours behind them. Jerome hadn't known what would happen to him – locked in Pembroke's cellar, cuffed and bound, he figured he was pretty much as good as dead.

Then the cellar door had been opened by none other than Hank.

And Gloria.

She had explained everything – Clara and Marcus getting together, Forrest's death and Pembroke's arrest. 'I'm just so glad you're safe,' Gloria had whispered, clinging to him. 'I couldn't live without you.'

'I put you both in danger, and I'm sorry,' Hank admitted. 'But we got our man. It's about as happy an ending as we could ask for.'

Not for Ruby or Forrest, Jerome found himself thinking, but he kept his mouth shut. Hank promised that Gloria wouldn't have to spend any more time in jail, and he'd even given the couple Pembroke's tickets to Paris to use if they wanted to.

So here they were.

Escaping – again – to start a new life together. Only this time would be different. They were older, smarter. Even more in love.

'Are you scared?' Jerome asked. 'You're taking a lot of risks escaping to Paris with a black pianist.'

The two leaned on the railing, staring at the water glistening in the quiet twilight. Soft waves brushed by the hull of the ship, and the breeze lightly blew Gloria's flame-red waves from her delicate face.

'Scared?' Gloria asked. 'Anything but! I'm tired of everyone telling me who to be. I'm tired of my parents thinking they can dictate my life.' She leaned her head on his shoulder. 'Paris will be a fresh start for us, Jerome. And it's gotta work out . . . I mean, the French even have Josephine Baker!'

Jerome laughed. He never could decide whether Glo's blind optimism made her sweetly naïve or one of the wisest people he'd ever met. Either way, it was highly infectious and was one of the things he loved most about her.

'You know that's not what I meant,' he said. 'I meant—'

'Fine,' Gloria said, and raised her head to look at him. 'I'll be serious.' She reached over to hold his hand tight. 'I was so worried when Pembroke revealed that he was holding you hostage, Jerome. You were in that situation because of me, and I was there because of Hank.'

'Gloria, you shouldn't blame yourself.'

'I don't want to have to hide anymore or playact for the police. I don't want to work for gangsters. I just want you, and me, together in a place where we might have a ghost of a chance.' She frowned and glanced at the retreating shore. 'I can't bear the thought of being like Ruby, finally getting the courage to be with the man she loves only to lose him.'

Jerome nodded and folded her into his arms. 'If we have love, the rest of life will take care of itself. In Paris, no one will tell us that we can't be together because of our skin color. No one will care. It'll just be you and me. Forever.'

At that, Gloria tilted her head back and kissed him softly, right in front of everyone on deck.

'In Paris we'll be able to follow our dreams,' Gloria said when she drew away from him. 'Not just in our careers, but everything else, too. Maybe we'll come back to New York someday . . . but for now, we're making the right decision, Jerome. I can feel it in my bones.' She was silent for a moment. 'I just hope you don't mind following me across the ocean.'

Jerome tightened his arms around her. 'Miss Gloria Carmody, I would follow you anywhere.'

They kissed again as the sun set and stars began to glint in the darkening sky. The golden-orange light gilded everything around them – the shrinking skyscrapers, the blue sea, and the gleaming floorboards of the deck. New York was giving them a truly golden send-off – that had to be good luck, right?

With Gloria in his arms as the ship steamed off into the fast-falling night, Jerome knew he already had all the good luck he would ever need.

EPILOGUE

CLARA KNOWLES GETS HER
HAPPILY-EVER-AFTER

By Parker Richards, for the *Manhattanite*
January 1, 1925

In a small but elegant ceremony this Saturday afternoon, Clara Knowles and Marcus Eastman said their vows at the Franklin Arms Hotel in Brooklyn.

Miss Knowles wore a beautifully beaded Lucien Lelong gown, while Mr. Eastman was dressed in a traditional Brooks Brothers tux. Miss Knowles's maid of honor was Lorraine Dyer, and Mr. Eastman's best man was his old prep school friend from Chicago, Charles Drakeman. Miss Dyer and the other bridesmaids wore sleeveless deep-burgundy dresses covered in floral-patterned beading.

The reception was a joyous affair, and Mr. and Mrs. Eastman seemed excited for all their future would bring. After a honeymoon to Paris, Mr. Eastman will continue his freshman year at Columbia University. Next fall, Mrs. Eastman will begin her freshman year at Sarah Lawrence College.

As our dear readers know, Mrs. Eastman has been with the *Manhattanite* since its very first issue, and her articles about her cousin, Gloria Johnson (now living in Paris and unable to attend the wedding), and her recent exposé on Deirdre Van Doren helped to make the magazine what it is today. We'll be sad to lose her when she heads off to school. But I know she will go on to do great things, and wish her and Marcus a lifetime of happiness!

This beautiful wedding was the perfect way to kick off a brand-new year in the greatest city in the world – where love is hiding around every corner, music is thriving in every club, and, of course, anything goes.

ACKNOWLEDGMENTS

The author wishes to acknowledge Lila Feinberg for her valuable contributions to the story and the characters of the Flappers series.

Writing the Flappers series has been the cat's pajamas, the eel's hips, the bee's knees. But just as the greatest jazz pieces of the Roaring Twenties could take months to write and seamstresses at Parisian fashion houses of the time might spend weeks on beadwork alone, this series has taken a lot of time and hard work. I never could've done it without a gifted orchestra behind me. Thank you to Ted Malawer and Michael Stearns at the Inkhouse for your faith in me. And thanks to Wendy Loggia, Beverly Horowitz, Krista Vitola, Lauren Donovan, Trish Parcell, and everyone at Delacorte Press and Random House Children's Books – you're all the berries. To my mother for reading every chapter of this book as I wrote it and making sure I knew which parts made you laugh. To Dan for your constant support. And to F. Scott and Zelda Fitzgerald, for providing so much of the inspiration for these books and making me fall in love with the Jazz Age.

Also available in The Flappers series

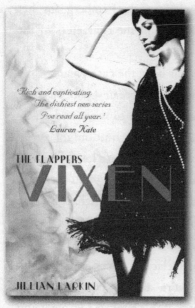 

Young. Wealthy. Beautiful.
Dangerous.
It's the roaring twenties . . .
and anything goes.